SWEET WILLIAM

Iain Maitland

CONTRABAND 🔒

Contraband

An imprint of Saraband,

Digital World Centre, 1 Lowry Plaza

The Quays, Salford, M50 3UB

www.saraband.net

ISBN: 9781910192917

ISBNe: 9781910192924

10 9 8 7 6 5 4 3 2 1

Typeset by Iolaire Typography Ltd.

Printed and bound in the EU on sustainably sourced paper.

For Tracey

Part 1

THE ESCAPE

11.10PM FRIDAY 30 OCTOBER

If I move, even ever so slightly, this stair will creak and they will hear me. They're all around me and one of them will cry out, that's for sure. Bound to. Then I'm done for. I'll never get another chance like this to get away. And I need to get away tonight, come what may. No matter what.

If I turn my head oh-so-slowly to the right and look up, I can see three doors on the first-floor landing just above me. All shut. Ainsley is in the room at this end of the landing, closest to the stairs. He'll be sitting there now, rocking gently back and forth and mumbling to himself. He's sharper than you'd think, though. If he hears me, he'll shout out, "Who's there?" at the top of his thin, whiny voice. And he'll do it over and over, each time louder than the last.

Sprake is in the middle room. He'll be staring out of the window across the lawn. Absolutely motionless, he'll be. I know. I've seen him. He sits that way for hours at a time. Like he's in a trance. If I get out of here, I'll have to stay round the side of the building to get away. If Sprake sees me he'll start shouting and banging on the walls with his fists. He turns quickly, that one. He's mad, proper mad. I've even seen him biting his toenails until they bleed.

The last room on this landing is mine. It'll be 'was mine' in a few minutes. I'll be glad to see the back of it, to tell you the truth. I've been in the annexe for six months now and you can only take so much, even if you're not locked and bolted in like you are in the big house. You're still not free, whatever way you look at it.

All of my weight is on this step. I'm four steps down now. Nine to go. Then four to the corridor and away with a bit of luck. Security's piss-poor at the best of times, but it's been non-existent during the renovations. And it just about disappears in the annexe at this time of night when we're all supposed to be drugged up and in bed. Those who take the medication probably are. But I've been tucking my tablets under my tongue and spitting them out afterwards when I go to the toilet. They never notice. They think we're all stupid in here.

I've got to move my left leg down ever so carefully onto the next step. To do that, I've first got to shift all of my weight over to the right foot. I daren't move the right foot yet. It's got the creak waiting underneath it. I can feel it there ready to screech out.

There, I've done it. I'm on the next step. And all without a single sound.

They all wondered why I spent so much time moving up and down these stairs over and over. I spent ages on each step, just rocking to and fro. They think I'm as mad as buggery. I'm not, though. I know which stairs creak and which ones don't. That's why I'm going to get away tonight and the rest of these poor stupid bastards will be rotting here for years to come.

The next three steps don't creak at all. I know. I've tested them.

One.

Two.

Three.

There. I'm now just five steps from the bottom. Easy as pie that was.

Smith the warden is at the bottom of the stairs, sitting in his so-called office on the left. He's supposed to be security but he's short and fat and bald and looks 70 if he's a day. He'll be sitting there with his back to the door, the lamp on and his paper spread out. Humming to himself and jangling his keys, he'll be. I know.

I've heard him night after night. World of his own, the lazy pig. He'll never notice me slipping by; not if I'm quiet.

On the right is the residents' lounge. We're 'residents' nowadays out of respect. 'Human Rights', that's what we've all got. The press don't call us residents, mind. Nor the locals. They call us psychos – and worse. They don't respect our human rights at all. There's always a huge hoo-hah whenever someone new arrives, especially if they've been in the papers like me. We've had demonstrations at the gates even though we're medicals not criminals. That's official, that is. Medicals.

There won't be any of us residents in the lounge at this time of night. It's way too late. I know who will be in there, though. Maureen Fucking Spink and her crony, Fat-Arsed Eileen. That's my names for them, by the way, not anybody else's. They'll be smoking. They're not supposed to, it's a fire hazard. That's why they hide away in there. And they'll be talking quietly under their breath about us.

Spink will be out of that lounge like a shot if she hears anything. And she won't hold back, I can tell you. I've seen her hit Tosser Gibson when no one was looking. Really hit him, not just pushing and pulling him about like she does with the rest. She thought no one was around at the time. But I was and I saw it all. I keep my eyes open, see? Eyes open, mouth shut, that's me. I take it all in. I'm clever like that. I'm smart. Dead smart. Just you wait and see how smart I am.

These final few steps don't creak at all, except for the second to last one. I move down. Onto step five, then four and then three. I pause, miss step two to get to one and then I'm on the ground floor. Corridor straight opposite and down there at the end to the left is the unlocked side door.

There's no one down that corridor. Nobody to hear me. Just walk along and open that side door and I've another corridor and a locked door, maybe two locked doors, to get through after that and then I'm out and running for the wall and freedom.

I've never seen much beyond the side door to be honest. I only dared open it and look down the next corridor once. Couldn't risk being spotted checking it all out. It will be all quiet there though for sure. No one about. Once I've gone through the side door, I can force open as many other doors as I have to and I'm away – too late for Spink or anyone else to stop me.

I pause.

Draw breath.

Think for a moment.

I'm leaving because of William. My little boy. My wife died, you see. 'A tragedy', the papers called it – 'a shocking waste of a young mother's life'. That was the quote. Horrible it was. Really horrible. And they blamed me for it. That's why I'm in here. One year in the big house, six months in the annexe so far. Lots more to come if I stayed.

The judge didn't send me to prison, though. I fooled him good and proper. I'm smart. I told you, didn't I? Sectioned and assessed under what's called section 37, that's what I got. A cushy enough number. Being here's better than prison, I can tell you. Easier to get out, too. You just wait.

Since the wife died, her sister and the husband have been bringing up my little William. I've got to go and get him now, though. Tonight. Right now. It has to be this weekend, see? Halloween. It's the time the family gets together at Aldeburgh in Suffolk. Nice, quiet, back-of-your-arse Aldeburgh.

Just the sister-in-law and her husband, his fat old father and that bitch of a mother. And my lovely little William. Saturday night they go to the Halloween carnival parade on the seafront. I move in from the shadows. I take William. I move out and off we go to a new life. And it'll leave the sister-in-law and that husband back where they started. Childless.

As I told you, I'm smart.

Dead smart, me.

You'll soon find out just how smart I am.

Me and the little one can get away somewhere. Europe. France, maybe. It's nice there, especially in the south. I've seen pictures. And it's very sunny, so I'm told. I can get a job cleaning or something, and we can start a new life together. I've worked it all out in my head. Got it all planned. I've thought it through good and proper.

I wait. Listening for old Smith in his room. I've got to be careful.

Still waiting. Yes, and still listening.

Got to wait. Be sure. Feel absolutely certain.

It's okay. He's quiet, not moving at all. He must be reading. Just like I told you he would be. I take two steps. One to the door, which is open no more than an inch.

He's not there.

Smith.

Must have gone for a smoke.

The second step takes me to the corridor. I want to run, just go as fast as I can. I daren't, though. Not yet. I force down the panic surging up inside of me.

I hear a door open.

Voices. Women's voices.

It's Spink and her fat-arsed mate coming out of the residents' lounge.

I wait. There's nothing I can do. If they turn and come towards this corridor, I'm fucked. Well and truly. I've no reason to be here. No reason at all. Not at this time of night. They'll know what I'm doing. They'll shout out.

Spink? I could take her if I had to. Easy. But I couldn't keep both of them quiet. And Old Smith as well. Not three of them. He's got some sort of truncheon he carries round with him. From when he was in the force. He's the sort who'd use it too. Bastard.

They've turned left. To the bottom of the stairs. 13 steps up and another turn onto the landing, that's what. No, sounds like they've stopped. They're saying something about someone. Me, probably. Can't make it out. They're speaking softly. One of them chuckles. A piss-taking sound, that. They've said something nasty about me for sure. They don't like me much. I don't kow-tow to them like the rest of the dribblers.

I can hear them at the top of the stairs.

It's 18 steps down this corridor. I have to walk normally. Not panic. 18 ... 17 ... 16 ... 15 ... 14 ...

Spink will go to Ainsley's room first.

Opening his door.

Checking him.

Spink will stand there looking at Ainsley.

Maybe say something clever to him, wanting to make Fat-Arsed Eileen laugh.

"And h-h-how are you, Mr Ainsley?" mocking his stutter, most likely.

I walk, one step at a time, down the corridor, slowly, quietly, so I can hear what's happening upstairs. 13 ... 12 ... 11 ... 10 ...

Spink and Fat-Arsed Eileen will then move to the next room.

Checking on Sprake, I wouldn't wonder.

I pause, wait, straining to hear.

I know Sprake, the stupid fucker. He'll try and engage them in conversation. Like he's normal. But what he says is gibberish. I know. He talks to me sometimes. You can't understand a word. Spink and her mate will listen and she'll smile and nod for a moment or two, taking the piss. Then she'll put on that sneering smile of hers and say, "Well, we can't stand here all night talking with you, Mr Sprake", and all with that exaggerated politeness. She'll snigger and slam the door in his face and they'll all have a right good laugh at the poor confused prick.

I'm more than halfway to that side door. 9 ... 8 ... 7 ... 6 ... 5 ... 4 ...

They'll turn and go to my room. Spink will be thinking of something clever to say to me. She tries hard to make me react, I'll give her that. Very hard. But it never works, not with me. I just smile and act polite, like nothing ever bothers me. She'll have some snide comment ready as she walks up, puts her hand on the handle and opens the door.

I take the final steps to the side door, 3 ... 2 ... 1 ...

I put my hand on the handle, pull down, step through. Breathe a sigh of relief. Ready to break down the next door ... and the next ... and the next. No matter what, no matter how many doors, I have to get away.

Now.

Tonight.

To get my sweet William.

Smith is leaning against a wall at the far end of the next corridor. He's near a half-open window, smoking, just like I said, and he's looking at something on his mobile phone, turning it first this way and then that. He glances up and I see the shock on his face as he recognises me.

I look at him and his keys.

The keys to my freedom.

And I give him a lovely big smile.

11.25PM FRIDAY 30 OCTOBER

"All done?" the young man asked, rolling over and putting his glasses next to the newly opened paperback on the bedside table.

"Almost," the young woman replied, walking into the room and pushing the door to behind her. "He struggled a bit, as usual, but then nodded off ... his levels are still high, a bit more than yesterday. We just need to pack all the paraphernalia in the morning – and find Mr Jolly."

"I think you'll find Mr Jolly's here, ready and waiting for you."

"Ha ha, not now, Rick, exhausting day, long drive tomorrow – what time do you want to leave?" She sat down on the side of the bed.

He sat up, reaching out for her, "I don't know, Nat. My dad really wanted us to go up tonight to get the place ready. If they're going to arrive at lunchtime, we should get there for, what, 11.00, just to freshen things up? So how about we leave at 8.00 and stop on the way to get something to eat?"

"Seriously?" She laid down, pushing his hands away, "Not now … I want Will to lie in as long as possible and then check him again and get him jabbed and fed before we leave … at 10.00."

"9.00."

"9.30 at the earliest, and you're doing the 'freshening up' if we get there before them. I want everything calm and peaceful, otherwise he'll just get agitated and fretful and it'll be hell for all of us, especially with your mother sitting there taking it all in. Have you told them about Will yet?"

He shook his head.

"We'll have to over the weekend, early on, when we get there, otherwise it'll just be a nightmare and he'll be edgy and tired and hungry and God knows what and your mother will just give me that look of hers all the while … but if we tell her he's diabetic, she'll be sitting there thinking I've screwed up and don't look after him properly. Like I'm not a proper mother."

"Don't say that Nat, you couldn't be better."

She sat up straight, "I wish we weren't going. I'm not in the mood to play happy families this weekend."

"It'll be just fine; we'll get there, have lunch together, a stroll to see the fireworks, early night, breakfast, a cycle on the prom for Will when it's nice and quiet and we'll be on the way back mid-morning. You can get started on your OU work on Sunday evening, I'll sort Will out."

He sat up too, "Do I have to wait until Sunday night? You'll be even more tired then, especially if the journey sets him off."

"God's sake," she said, pulling her T-shirt up and over her head, "get on with it then."

They both laughed.

12.19AM SATURDAY 31 OCTOBER

Got to keep moving.

They will have called the police straightaway, had to. 11.25 I'd guess. What happens then? I don't know. Does it go straight to CID or does the local plod come in first? Plod, I reckon. How long's that take? 20 minutes? They'd have arrived at 11.45 then.

Must keep running as best as I can.

Spink would take charge when the coppers turned up. She's like that. She'd explain what's happened. Who I am. Why I was there. Probably show them the newspaper clippings, knowing her. She'd have no mercy, that's for sure. So the coppers call for assistance? When? 11.55?

Have to keep going as fast as possible.

How soon before the police are all over the roads? 12.15? 12.45? Am I too late already? Will they set up roadblocks? They'll have to, won't they? Especially when they know who I am. Spink will make me sound evil. She'll say I'm dangerous without the tablets. Nonsense of course – I don't really need them at all. They'll have to put up a show to placate the locals, though. Lots of cars. Loads of roadblocks everywhere.

Got to get to a main road, hitch a lift and get well away before they can do all that.

Will they send in dogs? I can't outrun dogs, can I? I wouldn't know how. Could hide up a tree. But they'd have the scent, wouldn't they? No rivers round here to wash it off.

Just have to keep going, got to run flat out.

12.15 now I'd guess, has to be. Been running for an hour at least. It's killing me.

I'm still in the woods. What would have been Sherwood Forest I reckon, hundreds of years ago anyway. Not much of it left these days. I'm sticking to the wooded parts, going as quickly as I can, and keeping under cover. I don't think they'd use a helicopter, but you never know. Best be careful.

I can't run fast. Not as I'd like. It's dark and there's only a half-moon. And I'm only shuffling along really. Trotting at best – in bedroom fucking slippers. Thing is, I had to break out wearing my dressing gown over a T-shirt and trousers and my usual slippers – think about it, if anyone had seen me on my way out in proper clothes, with a coat and shoes, they'd have known what I was up to, wouldn't they?

Got to stop for a moment.

Get my breath.

I'm drenched in sweat.

Shouldn't be hot in October. Late October at that. The clocks have gone back. It's the dressing gown that's doing it really. It's making me sweat. But I can't ditch it. The dogs will find it. They'll know where I've been. And you can't hitch a lift just in a tee shirt, trousers and slippers, can you? No matter how respectable you look, who's going to stop for someone looking like that in the early hours of the morning? My dressing gown could be mistaken for a mac, in the dark anyway, if I pull it round me tight.

I just need to catch my breath. I'm taking huge great gulps as I run. I'm trying to breathe in time with my strides. But it's too much. Way too much for me. I'm not used to this. Not used to this at all. I'm 39. I've looked after myself as best I can. But I've not run like this for years. I've never run for my life before.

Three miles to go, I'd guess. Three miles to the big road. I'll flag down a lorry on the way to Nottingham. Get into town before the roadblocks go up. I can disappear into the clubs in Nottingham. Get myself cleaned up. Hack this gingery fluff off my face, sort myself out. Get myself tidy. Then go down to Suffolk to get William.

Easy.

Just got to reach that big road first.

Have to keep running. Must be 12.20 now . . .

12.40?

Got to keep moving, slow as I am.

12.50?

I've made it. At last.

I've done it.

I'm out of the woods.

I'm now in a ditch. It's okay, though. It isn't as bad as it sounds. It's clean and dry and full of bracken. I could sleep here if I had to. I can't, though. No time. Got to get away. Just need to get my breath back.

Just a moment, that's all.

Give me a minute or two, that's what I need.

The ditch is in a lay-by by the side of the big road. I'm well placed to hitch a lift. I just need to get my breath.

I'm alright now. I'm sitting up. In the ditch.

Getting myself ready to go.

I'm just taking a minute or two to compose myself.

I can see out of the ditch and up along the road, both ways. It's quiet at this time of night. Just a few cars racing by now and then. Boy racers coming back from the clubs, I'd guess. No coppers yet. No flashing lights or wailing sirens, like I'd expected. I duck down whenever a car comes by, though. Just in case.

You can't be too careful.

And I'm that, alright.

Dead careful.

Christ almighty, a car's signalling that it's pulling into my lay-by. And it looks like a police car by the shape of it. Jesus Christ. They can't have seen me, can they? I duck down. Daren't be seen. If they've not seen me, I'll be okay.

I hold my breath and wait.

Trapped, I am. I can't move. Carpet slippers, see? I'd never outrun two fit young coppers. Not in these. The slippers. You can't run in them, not really. Not properly anyway. I've tried. You can shuffle well enough. And I even got to do some longish strides after a while. But you can't proper sprint. So I've just got to hold tight and hope I'm mistaken.

The car rolls into the lay-by. Level with me, then goes slowly by and stops. It's just above me, to my left. I'm about level with the back wheels I guess.

I crouch down, pressing myself against the side of the ditch so I won't be seen. I can hear myself breathing, though. In and out. In and out. In and fucking out. Never mind the cars. All I can hear is my lungs pumping back and forth like great big bellows. Thumping in my ears, they are. Louder and louder. I can't stop them.

Is it the police? I can't tell. I daren't look up. I can't be caught like this. Bent double in a ditch in my dressing gown and stupid paisley slippers. I can't be caught so soon, so easily.

There's no traffic going by now. I can hear the car engine and it's still running. Maybe they're checking a map. Directions to the big house? A roadblock, perhaps. Wouldn't set it up here, though, would they? In the middle of a road?

God help me, they've turned the engine off. It's silent now. Totally quiet except for my breathing. I'm doing that through my nose. It's less noisy than my mouth. But I can't get enough air this way. I have to keep taking in these great long breaths. Gasping and wheezing I am. They're sure to hear me.

A door's opening. Sounds like it's on my side. The passenger side. Coppers? They'd both get out surely. Especially if they'd seen me. Maybe they've been told to search ditches. They're taking it in turns?

I don't know what's happening.

I don't know what to do.

I'm waiting. Just waiting endlessly.

Well I can tell you this - it's a man who's got out.

Yes, a man for certain.

A dirty man who is now relieving himself in the ditch up and away a little to my left.

He went towards the front of the car to do it, thank God, not towards me. I crouch down further. I don't think he can see me. Dirty bastard can't even be shielding himself. Anyone driving by could see him for sure. Must have been on the piss all night. Not an on-duty copper then. He must be a clubber.

Is this my chance? Can I get into the car before he's finished? He got out of the passenger side for certain. Cars are going from my right to my left. That means there's a driver? A girlfriend? Another man? A girlfriend, I'd say. If it were another man, he'd get out for a piss too. It's the pack instinct.

I reckon there's just the two of them. Him pissing in the ditch, her waiting in the car, tut-tutting over her watch. If I'm fast, I can get out of here. Jump up suddenly beside him. He'll turn, all startled like, and I'll just nudge him, that's all. Nothing heavy. Nothing violent or dangerous. I'm not like that, not really, no matter what they said about me in the papers. But you know that already, don't you? I'm sure I told you. Sometimes I can't remember things, small things anyway. It gets fuzzy.

Just a little push. He'll stumble back and fall in the ditch. That'll give me a few seconds. I'll pull open the passenger door. I don't think it's even been shut. I'll get in the car next to her. I'll smile warmly. They say I've a wonderful smile. Let her know I'm friendly. Normal. Then ask her to drive me to Nottingham.

Easy.

Should I wait until he's back in the car? That would be better, I think. More normal. I could knock on the window. He'll jump, surprised. But I'll smile. One of my big reassuring smiles. Like I give the doctors back at the big house when they do the annual review. It was one of my smiles that got me out of the big house and into the annexe last time round.

The pisser will see I'm respectable. I've got a kind face, after all. I was told that once too, years ago. By a woman. And I can pull the dressing gown round me. I did have a cord for it, with tassels, but I left that behind in the annexe corridor. Did I say? It doesn't matter – I can simply hold the dressing gown tight. They'll think I'm in a mac. That my car's broken down.

"Excuse me," I'll say, all nice and polite. "Can you take me into Nottingham? My car's packed up." I could make out I've walked from the last lay-by. That would explain why I'm sweaty.

But what if they're stopped at a roadblock? And they've put child locks on the door. And I'm sitting there in my dressing gown and slippers? I'm done for, aren't I?

They'd remember me anyway, wouldn't they? Even if there weren't any roadblocks. I'll be in the papers again for sure tomorrow, or the day after.

They'll tell the police they took me to Nottingham. That gives the coppers a lead. Can't have that, can I? But I'd be long gone from Nottingham by then though, wouldn't I? Probably into Suffolk and away with little William.

What do I do?

Well, what the fuck should I do?

What would you do?

He's stopped, the dirty pisser. He's zipped himself up. Must be going back to the car.

I've got to decide. Do something now. Got to take a chance. Ask for a lift. Hope they don't think anything's odd.

He's in the car, shutting the door.

I've got to move.

Have to do it now.

I stand up and haul myself over the edge of the ditch. Roll into the lay-by. She's started the engine. I can do this if I'm quick. Bang on the window and shout "Excuse me". Got to be fast, mind. She's signalling and the car's moving, pulling out now. It's my last chance.

I'm up and running alongside the car, level with the back window. I bang on it with my fist. Harder than I mean to. He turns. I can see his face. He looks shocked, scared even. He's saying something, his face twisting in fear. Shouting at her. The car's away, accelerating fast.

He sits there, not moving, just staring back at me. Then he turns, as if coming awake, towards her. She looks to be passing something to him. And then it strikes me what she'd have been doing while he was having his piss. She'd have been sitting there, playing with her mobile phone.

Now she's passing it to him and screaming at him to call 999 . . .

12.57ᴀᴍ SATURDAY 31 OCTOBER

"We should've stayed the night in that Travelodge once we hit the traffic," snapped the old man, dragging a suitcase up the path to the cottage. "I'm too old for these late nights . . . it's early morning already." He sighed.

"Shh, you'll wake the Simmons," hushed the old woman,

following close behind. "We could have come up this afternoon if it wasn't for your silly bowls game. And even then, we'd have been here by 10.00 if it hadn't been for that pile-up and your so-called short cut for goodness knows how many miles."

"We shouldn't even have come here this evening in the first…" The old man stepped back as he opened the front door, "Oh, it smells … we can't go to sleep with it like this. Why couldn't we just have come up in the morning like everyone else … like other people?" His voice rose again in irritation.

The old woman pushed by him, turning on a light, "Because if we don't come and give it a clean-through, no one will and we'll have to spend all weekend with the place as a pig sty. She won't do any cleaning, she'll just spend all the time fawning over the child."

"Don't start on that again, he's a sweet little thing."

"Sweet little thing," the woman snorted derisively, moving from room to room turning on the lights. "It's all well and good when it's little. And … and the sister was a drug addict and the husband, well … how do you think it'll turn out when it's older?"

"It? He's a … it's not his fault … and he's being brought up properly – doesn't want for anything." The old man stood there defiantly, blinking in the light. "It's not his fault, is it? And she was on anti-depressants, not drug-drugs."

"She wasn't right in the head, that's for certain. Richard will do his best for the child, we know that, but they should have adopted properly, through the channels, not taken her sister's leftover. They're just asking for trouble."

The old woman opened kitchen cupboards, pulling out various cleaning items. "Go and get the hoover from upstairs and run it round the bedroom while I clean the bathroom and I'll get the bedroom wiped over and we can get to bed. We'll do the rest in the morning before they arrive, show her how to keep a place clean and tidy."

He sighed again and made for the stairs. "This is going to be a hell of a weekend," he muttered, just loud enough for her to hear.

1.12AM SATURDAY 31 OCTOBER

I've been heading towards Nottingham for about 20 minutes or so now. Nice and quiet. No fuss, no bother.

The traffic's eased off. Time of night, see? I'd guess it was really busy early on.

I'm keeping close to the side of the road. Just in case the dirty pisser has phoned the police. They won't know which way I've gone, though, and I can slip out of sight if need be. Of course, I duck off whenever I see a car's lights in the distance. They come by very fast in places. Might be the coppers, might not. I can't take any chances, though, can I?

Actually, if I'm honest with you, I'm not really worried that the filthy bastard saw me. In fact, I'm not worried at all. Not really.

But it's best to be careful, see? That's what I am, you know. Calm and careful. But you know that by now, don't you? Of course you do.

I reckon, thinking about it a little more, that they'll just assume I was a down-and-out. Probably won't report it. No harm done. I only banged on the window, after all. And that was only because I was desperate to get a lift. No crime in that, is there? No crime at all. They'll have forgotten all about it in a few minutes, mark my words.

All I've got to do is stay calm and keep walking.

Nice and steady, nice and cool. That's me.

Let's just keep everything in proportion and see what happens.

A few minutes more and I walk over a hill and look down at what's in front of me. Ahead, at the side of the road, I can see an old Peugeot. Broken down, I'd guess.

As I get closer I can see from the plate that it's five or six years old. Not that old, really. It's empty. Abandoned? No one's in sight, that's for certain.

I stand still and listen. All quiet. No one around. Not been here long, I reckon. It's not been stripped or torched yet. Maybe too far out of Nottingham for the joyriders to get it.

No 'Police Aware' sign either.

I scout round, trying each door handle in turn. Might have some money in there. Some loose change in the ashtray, kept for parking. I'll need money soon. I've nothing on me. I'll need clothes as well, although I'd be lucky to find anything in here. Not unless it's a salesman's car, with a change of clothes packed away in a neat little hold-all in the boot.

I try the boot. No luck. That's locked too.

I could force my way in if I had something to use as a lever. But I've nothing like that on me. And maybe there'd be some sort of alarm on it anyway. Guess that wouldn't make much difference as there's no one within hearing distance, but you never know. If a cop car came over the hill at that precise moment, I'd be fucked, wouldn't I? Alarm flashing on and off and wailing away. Could hardly miss that, could they?

And then I suddenly hear it climbing up the hill from behind me, the driver changing down and clunking heavily though his gears. A lorry. Must be on its way to Nottingham.

I'd be safe in that, I'm sure. I'm on a roll, you know. Lady Luck is on my side. She most certainly is.

I'll be in Nottingham in 20 minutes. High up and safe, the police cars (if there are any) far down below. Maybe even going the other way if that dirty pisser has reported me.

I step out, throw up my arms and wave frantically. He blasts the horn once and then twice. What's that mean? Two blasts. Fuck off? I stop waving and step back. Is he stopping? For a second or two, I'm not sure. Then I hear the great whoosh of the brakes as the lorry starts to slow. It comes to a halt with the cabin door just up above me.

I reach for the handle, pulling the door open. I put my left foot on the step and lift myself up so I can see into the cabin. The driver looks across at me. Blank-faced – no welcoming smile, but no scowl neither. He's a big man, heavy-set. Not fat, just solid. 6' 2", I'd guess. Dark hair cut short. Thick stubble, all peppery. Trucker's uniform of checked shirt and jeans. He looks tired, worn out.

"Are you going to Nottingham?" I ask. "The car's packed up. I'm supposed to be picking up my daughter from the Roxy."

He nods, beckons me in with a movement of his head.

I sit, reaching for the seatbelt and pulling it around me. The lorry driver turns from me, checking his mirrors as the brakes whoosh again and the lorry pulls slowly away.

Silence.

Absolute silence.

Total fucking silence.

Should I have said the Roxy? It sounded stupid as I said it. But it was the first name that came into my head. And straight out through my big fat mouth. I'd no time to rehearse, see?

Is there a club in Nottingham called the Roxy? I've no idea. Do they even call clubs the Roxy these days? Did they ever? I don't think so. Not in Nottingham anyhow. America maybe. The Deep South.

Would he realise, though? That there's no Roxy. No club. No daughter. No concerned father sitting next to him in a dressing gown and stupid fucking slippers.

"Are you from Nottingham?" I say at last.

He sits quiet for a moment, concentrating on the road ahead. I'm not sure he heard me. Should I say it again? Maybe I didn't say it loud enough. Maybe I'm mumbling.

Does he think I'm mad, just talking to myself? A madman, muttering and twitching like those stupid fuckers back in the annexe.

Then he shakes his head, says something in reply. I don't catch all of it. Guess he's not from Nottingham by the headshake. That he's telling me where he's from. Hessle-something? Up North by the accent. I can't place it. Maybe the North-East. Doesn't matter. He doesn't know the Nottingham clubs. Doesn't realise there's no Roxy.

It's silent again. And dark outside. The road through the trees half-lit by far-apart lights. It dips and weaves up and down so we can see some distance ahead.

I feel I should say something. Wouldn't you? Just to keep the conversation moving. Make it all seem natural. I'm not good at niceties, though. That's what comes from being in the annexe with Ainsley and Sprake sitting there twitching and jerking and pulling at themselves all day long. There's no polite conversation there, I can tell you. It's all grunts and moans and sudden cries.

"Do you have the time?" I ask finally.

He nods towards the front of the cabin. I'd not noticed. A couple of daily papers. A handful of sweets and wrappers. A small clock with illuminated hands. Says it's 1.31am. It's taken me longer than expected to get this far. Two hours? Must have been in that ditch longer than I thought. Walked farther too. No police cars now then. No roadblocks. They must have thought I'd gone the other way towards the M1.

Mugs.

"My daughter's missed the last bus ... I've got to pick her up." I can't think of a girl's name. What are 17-year-old girls called now? Stupid American names they have these days. Britney. And made-up ones. Kay-Leigh and Chavney. Tabitha Rainbow Fucking Trout.

What if he asks her name? What if he turns and says, "Oh yes, and what's your daughter called then?" Friendly like, not suspicious yet. What would I say?

Kelly. The name just came to me.

Just like that.

It simply popped into my head.

That Fat-Arsed Eileen has three daughters. One's Kelly or Kelly-Marie? Kylie? I don't know. I'll stick with Kelly. Easy to remember.

"Kelly," I say, nodding. "My daughter, Kelly. Got me out of bed, see?" I move my legs out from underneath me. Show him my slippers. Better to make a joke of them really. He looks down and smiles.

"You must have been in a hurry," he replies, "I'd have got dressed. At least put shoes on."

He thinks it's odd. Out of the ordinary. That I should be wearing slippers. Dressing gown's okay. That's normal. But slippers? Slippers are odd. Would anyone wear slippers to drive a car?

"I couldn't find my shoes. I drive easier in these anyway. Bad toes," I say, thinking fast.

Does that sound believable? Can you even drive with bad toes? I don't know. What are 'bad toes' anyway? I hope he doesn't ask me anything about my feet. Hope he doesn't have corns and stuff he wants to talk about. I don't want a conversation about cutting off bunions, that's for fucking sure.

Will he notice I've no keys? I'd have keys, wouldn't I, if I'd broken down? They'd be in my dressing-gown pocket. I'd have my hand on them now. Probably jangling them. And I'd maybe whistle too. They do that, don't they? People. Men, really. They jangle keys and whistle at the same time. Smith used to do that. I don't know why. I never have.

And I said she'd missed the last bus. But it's gone 1.30. What time's a last bus round these parts? 11.30? So how come I'm driving to pick her up two hours later. Has he noticed that too?

I'm giving myself away at every turn.

He coughs. Clears his throat. I think he's going to spit. Instead he half turns his head towards me and says, "How far you going? I'm turning back onto the M1 before Nottingham. I've just been and done a private drop-off."

I look at him, expecting a nod and a wink. Say no more. On the fiddle. A bit of cash on the side. But he doesn't add anything to it and I don't really know what to say next. I would have winked if he had looked at me, but he didn't.

"That's fine," I reply. "I can walk the last bit." I don't know how far the last bit is. A mile? Five? Does that sound strange? I'll walk the last five miles? He's not noticed anything, though. I'm sure of it. He's too tired, too worn out. Probably doesn't know or care anyway. I'm just someone to pass a few minutes with at the end of an eight-hour drive.

"You'll get some queer looks dressed like that. I'll take you in as far as I can go."

A kindness, a thoughtful gesture. He didn't have to offer. I'm touched. Really I am. Small kindnesses are rare. I'm not used to them. Not where I've come from. Not from Spink and her cronies, that's for sure. No small kindnesses at the annexe and certainly not in the big house. Quite the opposite, in fact.

"There's another of them," he says suddenly. I lean forward and see a police car overtaking, pulling in front and accelerating away. No flashing lights, but it's going at speed towards Nottingham.

"That must be the fifth that's gone by me in the past 20 minutes. Something's happening in Nottingham. They're all going that way."

And then we see it in the distance. Just as we come over a hill following the police car.

A crossroads down by the River Trent. Two police cars – one to the left and the other to the right of this side of the road. Flashing lights. They're stopping cars. It's a roadblock. Just like I knew there would be. CID has acted pretty fast.

I said, didn't I?

I fucking well told you.

Why don't you just listen?

I can see two cars pulled into a queue on this side of the road. Looks like a Mini and some sort of estate. Coppers all around them. The police car in front of us moving towards them. We're following behind, moving down. It's all half a mile away. A minute or so from being caught. I'll end up back inside. They'll lock me up good and proper this time. In prison. I'll never get a second chance to get away.

I've got to be quick. We've got woodlands to the left, opening up to scrubland down to the river, not so very far away. All wide-open scrubland as far as I can see to the right; no chance that way.

Have to act fast.

Now.

Do it right now.

"Stop," I shout, turning to the lorry driver. I'm pleading, I know I am. I can hear it in my voice. "Stop, please. Pull over here. I've been drinking. Before I came out. They're after me. The police. Quickly, stop here. Before they see."

He half turns. Looks at me. Checks me over.

The dressing gown.

The stupid paisley slippers.

He looks at my face. Can see I'm desperate. Knows I'm lying. He thinks for a moment. The lorry keeps moving. Another second. One more long one. Another timeless, everlasting second.

The lorry moves closer still.

Another few seconds and it'll be too late.

"Please..." I say again, and I'm really begging now.

And then I hear the whoosh of the brakes. He's going to stop. Let me out. Thank Christ. He's giving me a chance to get away.

The lorry shudders, slowly shaking itself down, and finally stops. I look ahead down the hill. I can see the coppers by the two cars in the queue. I can't see any of them looking up this way.

I turn to the lorry driver, smile, tell him I'm drunk, a little bit tipsy. My voice cracks, I'm talking nonsense. He looks at me, disbelieving. Then says something I don't catch. Something about not owing them any favours. What's he mean? The coppers? Has he been in prison? Maybe. I've no time to ask.

I nod my thanks. Open the door, jump down. I move quickly into the woods. The whoosh of the brakes signals the lorry is moving away again. It's going towards the roadblock – without me.

What now?

I wait in the woods, looking at the crossroads. I have a clear view from here. I can see three cop cars in all, including the one in front of the lorry. The Mini has been waved on its way. There are two coppers now, talking to the driver of the second car.

Another copper is peering through the windows. There may be another copper in one of the cop cars. Sitting by the radio, I guess. Makes four in all. Plus two more in the cop car that's just arrived? That makes six. The estate driver gets out, opening the back of the car. They're thorough, I'll give them that. Spink must have laid it on real thick about me. Then again, me leaving like I did would have been enough to get the roadblocks up.

Should I run? Hold my breath and start running like I did when I got out of the annexe? In carpet slippers? I don't know what to do. The coppers will get to the lorry driver in a minute. All he has to do is tell them about me. They'll come racing up the hill in their cars. Stopping, spreading out, searching these woods.

They'll find me, won't they? Easily. I'm fucked if he says anything, well and truly.

Let me think. Just let me gather my thoughts.

All I need is a moment. A chance to work out a plan.

Just give me a fucking minute, why won't you?

Will he say anything, though? The lorry driver? He mumbled something about not owing them any favours. If he doesn't like the coppers, he'll stay quiet. Won't want to get involved anyway, will he? He's not going to want to go to the copshop, give statements, shit like that.

Even if he says something, they've no dogs, have they? Not that I can see. Not yet anyhow. And they'll expect me to be running. They'll reckon I'll be half a mile away by now. Sprinting like crazy in the opposite direction. Not standing here 100 yards from where I got out of the lorry.

The estate's been waved on its way. So has the cop car, once the fourth copper had come across from one of the parked cop cars for a bit of yakety-yak. Comparing notes, yawning, saying what a waste of time all of this is. I watch as the cop car that's been waved on drives off to repeat the 'nothing happening' routine at the next roadblock down the road. There are now four coppers left standing there together, talking to each other.

One beckons the lorry forward. Two of the coppers move to the lorry. They're out of sight, on the other side. Round by the driver's door. Talking to the driver. The third copper is walking around the lorry. I can see him bending, looking underneath. He disappears out of sight too. Moving towards the driver. The fourth copper stands there looking up the hill, seeing if any other cars are coming down towards them.

It's deathly quiet.

I reckon the three other coppers are round by the driver's window, quizzing him, asking him if he's seen anyone walking, maybe thumbing a ride. Has sir stopped for anyone? Given someone a lift? That's what they'd be asking. And he'd just shake his head. No, no, he's not seen anyone.

What a pile of shit.

A complete and utter waste of time and that's a fact.

Let's be on our way, please.

I yawn as the three coppers reappear from round the front of the lorry. They're going back to speak to the fourth copper, who's obviously in charge. I ignore them, looking back towards the lorry, which is about to pull away and continue on its journey. Thank Christ he didn't say anything. He'll be gone any moment, and then I reckon these coppers will pack up and piss off. I can settle down in these woods for an hour or two's shut-eye and be on my way again before dawn.

Perfect.

Absolutely perfect.

Nice and easy, this is.

I glance back at the coppers. They're all in a huddle, all talking among themselves. They're in a circle, three coppers with their backs to me. They're lighting up, having a quick fag before they go home. There's a big fucker in the middle with his back towards me. I reckon he may be some plain-clothes CID wanker from one of the cars bossing these bobbies about, telling them what to do. I can see him moving, looks like he's lighting up each of their fags in turn. He stops, steps back and moves to the side.

And I realise what's really happening.

I see it's the lorry driver standing in the middle of the circle of coppers. I watch him shaking and nodding his head, his hands rising and falling as if to emphasise what he's saying. And then he lifts his right arm up. I expect all of the coppers to stand there listening to him. But they don't. One by one, they turn, each of them now looking up the hill towards me. And the lorry driver jabs out the index finger of his right hand. He looks up and it's as if, in that instant, he can see and is pointing straight at me ...

1.36AM SATURDAY 31 OCTOBER

The little boy lay in bed, watching the light on the ceiling. He had been woken by the sound of the toilet being flushed in the bathroom.

Drowsy at first, he had struggled up and called out faintly, "Mama ... Drink?" but no one heard him or came to his door like they sometimes did when he heard them moving about at night.

He called again, "Drink ... please?" and then lay back down and thought for a moment or two about getting up to go to the bathroom himself.

But the light had caught his attention. It was a strong light that shone in through the crack in the curtains from the street outside his bedroom window. It puzzled the little boy, the light, because he had not noticed it before.

His favourite film, right now at least, was *Mars Needs Moms* – he had a DVD he carried round under his arm during the day, constantly looking at the cover. It excited him in a way. It frightened him a little too, although he would never say that to his mama or papa. The light on his bedroom ceiling was exactly the same, or so he suddenly thought, as the one from the Martian spaceship on the front of the DVD.

He licked his lips, which felt cracked and dry, and turned his head slowly towards the curtains. The light stayed the same, strong and unwavering. It did not shake nor move about like papa's torch when they sometimes went outside to look at the stars at night.

The little boy knew, he just knew, that this was the spaceship from Mars outside his house.

"Go away," he said out loud, using the same firm voice his mama used when the big slobbery dog next door jumped up to lick his face.

He knew it had come for his mama. The scary spaceship with the beam of light. He knew he needed to get up. Go and find her. Tell the Martians to leave his mama alone.

Very slowly, he turned his head away from the window and looked at his door, open just a crack so he could see the dim but reassuring light on the landing.

It might be dark, pitch black, beyond that.

But he was going to have to go to his mama. He had to save her. He listened carefully for the sound of the Martians moving across the landing towards his mama's bedroom.

He was sure he could hear the slow but steady steps of the Martians outside his room.

He got up quietly out of bed and padded in his bare feet over to the chair in the corner.

He looked at his Batman costume, the one he wore whenever he played action heroes.

He pulled down his pyjama bottoms and stepped out of them.

He lifted up his top as best he could, over and above his head. Stumbling back and losing his balance, he fell to the floor with a thud.

He did not cry.

He was a brave little boy.

Getting to his feet, he pulled off his pyjama top and reached for his Batman costume.

He did not hesitate.

He did not falter.

He was in his suit and he was going to save his mama.

He shouted "G'onim-oo-ooo" at the top of his voice as he ran out onto the landing.

1.37AM SATURDAY 31 OCTOBER

Everything freezes for 10 to 20 seconds. The coppers stand and stare up the hill towards me. Not one of them moves. They all stand perfectly still. Like they're waiting for something to happen. Like I'm going to step out and wave at them. Maybe I'll set off some fireworks to show them where I am.

Then all hell breaks out. It's like watching the Keystone Cops. Two of the coppers turn and run into each other. Another looks like he's shouting at the lorry driver. The fourth copper stands staring at the one who's shouting.

The fourth copper suddenly takes charge. He steps back from the one who's shouting, and waves his hands for silence. Next, he's gesturing and pointing, stabbing a finger towards the two other coppers. I see him keep turning his head towards the lorry driver. Must be asking questions. I see the lorry driver nodding and shaking his head again, the oh-so-anxious-to-please bastard.

The two coppers are running towards their cop car. Doors slamming. I hear the engine roar as the car skids, turning round by the crossroads and racing back up the hill towards me.

I see the car coming, swerving behind the lorry and back on to the right side of the road again. Out of sight for a moment, then back again, accelerating up the hill. I lose sight of it once more behind the trees lining the road.

The trees hide the car from me.

The trees shelter me from them too, of course.

Little old me sitting here in my tree.

I'm clever. I told you, didn't I? No use running when that lorry driver gave the game away. They all looked up, the coppers. Stood there waiting. What did they expect to happen? Me to break cover and start running? No way. They'd be on to me within minutes, that's for sure.

I just stepped back behind this tree and lifted myself up into its branches.

Easy. Took seconds, that's all.

The cop car roars up, going faster and faster. Level with me now, and then away, moving 100, 200, 500 yards off and up the hill. I can't see it any more. But I hear it screech to a halt. It's some way up on the road behind me. I can't tell how far. Hard to judge.

Got to think quickly.

Act fast.

Do I stay or make a break for it?

I have to do something. There are two coppers coming up towards me on foot from below. There are two coppers now out of their cop car high above me, coming down towards me.

Piggy in the middle, that's me.

What do I do? You tell me.

Stay or go? Hurry.

To one side, it's scrubland – I'd be seen as soon as I broke cover from the trees. To the other, downwards, I can see the dark swirl of the River Trent.

The Trent – is that my best chance to get away? It has to be. Maybe my only chance.

The copper in charge and the other copper will be up into the woods in a minute or two. Moving slowly, searching. How long will it be before the other coppers arrive? Once that busybody copper in charge has radioed everything back to CID, they'll be drafting in cop cars from all around to come here.

So more coppers?

And dogs?

Have they already called for dogs?

If they bring the dogs, I'm done for. I'll never outrun them. They'll take the dogs to the lorry. Let them get the scent of me.

Then they'll bring the dogs up the hill. Barking, snarling, straining to be set free. To hunt me down. They'd be let loose when they picked up my scent again by the side of the road. Just where that bastard lorry driver let me out.

I'd stand no chance. They'd be on me in less than a minute. Scratching, tearing at my clothes, ripping them to shreds. They'd probably kill me if they got my throat. If the coppers didn't stop them. And they wouldn't, would they? They'd laugh and jeer and urge the dogs on. Because I'd led them a merry dance. Made them look like fools.

The river's my only option. If I get in the river, the dogs won't be able to track me. The river will wash off my scent. Dogs can't follow a scent through water. The coppers won't know where I've gone. To Nottingham? Towards Newark? Out towards Grantham? Good as lost me again then, haven't they?

All I've got to do is climb down from this tree. Keep my eyes on the crossroads, the road to my right, and listen out for the coppers. I'll move down to the edge of the woods close to the river. I've got to do it; got to take that chance.

Sitting upright, I slide my knees down. Stretch my legs out either side of a branch. My legs feel stiff. My bones ache. It's the tablets, see? I said before, didn't I? Yes, I told you that, remember? I've stopped taking them but they are still in my system. They should wear off in a day or two, though. I'll feel better then, much better, just you wait and see. I'll think straighter. Clearer too.

I pause.

Wait.

Listen.

I can't hear anything. The coppers are not close enough for me to hear a sound. I've got to go before I do.

I turn, lift my left leg over the branch. Slowly turn again and lower myself down to the next one. Hold tight, slide and sit on it. Hold on. Listen again. Still no noise.

Nothing. I turn and slip down once more, holding on to the branch. Lower my body. Not quite touching the ground. I look down. Only three or four feet. I drop, land and lose my balance. Fall forward onto my knees, my weight pulling me over.

Have I been heard?

I wait. Not breathing.

Still no sound.

It's almost as though I'm out on my own. It's dark down here, but I can still see some moonlight through the branches.

I move quickly. Between the trees. I'm making a noise. Slippers crunching on the undergrowth. Like running on gravel. No one nearby to hear though, so I just keep going.

I've got to get to the edge of the woods. Pause. Look out across to the crossroads and the river. Pause again.

I'll run as fast as I can. Down the hill, across the open scrubland. Over and down and into the river.

The lorry driver. He'll be in the cop car. He'll see me. He'll lean forward from the back seat. All he has to do is slam his palm down on the car horn. He'll hold it there. All the cops will hear. They'll see me before I can dive in. Could I still escape? No, too tired, too exhausted. I've been going so long now. Far too long. I'm near the end, I'll tell you that. I'm at the end of my rope already.

I move along the trees marking a line between the woods and the scrubland. Farther and farther to my left I move, as fast and as far as I can. I can't go too far. It looks marshy way over to my left. If I go much further, I could get stuck in it. I'm still under cover and well away from the crossroads, the road and the lorry - and the cop car with the lorry driver in it.

What I've got to do is simple. Dead simple. I've got to find some undergrowth that stretches down from the woods to the river. Somewhere I can crawl and keep crawling. Staying low, the lorry driver won't see me. He might not be watching anyway. Or maybe he'll be looking the other way. It's dark, of course. And I'll be low, flat as I can and crawling on my belly.

Is this far enough?

Here?

I can make out the lorry driver in the car, just.

Or am I imagining it? It's hard to tell from this distance. I can't see which way he's looking. I can't really make him out much at all. Surely he can't see me, though. And the coppers? Can they see me? Not yet. But they could when I break cover. Unless I keep low and crawl fast.

And then I hear it. In the distance. Behind me. From the road. Farther up, back from the way we came in on the lorry. Faint now. But becoming louder.

It's not an 'it', of course. It's a 'them'. I can hear them now, ever so clear they are. And it's not the coppers' police car sirens either.

Dogs is what it is.

Just like I fucking told you.

Fucking listen for once, why don't you?

The four coppers must have guessed I'd run back when I jumped from the lorry. Away from them at the crossroads. Back up the way we came. So they'd radioed CID for more coppers and dogs. To go two, three miles back up, come down and flush me out.

The coppers would come up from the crossroads. Moving up the hill. They'd keep driving me backwards, towards the new coppers and dogs. I'd be trapped in the middle, sure to be caught.

I've got to go now.

Right now.

I'm at the edge of the trees and about as far away as I can get without going onto the marshland. There's just 800 yards of scrub in front of me to crawl across and I'm at the river and away.

300 yards to freedom.

I drop to my knees. Lie down. Start crawling, moving forward as quickly as I can.

Dogs coming closer. Still some way away. But getting nearer. How far? How long have I got?

I've got to keep crawling. There's no noise from the cop car. Can the lorry driver see me? I must keep low.

The dogs are louder now. They're pulling on their leashes, eager to be released.

I look up.

200 yards?

No more, surely.

Have the dogs been let loose? They sound very loud. And spread out, too. They're all behind me and getting closer by the second. Have the dogs got my scent already?

Maybe they're already running free. They'll be here in minutes – maybe less than that.

Just keep going. Almost there now. Not far.

100 yards?

50?

Getting closer every second.

There's still no sound from the cop car. I want to look. Check he can't see me. I daren't, though. There's no time. The dogs are in the woods now. Their barking sounds different. Echoing almost. How soon before they're out and coming down behind me?

Less than a minute, I'd guess.

60 seconds is all I've got at most.

These clothes don't help. Dressing gown and slippers. I wish I could shake myself free of them.

I'm almost there. I lie still for two or three seconds. I can't wait.

Look left. Nothing.

Look right. All clear.

Still no noise from the cop car.

But the dogs are close now, very close. They're about to come racing out of the woods. They're almost on me.

I've got to break cover. Got to do it now.

I lift myself up, half crouching, half running. It seems incredibly far. I'm waiting for the sound of the cop car horn any moment.

Any second now.

Here it comes.

That terrible sound.

I've done it. I've fucking well done it. I'm on the bank of the river, slipping and sliding downwards into the water's edge. My feet are in the water. It's black and filthy. Stinks too.

I don't care.

I've made it.

The dogs are now in the open. Out of the woods, and spreading across. I can't tell, for sure. I'm gasping for breath as I drop into the water, the dressing gown billowing up around me.

The cold hits me; I gasp for breath, struggling to stand up. I pull the dressing gown tight around my waist. I'll lose it soon, though, as quickly as I can.

I drop back down and start swimming downstream and away.

I'm not sure where.

I keep close to the river's edge by the trees.

I'm away.

Free.

They'll not catch me now. Not tonight anyway. Even if they track me to the river, I'll be downstream and gone. They won't know which way I've swum. Up, down or across. But what next?

I'm in a freezing-cold river.

I'm in my dressing gown and slippers.

I'm cold and I'm wet and I'm exhausted.

I'm 150 fucking miles from Aldeburgh and my little William.

I've no money.

No proper clothes.

And I'll be all over the news tomorrow. Not just the press, TV too. The BBC, all of that.

So you tell me – what the fuck do I do next?

6.55AM SATURDAY 31 OCTOBER

"Can you really face this over and over this weekend . . . in front of your mother?" said the young woman, struggling to keep the little boy from wriggling out from beneath her legs and away. "Help me, why don't you?"

The young man stepped forward, "William John," he said sharply, using the boy's full names, "stop it. Lie still and behave yourself."

The boy took no notice. When he was fully awake, as he was now, he would always try just as hard as he could to avoid the injections. His legs and tummy were covered in bruises.

He knew he was being naughty.

He did not want to be.

But the injections hurt and made him feel sick.

He always hoped, if he wriggled hard for long enough, that his mama and papa might give up and leave him alone. But they never had. Not yet anyway.

His papa would say it was good for him.

To have the injections.

The little boy did not understand why.

The man pressed down on the boy's arms, which just made him twist his head more. He banged it against the floor, which stunned him for a moment, his large blue eyes staring up at the two adults now pinning him down.

"If your mother could see us now ... she probably will see us ... what will she say?" said the woman, trying to move the needle towards the top of the boy's leg without him seeing it. "I h-a-t-e this, really, it's too much."

As the man loosened his grip, the boy pushed at the needle, as he always did with his mama, knocking it away as it scratched his skin.

"Will," she shouted, "you need to let me do this, you need to be still."

Their eyes locked, hers full of anger, his close to tears.

He tried to smile at his mama.

Sometimes that would make her happy.

He liked to see his mama laugh.

"It'll be okay," said the man, suddenly sweeping the woman and the boy into his arms and hugging them clumsily. "Let's calm down and watch some cartoons for a while. Have some Weetabix. Do it after that. We have to do this together. That's all."

"There's just so much, all the time. It's non-stop."

"It'll get better ... as he gets older. He should be able to do some of it himself."

The boy smiled contentedly.

He liked it when they all hugged like this.

It made him happy.

7.42AM SATURDAY 31 OCTOBER

No need to worry about me.

Everything is fine.

All is well and good, thank you.

I'm downstream, did I say? Not as far as I'd have liked, but far enough away. I reckon I'm safe now. It's all quiet, has been for ages actually.

I started off well enough and the sounds of the dogs soon faded as I kept swimming farther and farther away. I swam on for as long as I could, hearing nothing except for the occasional noise of traffic far off in the distance.

But the water's cold, so fucking cold it freezes the blood in your bones.

After no more than 10 or 15 minutes at most, I had to stop. Get out.

Later, I tried to swim again.

And again.

One more time.

But the cold comes so close to paralyzing you that you think you're going to die and have to get out.

So I walked for a bit.

And the air, a chill breeze, seemed to dry me a little.

And I walked for a while longer by the edges of the water.

I knew I could not go on much more.

Then I got lucky.

The river, twisting and turning, led me to where I am now. Hidden in a dense mass of trees and bushes by the side of the river. Opposite me, woodland stretches out as far as I can see upstream and downstream.

I'm safe – no one will penetrate through that to get to this part of the river.

Why would they want to?

Behind me, up and on the bank a dozen feet away, is a fence. Several fences as a matter of fact. I've ended up behind of one of those new housing estates in the back of beyond. Lots of little boxes. Matchbox-sized gardens. Neat and tidy fences. Fucking suburban heaven for wankers in suits.

Four houses back up to the river where I am. I guess they're part of a cul-de-sac. The owners have each put up fences to close off their gardens from each other and the river. I can sit and watch what's happening at each house through the knots and tears in the wooden fences.

No one in the houses can see me.

I sit and watch and wait to see what happens. I've got ideas, you know. A plan, actually. A little plan of action. But I've got to think it all through first. It takes time to do that even if you're a cunning devil like me.

I can't wait here for long, mind you.

It's still cold, very cold.

I'll catch my death.

I've stripped down to my T-shirt and trousers. I've wrung them out of course (I'm not stupid). First the T-shirt, then the trousers. Gave them a good shaking before putting them back on again. They feel alright, I suppose. They're quite loose on me actually. I'm not fat. And there's a breeze. Still a chilly one as a matter of fact.

I got rid of that dressing gown way back upstream. I said, didn't I? I had to. It soaked up the water, dragging me down, slowing me up. I swam to the river bank, stood up, stripped it off and bundled it deep into the undergrowth. It'll never come loose, not in a hundred years. No one will ever find that, I can tell you.

Perfect.

Just perfect.

Things are taking shape.

I'm going to have to break into one of these houses. I don't want to but I've no choice. I can't hide here for much longer. It's just too cold. Far too cold. I need clean, dry clothes for a start. And money. I can't get far without money. And food, I must have some food. I'm starving.

I'm waiting to see when the owners of one of the houses will go out. Maybe to work. Lots of people do on a Saturday. Or maybe they'll go out for the day, to the shops or a garden centre. That's what middle-class people on housing estates do for fun. I'd rather put a fork in my eye, to tell the truth.

Won't be long now.

It must be getting on for nine o'clock. Someone will leave their house empty. I'll force the back door and slip in oh-so-quietly. Out again just as smoothly. No one will ever know.

It's an offence, of course it is. Someone as smart as me knows that. But the beauty is that nobody will ever realise I've been in and out. Not if I'm clever, which I am (as you know).

They've all got patio doors, these four houses. You can get in and out of a property with those dead easy. I'll put my shoulder against the doors and push in slow but hard. They'll pop open with barely a sound, just the bolt slipping out of its casing. You get a lot of noise and damage only when you shoulder it hard and fast. Or kick it in – that's when everything cracks and breaks. That's when you get all the noise. I can't afford none of that. Shoulder it slow and it all slides open nicely for you.

I'll slip quietly upstairs. Find some nice and clean, warm and dry men's clothes tucked away at the back of a wardrobe or maybe the bottom of a drawer. Stuff that's not worn any more. Clothes that won't be missed for ages and maybe never at all.

A shave would be a smart idea, if they've got one of those disposable razors they'd never miss. I need to get all this fuzz off my face. I'm told I look ten years younger without a beard. Spink told me that when I shaved it off before. Said she wouldn't have recognised me. She smirked (like she always does), so I wasn't sure if she was taking the piss.

But I'd look different anyway. Nothing like the photo they'll put in the papers. I know the one they'll use. The one where I jerked my head away at the last second. The one with the beard. No one who sees that in the papers would notice me without that big fuzzy beard; they'd never give me a second glance.

I've got to get some food too. I'm going to find that first, I have to. I'm hungry now, really hungry. It's been hours since I ate anything. One of Spink's stews. Was it only last night? 7 o'clock. 12, 13 hours ago? It seems longer, much longer. The tablets have been wearing off, been ages since I took them. It's giving me my appetite back. I feel ravenous.

Maybe I'll find some loose change as well. Not much, not so's anyone would notice. I'll rummage in the pockets of old jackets, the backs of drawers, places like that. Perhaps they'll have a bottle of old coins by the fireplace. Full of 20p and 50p pieces. I'll take a couple of handfuls so they'll not see. Two handfuls can add up. Maybe a fiver's worth or more. Enough to get a train ticket for one or two stops from Nottingham. Once you're on the train, you can go where you want in the system, it's easy. I'll hide in the toilets if one of the inspectors comes along. Then jump off at some isolated station in Suffolk. I can hitch from there.

I'm going to go for the house to my far left, at the end of the cul-de-sac. A professional couple live there by the look of it, and are getting ready for work. Mid- to late 20s, I'd guess. No kids – not that I can see. He's about my size and build. Close to six foot, quite solid but not fat. A smoothie, with his slicked-back hair and stupid goatee beard. Like Veitch, the oily fucker. A yuppie's what they call them. Or they used to anyway. You lose touch when you've been away, so to speak.

She's a skinny little thing. Not my type at all. About five six, I'd guess. Slight build. Boyish even. Blonde hair, cropped quite short. She's in a business suit now. (She wasn't to start with, I can tell you.) Black jacket, white top, short black skirt and heels. Very nice, some would say. If you like that sort of thing. I don't. Not particularly. No, not me.

Best of all, the house is on a corner plot. Trees down one side, all along my left. A nice tall fence between this house and the next one to my right. Just one neighbour, that's all. Very nice. All quiet and peaceful.

They're in the kitchen. She's at the sink, standing over it, holding a bowl of cereal and trying to eat it. He's behind her, pressed up tight. His hands are everywhere; I can see that very clearly. She's wriggling now and smiling. Putting her arms out to keep the cereal bowl away from her, stopping it from splashing milk down her front. His hands now up and round her breasts. She's laughing and I can see her mouthing "No!" as she twists and faces him. They kiss. Seems like forever.

I feel myself stirring.

It's been a long time.

A very long time.

It's been years since I was with a woman. I lower my eyes for a moment, thinking about the wife, Katie. Mustn't think about her or any of that. Daren't. Not yet. It upsets me. A lot. Got to hold it all together.

When I look up, they've gone. I move to my left, looking through a tear in the wood to see the room to the right; the lounge, I guess. They're not there, not as far as I can see. Have they gone upstairs? Would they do it before they went to work? I don't know. Maybe.

I move again, now back to my right, so I can look through and get a better view of upstairs. The frosted bathroom window to the left, the bedroom window to the right. The curtains, which they pulled back a good hour or so ago, are still wide open.

I wait. I'm sure they've gone.

I'll give it five minutes. Just to be on the safe side.

No, they're not there. No one's there any more.

Time to move. It's been a good five minutes, maybe more. I slip sideways to my right. Peer through next door's fence. Crouching, waiting for two, three, four more minutes. No signs of life there either. The curtains, top and bottom, are still pulled closed. All still in bed. Maybe a retired couple? Could be, looking at the poxy garden with its neat, trimmed borders and stupid fucking statuettes.

I move back to my left, pulling at two or three large clumps of loose turf by the bottom of the fence. They fall away easily. Enough room to crawl under, I think.

I lie flat, slide forward. No, not enough room, no way enough.

I slide out, dig again a little deeper. Try once more.

Still not enough room for me to slide under and through. I dig deeper still, wiping my hands clean on my trousers.

I've done it. I slide under. Wriggle. The fence catches in the small of my back. I pull, hard but steady. My full weight's tugging against the fence. For a moment, I think it will crack, the noise ricocheting around the close. Waking neighbours. Faces at windows. The old couple next door at their back window, looking down, seeing me, half in, half out of the garden. What a way to get caught. Trapped under a fence, for all to see.

I pull through, the fence snapping back into place behind me. A noise, for sure, but not enough to wake anyone, or attract attention. I move quickly up the path, keeping low and close to the fence between the two properties so I'll not be seen. Six, seven, eight strides and I'm at the patio doors. I'm up against them. It's too late to back out now. I've no excuses, no good explanation if I'm seen. Up to no good for sure.

I pause.

Catch my breath.

I feel the nerves rising.

I expect one of them to come into the lounge at any moment and see me standing there. I try to think of something to say. "I've come for the rubbish," is all I can think of. There's no chance of that sounding very likely. It's a Saturday. And I'm in a tee shirt and wet trousers, for Christ's sake. Binmen don't do their rounds looking like that.

No one is there, though.

It's all quiet.

No sounds, nothing.

I gather myself, calming my nerves. It's going to be alright. Easy. I've just got to remember what I'm going to do. Slip in. Get food. Clothes. Loose change. Slip out. Gone. That's it.

I put my fingers on the handle of the patio doors, still thinking, calming myself down. It opens, the door swinging away in front of me. I stand for what seems an age. Can you believe it? Jammy devil, that's me. I won't have to force the doors and risk the noise. I can just slip in, here and now. Get what I want. And slip out, shutting the door behind me.

I step in, pulling the door slowly shut. I hear it click into place. I wait for a moment, my head cocked at an angle, just listening. Nothing to hear. No sound at all. This is going to be oh-so-easy.

I move to the kitchen. Sink to the far right by the back door. Work surfaces. All nice and shiny. Fridge freezer to my immediate right behind the half-open door. To the left, there are work surfaces full of kitchen utensils, a knife rack and fancy dried flowers. Cupboards all along above, washing machine and tumble dryer below. And for the next ten minutes, I can do whatever I want.

I'm suddenly overwhelmed by hunger. It's been so long. 12, 14 hours? I push the door to behind me and stand in front of the fridge. My stomach's straining for food. I crouch down and pull open the fridge door to see what's inside.

I reach for a pot of yoghurt, pulling back the lid. It tears, splits in two, half off, half still attached to the pot. I push the remaining foil in with the back of my thumb, yoghurt spurting up over my fingers. I laugh out loud. At this moment, I really don't care. I'll clean it up afterwards. I just dip my fingers in, scooping the yoghurt out and pawing it into my mouth.

I flip the empty pot onto the work surface. Wipe my hand on the leg of my trousers. Look back in the fridge again. I'm pushing all the low-fat and fat-free shit to one side to find something halfway decent to eat at the back. Something they won't notice is gone.

I see various plastic containers. I open one or two. They're full of some sort of fancy vegetable stuff. Who eats that? There are other things wrapped in foil. Maybe cold sausages and meats?

I see a container of that squirty cream. I like that. You couldn't have it inside, not even on a Sunday. I've missed that. I grab it. Sit down in front of the fridge. I'm going to enjoy this. I whoosh a gulp into my mouth, swallowing and gagging on the stuff. I do it again, coughing and spluttering. It's good, fucking good. I've not had this for years. I do it once more, letting my head fall back this time, spraying the cream down into my throat.

I can't stop laughing.

I'm roaring my head off.

And then I freeze.

I hear a key in the front door. It's opening. Someone's coming in and moving quickly.

I drop the canister on the floor, start rising to my feet, turning to face the kitchen door.

It all seems to happen so fast. The kitchen door slams open. Hits me full on the shoulder. I stumble against the fridge. Regain my balance. Turn round. She's there, looking up at me. Her mouth wide open in shock.

No fear.

No anger.

Just disbelief.

I hit her across the face with the back of my hand as hard as I can. Panic, not anger. I can't help it. I don't mean to. It's the survival instinct kicking in. Like it was with Smith.

She flies back against the work surfaces, the top half of her body somehow folding backwards, scattering knives from the rack and God knows what all over everywhere. Then she dips towards me, convulses and hits the floor among the clatter of knives.

She lies still. All I can hear is the sound of my own fractured breathing.

God forgive me, what I have done?

Now what?

9.00ᴀᴍ SATURDAY 31 OCTOBER

"Ignore it, Nat," the man shouted, as he reached for some of the bags piled up at the foot of the staircase, "they'll just be selling something."

The phone rang on.

He pulled open the front door, carrying the bags down the path to the car.

How much did they need to take for an overnight stay? Not this much, surely.

The man returned, dumping the unwanted contents of the car boot in the hallway.

The phone was still ringing.

"Who rings a landline these days? It'll be PPI ... or worse. There's this thing now where you hear a click and it switches you to a premium-rate number in Costa ..."

He tailed off, shaking his head as he realised she probably wasn't listening to him anyway.

The phone stopped as he picked up the last few bags and the boy's little blue bicycle and headed out the door again.

Thank goodness he'd sold the Audi; they'd never have got all of this in that.

He came back into the house, now ready and waiting to leave. He checked his pockets for his spare pair of glasses and his wallet and keys.

The phone started ringing again.

"Oh for ... don't get it, Nat, we've got to go now or we'll never get there."

He paused and then chuckled to himself, realising how quickly be became irritated whenever he was stressed.

He waited, his foot tapping, as the phone seemed to ring on forever. He wasn't sure if he wasn't now just hearing an echo in his head, it had been going for so long.

It stopped.

He hoped she hadn't picked the phone up. If it were one of her friends, it could be at least another half an hour before they left.

He waited, not sure what was happening.

She appeared at the top of the stairs, smiling sweetly at him, carrying the little boy, who put his arms out towards the man for a hug.

"I thought you'd answered it; if it'd been Lana, you'd have been on for ages."

"Number withheld. I've set up a message on the answer phone – so if it is PPI or Costa whatever, they'll be calling your mobile."

He shrugged, "Not this weekend. It's meant to be my weekend off. I've left it by the bed. I can't be doing with pointless calls from the office that can just as easily wait until Monday. I assume you've got yours anyway for emergencies?" He reached out, taking the boy from her and rubbing their noses together to make him laugh. "Come on, let's go before it starts again. They're persistent, I'll give them that."

They left, shutting the door behind them, as the phone began its ringing again.

There was a click as the message played.

And then the clear and strong voice.

"Hello, this is a message for Mr and Mrs Veitch. As a matter of urgency, please call DS Flanagan at Notts CID on ..."

9.02AM SATURDAY 31 OCTOBER

I've just got to keep my focus. Concentrate on what I'm doing and where I'm going in my nice new shiny car.

I'm driving to Suffolk. To get my little boy, William.

We're going to get away to France and start a new life together.

I have it all worked out. I've got a plan. I just need to think about that. And that alone.

God save me, what did I do? I needed dry clothes, something to eat, some loose change, that's all. I wanted to feel human for a few minutes, then be on my way without causing any trouble.

I panicked, see? I panicked, and hit her. That's all it was. I wasn't angry and I wasn't violent. Haven't been for ages. Never was, really. This was just blind panic. Instinct. I lashed out. She didn't give me a chance to think, to work things out, not even a second or two. I could have talked my way out of it if only I'd had a few moments to work out what to say.

I'd have made some excuse. I'd have thought quickly. On my feet. I'm good at that, usually. I've had tests to prove it. Psycho-something. I'd have said I thought it was my sister's house. A week off work. Got lost. Mislaid the address. Came to this close, this house, by mistake. Then I'd have smiled. That would have worked, for sure. I have such a lovely smile.

She didn't give me a chance, though, did she? Even after I'd hit her in a panic, I'd not have done anything else. I was going to go quietly even then. Just slip out the back, the way I came in. Leave her there in the kitchen. She'd have been okay. Might not even have remembered what had happened, it was all so fast.

But I hesitated. I didn't know what to do. I was trying to think what the best thing would be. Was trying to clear things up, put them away, straighten it all up.

And then she came round and went for me, didn't she? Mad she was, real mad. Even then it wasn't too late, not really. I could have explained and spun her a story. Said something that would have sorted it. Made it sound believable. Maybe said I was a down-and-out, down on my luck. Christ, I don't know. How do I know? Something, anyway. An alkie, anything. Just to quieten her. Give me a chance. A moment. An opportunity to get out of there. No harm done.

She went for me. With one of the big knives she'd knocked over on the floor. And she'd have stabbed me. I could see it in her eyes. She was past talking, she was. She was going to kill me for certain. It was her that was angry and violent, not me. She wouldn't even give me a chance to explain. To say something, anything. I was rummaging for food, that's all. Not much to ask for, is it? Even as we struggled with the knife, it might not have been too late. I could have said something then. I should have said something. I know I should. You don't have to tell me that.

I've got to blot out what happened. Ignore it. Make it all disappear. Just keep driving. I'm doing well, really well. Must be 30, 40 minutes from the house now. 20 or 30 miles away from what happened.

I'm in her car. Did I say? The woman's car. A blue Renault. The one she had on the driveway. She'd left the driver's door open and the keys in the ignition. So all I had to do was a quick check that no one was watching and I was in it and away. And a full tank of petrol too, give or take. Enough to get to Suffolk anyway. My lucky day.

I'm two hours from Suffolk now, two and a half at most.

And I've got new clothes, nice and dry they are. I should have said. I picked out a black jumper from the man's wardrobe. And some black jogging bottoms he had rolled up in a chest of drawers. I'd have had trousers, but I couldn't find any trousers I liked; a bit too smarmy for my liking. A jacket too, black, with big pockets. They're useful, they are, big pockets. And I've some trainers of his as well from the cupboard under the stairs. He's a size 11 and I'm only an eight so they're not a perfect fit, but still. They're better than stupid fucking slippers.

Just got to keep my focus.

Nice and cool, nice and calm.

Just have to keep going.

I don't know how long I've got until they find her. She'll have been going to work, I reckon. Will her boss or colleagues call when she doesn't turn up? Then what – will they call her at home or on her mobile? I never thought to check if she had one. Never occurred to me, but they all have mobiles these days, don't they? They'd give her until 10.00 for sure. They'd assume she was delayed in traffic, that's all.

Would they wait until 10.30 maybe? Then they'd call, surely. Get no reply. They'd shrug, agree she was ill. They'd send someone round at lunchtime or on their way home after work, perhaps. Make sure she was okay. Then again, maybe they'd not bother, what with it being a Saturday. Perhaps they'd leave it until Monday? I reckon I've got until lunchtime at the very least. That's enough time to get to Suffolk.

I've gone by Grantham now, and am heading towards Stamford, or so the signs say. Doing well. Just keeping the car going nice and steady. I'm sat in the inside lane, going at a level 50. Nobody will notice me. No one at all. I'm not drawing attention to myself, see? I look like a regular Joe on a day out.

I can see her now lying on the kitchen floor. I'd twisted the knife out of her hand and slashed desperately at her with it. Just once. That's all. To scare her off. No more than that. But I misjudged it and sliced her neck open. I did not mean to do it.

She looked up at me, her eyes trying to focus. All I could see was the blood. And I could hear her gurgling as she fought to get her breath. Her eyes, looking past me, then centred. Focused. Fixed on me. Uncomprehending.

Cars go by, 70, 80, even 90, some of them. But not me. I'm concentrating. And I'm a careful driver, even though it's been a year or two since I've been in a car. I was always a good driver, me. Careful and thoughtful, just like the perfect driver should be.

Her eyes focused, then seemed to blur and lose their sight. Her head lolled back. Eyes rolling upwards. I stood there for what seemed an age. A minute probably. No more than that.

Did I say she gurgled?

Like a baby.

I did, didn't I?

Her skirt, that short black skirt, had ridden up towards the top of her thighs. I could see underneath, could see what she was wearing. I looked. Stared. God help me, I looked. I couldn't help myself. It had been so long. But I knew I mustn't touch, I mustn't touch, I mustn't touch.

I reached for a tea towel.

To cover her face.

I pushed her head to one side.

I have to keep driving, nice and steady. Just got to put it all out of my mind. I need to start thinking straight. Focus. Do what I have to do. What's done is done. I can't do anything about it now. Too late.

I've just got to get to Suffolk as quickly as I can. Before she might be found. Before the car's reported missing.

Not so long now. Not if I keep going at a nice level 50.

I tried to tidy her up afterwards, leaving her there neatly, arms and legs by her sides. Mopped around with tea towels as best I could. Shoved them and the knife at the back of the cupboard, behind everything else, underneath the sink. Pushed her body towards the fridge so that the blood might run away under it.

There was a lot of blood.

So much of it everywhere.

All over me too.

I pushed my old clothes, drenched red, as far back in the cupboard under the sink as I could.

I did my best to put things right. There's not much I could do though. Just so much mess. I may have left bloodied footprints as I went upstairs to find clothes. I washed myself clean in the bathroom. I may even have left some mess there too. And nothing will disguise what else I've done. No, not at all. Too late now. They have forensics. They'll know. Yes, they'll know alright.

No use being sorry about it, though.

Sorry won't help.

No, not one little bit.

There's a police car behind me. Inside lane. About three cars back. It's going at a steady speed too. About 50 miles an hour. It's just keeping pace with me. No more, no less.

I slow down from 50 to 47, 43, 40, 39; too slow, too obvious? Three cars between us. I keep my head level and facing straight ahead. But my eyes watch in the mirror.

I keep the car steady, moving along nicely at 40. One, two cars coming by me in the outside lane. Looks like they've all clocked the cop car. They all go by on the dot of 70, I reckon.

Not the cars behind me, though. They're still there. The same three cars between me and the police. Not one of them is willing to overtake with the cop car right there, watching.

I accelerate slowly, nudging the car carefully back up towards 50. Nice straight run. All three cars come with me, keeping pace. All in a line. None of them pulls out. Not one.

And still the police car stays put. Tailing me. Watching me. I try to see how many coppers there are in the car. Looks like two to me. Men. Both in the front, I think. I can't see anyone in the back. Hard to tell, though. Too far to see clearly. Too many cars in between.

One driving, following me? The other radioing CID. Calling for more coppers. Just tailing me until the other cop cars are in place. Somewhere ahead of me. Pulled into a lay-by. Two cars? They'll pull out in front of me. Sirens wailing as I approach. Two ahead, blocking the road. One behind, closing me down. Forcing me in. Trapping me.

Is that what's going to happen?

I can see ahead of me. Two, three miles of clear, straight road. Two lanes this side. Barrier in the middle. Two lanes the other side of the road. Nothing but fields everywhere else. There's no way I can pull over and make a run for it. I'm not going to outrun two fit young men. That's how it would end, wouldn't it? Me stumbling and staggering across a field and being brought down by some baby-faced coppers. They'd pin me down. Cuff me. I can't have that. Not that. Never again. I'd rather take the car up to 70, 80, 90, 100 and go straight through the roadblocks and take any coppers on the other side out with me.

If I have to, I will.

Hear my words.

I'll die rather than be captured.

This side of the road's still clear. I can see cars coming towards me the other way. But nothing this side at all. Not as far ahead as I can see.

Just the five of us now. Me. The three cars in between. And

the cop car. All in a procession. Me in front. Clapped-out Beetle behind. Green Fiesta. A beat-up old farm truck. The cop car. All of us going at a nice steady 50.

And still we keep going. I can feel the beads of sweat trickling down the sides of my face. One rolls and hangs for a second below my cheek. I want to dab it, brush it, wipe it away. But I daren't. I don't want to move. I just need to act normal. Like this is a regular journey. An ordinary fellow wouldn't be sweating like this. Not in October. Not when it's cold.

Head facing forward.

Keeping it still.

Nice and steady pace.

The Beetle pulls out. I see it coming by me. Accelerating away, up to 70. Seems to take an age to reach me and pass me by. Signals left, pulls in, moving ahead and slowly away. Textbook driving. He knows the cop car is there. He thinks he's being watched. You stupid fucker. It's me they're after.

The Fiesta does the same. Must have been waiting for someone else to move first, to see if the coppers respond. It pulls out, comes up next to me, and accelerates away, following the Beetle.

Now the old farm truck moves up behind me. Police car keeps pace. Just the truck between us now. They're waiting, the coppers. Getting ready for me to panic. Put my foot down and accelerate off and away. They'll pull out, moving up smoothly to 70, 80, 90 behind me. I can't outpace them and that's a fact. Not in this tinpot little car. It's like driving a can on wheels. The police car will move up, siren wailing, as we move on and over the hill that's coming up now.

What's on the other side? A lay-by, I'd guess. Two police cars there waiting for me. Did I say? Yes, I did. I'm sure. They're just sitting and waiting for me to make my move.

Here it comes.

Here it comes.

The truck. Pulling out. Puffing and wheezing by the look of it. Moves alongside me, takes an age to go by.

The police car's right behind me now, and close. I can see the copper driving. He's looking at me, watching me, seeing what I'm going to do. The copper next to him – it's a woman, I can see now – is talking into something, a radio, I'd guess. Radioing ahead. To the police cars just over the hill.

Got to keep calm.

Just stay calm.

Think what to do.

Over the hill, there'll be a lay-by. I told you, didn't I? Another cop car there, maybe two. They'll be a little way ahead. Will pull out as they see me. Get in place to force me over and slow me down. I'm trapped, so help me God.

Here we go.

To the top of the hill.

We're almost there. At the top. Up we go, up and almost over.

What am I going to do?

Tell me. Please.

What the fuck am I going to do?

11.07AM SATURDAY 31 OCTOBER

The old woman, sitting in a high-backed armchair in the front room of the tiny cottage, turned her head slowly to the window and watched the old man struggling up the path with handfuls of carrier bags. She listened as he dumped them on the doorstep, coughed and then rattled repeatedly through his pockets for his keys. As she heard the door opening at last, she spoke, her voice raised.

"You've been ages … did you get everything? They'll be here soon."

The old man drew in his breath. "I had to go to the other bakers, they didn't do kiddie things at the usual, only croissants and scones. I've got some biscuits with those sprinkles on top and eclairs and a nice Chelsea bun for Richard. We've got scones ... or we can share one if you prefer, they're quite large."

She sat back, waiting for him to put things away in the kitchen. She heard him turning the kettle on and clattering cups and saucers out of the cupboards, making a pot of tea.

"Do you want a pot ...?" he asked, looking in on her. "Oh ... I'll just use a bag then ... you've started early."

She held her glass up. "It's gone 11.00; it's just to get me warmed through. It's so cold."

He came in with a cup of tea and sat opposite her, so he could see out the window and up the path, wanting to watch for the son and daughter-in-law and the small boy to arrive in their new car. From here, he could see out and across the car park where they'd arrive.

"I've been thinking. While you were out. I've had enough of this place and the North Sea wind," she said, looking at him. "It's always so cold and it's just so remote." She thought for a moment or two and added, "We should sell it and buy an apartment or something somewhere warm, Majorca or that other island ... not Ibiza. The one we went to once when you were working in Belgium, France, wherever it was."

"Menorca ... It's not so bad here ... it's been a long time now. You used to love coming up here when Richard was young." He hesitated for a moment or two, watching her expression. "And Roger, Roger loved this place too. With the boats. He did love his boats."

She nodded once, twice, several times, as if thinking to herself. "We did. Roger did like the boats. But it was so long ago. And we're old and this place is a ruin. Look at it." She gestured at her armchair and to his sofa across the room. "It's got so tatty."

"It's how you wanted it kept. Like it used to be when ... in the old days. We can do the place up if you like. Get satellite television in. If we get a phone installed, they can run it off that I think. Maybe some double glazing."

"The cottage is so cold, it's always so cold here." She went quiet.

"The radiators just need bleeding, that's all. I'll do it later, this afternoon, if the kiddie has a sleep. I can get one of those keys from that shop opposite the bakers."

Her head had dropped down and she was silent. He could kick himself. He knew he shouldn't have mentioned Roger. It was still raw, even now. He thought perhaps it always would be. And the drinking didn't help. She didn't have the head for it. Drink, when she had it, made her less angry but more melancholy. Spiteful sometimes, when the mood took her.

"Come on, old girl," he said. "Chin up ... look, they're here already," he added at the flash of a blue car pulling up outside. "Sort yourself out while I get the door. You don't want the kiddie to see you upset. Let's give them a weekend to remember."

11.15ᴀᴍ SATURDAY 31 OCTOBER

The little boy stood on the doorstep of the cottage, holding an African violet in his cupped hands.

He looked at the brass door knocker shaped like a lion's face on the door, far above his head.

It was a friendly face, like the smiley lion in *Madagascar*.

He remembered seeing it before and thought about how his mama had laughed when he had growled like a lion upon seeing it.

He did it again.

"Grrr-rrr-rrr."

But his mama did not say anything, nor his papa.

"Grrr-rrr-rrr."

They stood there, behind him, waiting quietly.

He smiled anyway, remembering his mama's words as they got out of the car and she handed him the plant: "Smile little soldier, say cheese, big smile." He did not really know what all of that meant but he knew he had to smile. And he held the plant as high as he could, raising it up above his head as the door swung open and he listened to the hubbub of adults' voices.

The white-haired man leaned forward and bent down, his face appearing inches in front of the little boy. "Is that for Grand-Mama? Thank you very much." The old man took the plant from the little boy's outstretched hands and went to ruffle his hair.

The little boy smiled again, not sure what to say or do, and whether he should attempt another lion's roar. He put his face into his mama's skirt, but she pulled him out gently and moved him forward into the cottage.

He smelled a smell, something that reminded him of his papa's breath sometimes late at night when he came to say goodnight. He did not like the smell at all.

Moving into the cramped front room, the old man sat in an armchair by the window, opposite his mama and papa on the faded sofa. The small boy sat between them, laying down across them at first and then, when they kept pushing him up, pressing his head against his mama. She pulled him out, softly the first time, but more firmly after that.

"Do you remember me, Willie," the old man smiled. "Is it Willie? Or Billy? Or do they now call you a very grown-up William?"

"Will," answered the young woman, "we always call him Will."

"Will it is then," said the old man, winking and smiling at the little boy.

They sat there for a few moments as the younger man talked of distances and speeds and miles per gallon: "Litres, these days, of course."

And then the old woman came back into the room, pushing an aged silver tea trolley with a pot of tea and cups and saucers on the top and a range of pastries underneath, all arranged neatly on bone china plates.

The little boy sat up, pointing at the chocolate éclair he had spotted. He had eaten these before, one after another, at a party. He liked them a lot. But he also remembered when his mama had come to collect him and there were raised voices, mainly Mama's. She had taken his hand and walked him away. He tried to smile bravely as they went, knowing he would not now get a present as the other children did at the end of a party.

"Mama?" he said, turning towards her. He pointed towards the éclair.

"That's my favourite," said the old man, leaning down to pick up the plate. "But you can have it this time."

The boy smiled and went to reach out for the éclair as the younger man and woman looked at each other. He pulled a face. She grimaced back. There was a moment's silence as the older couple watched on.

The younger woman spoke, leaning forward to take the éclair from the boy.

"Thing is ..." She hesitated, looking again at the younger man, who glanced away. She spoke more firmly then, "Will is type one. I mean he's diabetic. He can have the occasional treat but we then have to change his insulin dosage, so it would be easier all round ... just for now ... if he didn't ..."

The little boy let out a cry.

12.03PM SATURDAY 31 OCTOBER

Want to know where I am?

I'm in Aldeburgh.

Too fucking right.

You'll never believe it. What happened? I'll tell you what happened.

Nothing.

Jack squit.

I came up over the hill and that was it. Sweet FA. Nothing on the other side at all. Not on the left. Nor on the right. No cop car in a lay-by. Just that long A1 road stretching out and away again in front of me.

I kept the car at a nice pace, mind you. Because I still had the police car behind me at this point, remember? So I couldn't be sure I was safe. Not 100 per cent anyway. I just kept on going on. Cool, that's me. Dead cool.

I went on and on to Suffolk. Easy it was. The petrol light flashed up with a little way to go. But I held my nerve. And I arrived in Aldeburgh, turned right by the bookshop and the cinema, and made my way through to the other side of town.

I'm sitting here now. Stretched out and relaxed. I'm just lying here, watching. I've tipped my seat back a touch. I'm taking a breather. Well, you've got to, haven't you? Not for too long, mind. Because it's all going to happen soon. It's all going to kick off big-time.

My plan's worked just perfect so far.

Just perfect.

Did I tell you about my plan? I did, didn't I? Yes, I'm sure I must have done.

It's why I got out last night. Friday 30 October.

And late – too late for the Saturday papers, see? Probably the Sundays too, if truth be told.

I had to get to Aldeburgh for Saturday 31 October. Where the Veitchs are. And the grandparents. And my little William, of course.

The Veitchs won't be at home in London, see – so the cops can't warn them I'm out.

And I reckon the cops won't know about the grandparents' place in Aldeburgh.

And they certainly won't know they all get together here at this time of year.

In a seaside cottage with no television and no telephone.

Perfect.

Just fucking perfect.

Now I'm here.

In Aldeburgh.

On Saturday 31 October.

It's the day that's the key. It's the Halloween festival tonight.

That's why little William's here. And the Veitchs. And the grandparents. The family all get together for the Halloween festival. I know exactly what they do. I used to come here with them, see? Years ago, when I was with, well, you know. The wife. They do like their routines, I'll tell you that for nothing.

They spend the morning on the beach, usually. Or at least they used to do – they walk up to the town and back along the seashore. I reckon they might still be doing that. Little William would be collecting shells by now. They do that, you know. Small children. Collect shells.

I couldn't take William straight off the beach, not in front of them. Veitch would put up a fight. Too many people around to see, maybe even stop me as they all cried out for help. No, the beach is too risky, far too risky.

But you know, I'm smarter than that.

I've got a better idea. Two, actually. Alternatives you might call them.

I've thought them both through.

They go back to the cottage for lunch. The old biddy fusses

around with cold meats and pickles and her plates of bread and butter. The old bloke will be opening his home-made bottles of wine and making a right to-do if any of the cork gets into any of the glasses. Sometimes, they eat in the back garden. If the weather's alright. Maybe, just maybe, William might wander into the front room or perhaps even into the front garden while they are out the back.

Well, who knows?

Did I say where I am now?

Right fucking now?

I'm in Aldeburgh. I said, didn't I?

But not just in Aldeburgh. Not just anywhere in Aldeburgh. I've parked the car in a car park at the end of the seafront, opposite the cottage. It's just over there, about 30 yards away, that's all. Just a couple of other cars. And there's nobody in sight but me. Not anywhere. I know, I've looked all around, back up the beach towards the town, everywhere.

I'm just lying back and waiting, like I said.

Just to see what happens.

Who knows, I might get lucky if the little fellow happens to wander outside unnoticed.

If not, there's always later on. As it gets dark, they walk to the funfair on the seafront by the town, a half-mile to a mile or so away. And here's the clever part. They'll all stop for a hot chocolate or an ice cream when they arrive. Veitch will probably wander off to look at the boats. The sister-in-law may sit and look out to sea. And Granny and Grandad might take William on some rides. Or will they think he's with Veitch or the sister-in-law? And vice versa?

"Who's got little William?" one of them will say suddenly. "Oh, he's with the others," will be the answer. No, he isn't. He's not with Veitch or the sister-in-law or the old biddy or the fat old fart. He'll be with his real daddy, heading back to the car and away.

It will all be very crowded tonight. Lots of teenagers. All pushing and shoving and swearing their heads off. Loads of families with the occasional "Excuse me" as they bump into each other. Queues everywhere for burgers and chips or teas and coffees or sweets and candy floss. Lots of chances for me to stroll up, cool as you like, when someone's not looking, and I'll be off and away with William.

I'd bet they won't even notice he's gone for 20 minutes or so. They'll all be waiting for the others to turn up with him. And when they've all got together, they'll then realise he's gone. Wandered off, they'll think. Maybe towards the sea. They'll panic, especially if little William can't swim. They'll go down to the shore, running this way and that. It will take them ages to actually call the police.

And old plod won't take it seriously, not locally, not immediately. They'll assume he's wandering in among the crowds. Then they'll reckon he's tagged on the end of another family. At 7.00 there's the torchlight procession along the main street, where everyone brings lanterns or torches or whatever they've got and walks along. Families, mostly. A few older people. Some teenagers too. And lots of little kids. The beat bobbies will tell the Veitchs to stand somewhere and watch the procession go by to see if they can spot William.

And where do you reckon we'll be by then?

By that time, of course, we'll be long gone. Me and the little 'un. We'll be on our way to a new life somewhere nice and warm in the south of France.

Just you wait and see.

2.12PM SATURDAY 31 OCTOBER

Shit.

I've been asleep.

I sit up, disorientated.

Christ, what time is it? I turn the key in the ignition. It's gone two o'clock, moving towards quarter-past.

I may be too late.

The car park has filled up. No longer just two or three cars in it; 10, 12 cars are now parked all around me. People getting in and out, unfolding coats, unpacking buggies, taking out just-in-case umbrellas, moving towards the prom and the beach.

No one seems to have noticed me here, though. Nobody turns and looks towards me. I'm just some bloke having a kip while his kids go and find sweets.

I look back along the beach. It's packing out now with people. In the distance, I can hear the tinkling music of the funfair that's started up way back towards the town.

I rub my eyes. Maybe I've just left it too late to get little William.

The thought fills me with panic. I can't come all this way, get so close but yet so far.

Somehow, whatever happens, no matter what, I have to have him and get away.

I can still see the cottage over on the far side of the car park. There's a big blue car between me and most of the cottage.

Perfect, they can't really see me from the cottage. But I can see the front door well enough. Can't see much beyond it, though. Can't tell if anyone's inside or not.

They should be back there by now. Should be back from the beach walk and have had lunch. After that, they read the newspapers until it starts to get dark. Then they walk along the seafront to the funfair.

Remember?

I told you, I'm sure.

Listen.

I wonder what's happening now back at the annexe, back at the big house. Spink definitely called the cops faster than I'd expected.

CID got the roadblocks up quick enough, that's for sure. But I was clever, see, and got away. They'd have no idea where I was going.

Even if they assumed I'd come for William, they'd not know about Aldeburgh.

Fact is, I'm probably as safe here as anywhere in the country. Who'd expect me to come here, to shitty old Aldeburgh? A man on the run disappears into a city. Manchester, Birmingham, maybe even London.

I watch and wait.

That woman. Christ, from that house. Would they have found her by now? Must have done. Unless the husband was out at work all day. And then on the piss with the lads in the evening. Who knows? They might not find her until later tonight.

Even then, they might not link her with me straightaway. Not necessarily. There was no sign of a break-in. Maybe they'd think it was the husband anyway. He's the obvious suspect. What the police call your prime suspect. Yes, they'll go for him. No doubt about that.

It's going to be a long haul sitting here. I've just got to be patient.

They'd question him first, I reckon. Before doing anything else. And that all takes time. They hold suspects – prime suspects is what they call them these days, did I tell you? – for 24 or maybe even 48 hours.

Even at the very worst, even if they do believe him and they do pin it on me, I've got until tonight for sure. A good ten hours or so to get William and make our escape. And anyway, they don't know where I am, do they?

I've just got to wait.

There are plenty of comings and goings. To and from the car park. Some old woman has just let her dog out the back of her car. A greyhound, it is. Dirty, filthy things, dogs. I watch it for a minute or two. It's running round her all excited. She's trying to put a lead on it. I hope it doesn't come over here.

The door's opening. The cottage. I told you I could see it, didn't I?

It's opening.

Sweet Jesus, it's little William with the old woman. She's standing in the doorway with him, looking out towards the boats at sea.

It's William, my sweet little William.

It's all I can do to stop myself sobbing.

It's been so long.

I'm crying, shit, I'm crying. I couldn't help it, really I couldn't. My eyes just welled up with tears. They're now running down my face. I can't help myself. It's just too much for me.

I've got to control myself. Someone might see. There are just so many people about now.

I can't cry, not like this, not great big sobs one after the other.

I've got to pull myself together.

I mustn't keep crying with big fat tears running down my cheeks.

I've got to stop. Now. I'm making a fool of myself. And I wouldn't want William to see me like this. It's no way for a daddy to behave. No way at all.

There, there. I'm okay now. I've got it. I mop my eyes with my sleeve. First one, then the other. No one's noticed. I've not attracted attention. I'm okay now.

My eyes mist up again.

I mop at them furiously. Angry with myself and my softness. I've got to stay calm. I've got to think. Not get emotional. Just sit quietly and think carefully what to do.

I could get out of the car right now.

This very moment.

I could go and get him right away.

Run across the car park, snatch him up in my hands. Lift him high above my head into the air with a great big "Wee-eeh". Tell him his daddy is back. Back to look after him. Like it should always have been. Like it always will be from now on until the day we die.

Then we'd turn, go straight to the car and drive away. Not to Dover, the ferries and motorways across the other side. No, I've thought of a better idea. We're going to drive down to Thurrock, the other side of the M25 near Dartford. They have coaches there that go all over the place, right across the world probably.

We're going to find ourselves a trip to France. Disneyland, maybe. Lots of dads and their sons on those coaches. Plenty of coaches everywhere, row after row. Everyone pushing. All the little children excited. No one quite knowing where they're meant to be. And none of the drivers will be paying too much attention to tickets and passports.

"They're with the wife," I'd tell the driver, laughing cheerily. "She's on the other coach, that one." And I'd point to a really full coach alongside ours. Maybe I'd even wave at a woman and she, not knowing what to do, would wave back instinctively. Well, it would fool the driver, wouldn't it?

"There wasn't enough room for us over there. We'll get the tickets when we get to Dover." I'd smile at him and William would as well. A right good little team we'll make. The driver would shrug, shake his head and laugh and probably pat little William on the head for good measure. We'd soon be on the way.

But right here and now, the old woman's with him, see? I told you that, if you fucking listened for once. She'd not let me take him without a fight. She'd grip his little arm with her bony old hand and hiss at me to go away. And that would upset William, that would, seeing his daddy pushing and pulling. It's not nice.

Not nice at all. And people would see and hear and come running across from the beach. And Veitch too, no doubt, from within the cottage. And the sister-in-law.

No, I can't do that. Much as I want to do it right here and now. Can't even think about doing it. Can I?

What do you think? I think I could do it, if I were quick?

I've got to take him when it's least expected. When no one will see. And nobody will realise. And when they'd spend ages looking for him while me and the little fellow get well away from here.

That's got to be later, at six o'clock or so. When they're at the funfair on the seafront and it's mad busy and dark. It'd be easy for a little chap to wander off.

But William's standing there right now, pointing out to sea, and laughing delightedly. He's a handsome devil is William. Blond hair, cut into a neat little bob. A happy, smiley face. He looks as though he has some sort of fisherman's outfit on. A dark chunky jumper and a pair of dark green chinos, by the look of things.

You know what?

I like it.

I like it a lot.

And that smile, it's just like his daddy's. It's a heart-breaker, that is. He's pointing and laughing. Almost doubled up. I bet he's got a lovely laugh like me. I can't see what it is he's looking at. I move sideways, leaning over towards the passenger seat, wiping the misted-up window to see out of it.

There are two clowns on the beach. Pierrots – those poncy French clowns that do the silly mimes. Looks like a man and a woman. They've got a crowd around them, that's for sure. Kids and mums and dads and a few grandparents. I watch for a moment as they do some sort of ballet routine, gurning and staggering about. I wind down the passenger window a touch and can hear the children's tinkling laughter.

But not William's.

I look back. My God, William's off, trotting along the track by the side of the car park. It takes him to the beach and the pierrots' display. I hear the old woman call after him, "Wait, boy," she cries, "wait while I get my coat" and she turns to go back into the cottage. The front door is wide open. I watch as she disappears from view. That'll take time, especially with the old man and his arthritis and all.

I've got time. If I'm fast.

If I do it now.

Should I?

If she's in the cottage and he's walking towards the beach, I can for sure.

If I'm quick.

I've got to take a chance.

Do it right now.

All I need to do is to jump out of the car, follow him down to the beach and mingle in behind him in the crowd. Then I move up, take his hand and walk him away along the beach before the old woman and the rest of them come out of the cottage and spot me.

"I'm Daddy," I'll say.

And he'll look up at me and smile with that sweet little face of his.

And my heart will melt.

I wouldn't be able to get him back to the car and away without them seeing me, though. I'd have to walk right by them. I'd have no choice. Maybe they'd not notice me if they saw me walking away from them on the beach with the boy wrapped up in my arms. Not until it was too late anyway. But there's no way I could walk by them face-to-face; they'd spot me and the little chap in an instant.

I'll have to take my chances with him in the town, maybe see if I can get on a bus with him and away to the railway station in Ipswich.

But that won't work, will it? I've got to get to Thurrock. Blag my way onto a coach and away. I've fuck all money to get all the way to Thurrock by bus and train. Just this car and half a cup of petrol.

What do I do? Tell me, what do I do?

I don't know.

I just need to think. But I haven't time.

I can't wait any longer. If I'm going to do it, I've got to do it now.

I swing the car door open and slam it shut behind me. I walk briskly towards the beach, parallel with the cottage and the little path that William just took.

I go by one car, two cars, three cars, parked in a line.

I'm now on the edge of the beach, can see the clowns ahead of me, halfway between me and the shoreline. It's a gently sloping, pebbled beach and the clowns have laid out some sort of seating area where people can sit down.

I daren't look round; the old woman may be behind me.

And Veitch. And the wife and the old man hobbling along.

If I turn and they see my face, I'm fucked.

From behind, I'm just another daddy, walking fast to catch up with his little boy on the beach.

I move up to the crowd, 15 or 20 of them. Mums and dads and grandparents at the back. Children sitting cross-legged at the front. I watch, hold back and hesitate as William, my little William, picks his way delicately through the adults and makes his way quietly to the front. One of the clowns turns towards him, bends over and offers him an imaginary flower. I see William's tiny hand go up and take it. Then, guess what? He pretends to smell it! And all the mums and dads and grandparents, they all clap and coo and make a fuss over him.

He's a clever boy, see? Joining in with a mime like that. Not many little 'uns would do that. They'd just stare or maybe even cry. But William's clever - just like his daddy.

Now.

Right now.

I've got to do it.

I have to push my way through, stepping over the adults at the back with an "Excuse me" and a "Sorry" as I zig-zag my way towards William. I'll put my hand out towards him and just say, "William?" in a quiet and friendly voice. He'll turn and smile that heart-rending smile and I'll say, "Come on William, come to Daddy. Come and see what Daddy's got for you." And you know what? He'll get up and come. I know he will. He's his daddy's little boy. I'm going to do it now. Right now.

"William?"

"William?"

"Will!"

Jesus. I can hear the panic in the voices from behind me. From the cottage. The first two calls are from the old woman. I recognise her old quivering voice. She sounds worried and awkward about calling out. The third call is a sharper, fiercer kind of voice.

The sister-in-law.

Everyone in the crowd turns towards the voices. The old biddy will be struggling along towards the beach and the crowd. She can't walk properly either, not really. The sister-in-law will be striding out, marching towards William.

I'd like to get her by the ... well, I can't. Don't even think about that. Not now. Later, if I can. But I daren't be seen now. I sit down, looking towards the clowns, who stand frozen, their faces long and droopy, shoulders sloping down as if they have been told off. They know how to work a crowd, that's for sure.

They're all looking towards the old woman and the sister-in-law. All except me and little William. (That's my boy.) I can see him five or six rows in front of me, over to my right. He sits with his arms and legs crossed, just staring at the clowns. I can't tell if he's mesmerised by them or is pretending to be.

He's scared of the sister-in-law, I'm sure of it.

She's in the crowd now, having left the old woman behind. She comes in from the right side, her eyes fixed on little William ahead of her. If she turned to the left, right now, she'd see me. God, how I hate that fucking bitch. There are only seven or eight people between her and me. She'd see me for sure. She'd look into my eyes and she'd see the hatred I have for her and all of them who took William away from me. It'd be all I could do to stop myself getting up and strangling her there and then.

I'd like to do that.

And why not? If I'm spotted, I'd have nothing to lose. I'd never get away from the big house ever again. Not after what happened in the annexe. And that woman in Nottingham. And the sister-in-law. Because I sure as hell would kill her too.

Why not do it?

Well?

William, that's why.

I've just got to sit here, and not be seen and wait until later when I can do this properly. Take William and get away. I dip my head down a touch, while still being able to see what's going on.

She's got William by the arm now, I can see if I bring my head up slightly. Not by the hand, all loving like a real mummy would have. By the arm, almost dragging him along, back out of the crowd. Her fingers pressed tight and hard and into his skin so that, when she takes her hand away, there'll be an angry white imprint on it. Disgusting it is, really disgusting.

Of course, they're all ignoring her. The crowd. Pretending nothing's happening. They're all watching the clowns again. As if there's no hard-faced cow dragging a poor little boy away by the arm. Even the clowns are acting again now, pulling their silly faces and pretending to have an argument with each other. All in fucking silence of course.

And then, oh then, it happens. Just like a dream.

Just as they go by, little William – who'd been staring fixedly ahead – turns his head slightly towards me.

Our eyes meet.

I smile at him. A soft and gentle smile.

As if it were meant to be.

And it is, you see. Because in three or four hours, when it's all dark and crowded on Aldeburgh seafront and people are pushing and shoving and the funfair noise is all around, I will come back for you my little boy and I will smile at you again and tell you I'm your daddy and then we'll go away together hand in hand and we'll live happily ever after.

Just you see if we don't.

2.35PM SATURDAY 31 OCTOBER

"You have to watch him all the time," the young woman said, sitting back down on the sofa and pulling the little boy close to her. "You can't just leave him to do what he wants."

The old woman, breathless but still standing, replied, "He should be old enough by now to know he shouldn't run out like that. When Richard was young, they were taught the Green Cross Code."

"No harm done," said the old man. "The rascal only went

because he saw the clowns. It's not as though he was running away. He didn't go into the car park and he wouldn't have gone down to the sea. He can't swim, can he? He's too young, I suppose."

The younger man shook his head. "There's a swimming pool up by West Norwood station but we've not taken him there regularly enough to learn. We're going to do it in the summer."

"That's not the point," answered the young woman, her voice rising. "About the Green Cross Code ..." She hesitated, and her voice tailed off.

The old woman looked across, "I suppose, as a diabetic, he's not like other children."

The younger man spoke up, "He is like other children of this age, really ... full of life and up to mischief ... it's just that with type one, we have to be extra careful. We have to do the blood glucose checks and some injections and just keep everything within the safe range."

The little boy sat quietly, kicking his legs contentedly back and forth against the settee. He liked the thumping noise they made. He started doing first one and then the other ... boom boom ... boom boom ... boom boom. Then he did them together again ... boom ... boom ... boom.

"Stop it, Will," said the younger woman, reaching down to still his legs. She looked over at the older couple. "It's not easy, it's a full-time job. You have to be on your guard all the time."

The younger man interrupted her, "His levels have been all over the place lately. You have to watch for signs that he's not well, so he doesn't get hypoglycaemia, which can be fatal if it's not treated. It's not always simple to spot; sometimes he can be a bit lethargic. You have to try and work out whether any changes are just him being a growing child or him becoming ill."

"Hypo ... what?" asked the old man, standing up and leaning over to pat the little boy on the shoulder. He looked up and smiled. The old man smiled back.

"Hypoglycaemia … g-l-y-c-a-e-m-i-a. You can Google it. Well, you could if you had the internet here. There's loads about it. It can be dangerous with small children, well, anyone really, I imagine. If it's not dealt with quickly, it can lead to convulsions and even coma. That's why we're protective. We may seem over-protective but we just have to be so careful all of the time."

For a moment or two, the four adults looked at each other, none of them seeming to know what to say next.

The young man went on talking, "And then there's hypergly-caemia. Hypoglycaemia – 'hypo' – is to do with low blood sugar. Hyperglycaemia – 'hyper' – is to do with high blood sugar. If he's not getting his insulin and has high blood sugar levels, it can be fatal. At the moment, that's something of an issue for us."

The old woman made a tutting noise, as if to herself.

The old man went to say something but stopped himself.

The little boy, noticing his mama had moved her hand away from his legs, started the thumping again … boom boom … boom boom.

"Well," said the older man finally, getting up and going out of the room, "maybe we should have some quiet time after all this excitement. We've some board games somewhere. What can he play? We've probably got a Ludo and a snakes and ladders in the loft from when the boys were small. Snakes and ladders can be fun."

"Oh no," said the younger woman, "there's no need to…"

But the older man was already gone and moving up the stairs.

4.35PM SATURDAY 31 OCTOBER

I'm sitting on a bench on the front. It's facing out to sea but perfectly placed so I can spot the Veitchs as they walk by on their way to the funfair in an hour or so's time. They'll come along the prom to the attractions. It's the quickest way to the funfair.

Yes, it's very nice and quiet and peaceful for sure.

I'm going to have a little snooze for half an hour. Recharge the batteries, so to speak. I'll be awake and ready for them by six o'clock.

I'll wait for them to go by. And when I spot them I will put my head down. Let them walk past. Give them a minute or two. Then get up and follow them.

After that?

Well, you know what happens next. I've told you.

I've told you that several times already.

You just need to keep up for once, don't you?

It must be moving towards five now. And it's just starting to get dark.

And I'm waiting.

Still waiting.

Always fucking waiting.

Then, just as I hear a clock striking five, this woman comes and sits down on the bench just as cool as you please. No "Excuse me" or "Do you mind?". Just plonks herself down to my right. Like she owns the place.

She's got a dog with her, the woman. One of them German sausages. I don't like Germans as a rule, nor anything to do with them, to tell the truth. And I don't like dogs either, smelly, dirty things. And small dogs can be nasty, yappy little fuckers.

This one's alright though.

The dog.

As dogs go, that is.

When the woman sat down, the dog sat obediently by her feet, without prompting. That shows it's been taught proper. Trained. She's then rummaging in a little brown bag and feeding titbits from it to the dog.

I'm just going to sit here and ignore her. I can't have any

distractions, not now, not so close to getting little William back. Any other time, well, you know - but not at the moment. There's no time. No time at all for any of that sort of thing.

She's okay, though, I can tell you. I don't turn and look at her. Not full on, like. But I can see her quite clearly if I move my head a little and make out I'm watching the sparkly lights that are coming on all along the seafront.

I feel myself stirring.

Down there.

Just like I did with that woman in Nottingham.

Can't think about that now. Daren't. Not now. No time for any of that. It will get me into trouble, that will. An awful lot. That's what got me into trouble in the first place. That and the other. But you don't really want to know about any of that.

I'm guessing she's about my age, mid-30s I'd say, maybe a bit older. (Well, I can't be fussy, can I?) She's wearing a sea green-coloured dress, plain and simple. Classy like. And she's got some sort of creamy-green coat on too.

Not too much meat on her. But nice, if you know what I mean.

What you'd call top-heavy.

Not that I've time for any of that. Not really.

I've just got to sit here and keep my head down and wait for the Veitchs to go by. With the cheeky chappie. My little William.

The dog sits patiently, waiting for another treat as, out of the corner of my eye, I see her fold the bag away and put it in a coat pocket. She takes a packet of cigarettes out of the other pocket and then rummages for a lighter. She sighs. I know what's coming next. I can just tell.

"Excuse me, do you have a light?"

But I don't smoke, never have. It's a filthy habit and makes you smell. The wife, Katie, she smoked all the time. And, as I used to tell her, she had caramel-coloured teeth because of it. My teeth, according to a dentist, are B1, whatever that means. Film-star teeth, I reckon. To go with my perfect smile.

I shake my head, no, I don't have a light.

She sighs again as she puts the packet of cigarettes away. We sit in silence, although I can tell she is about to say something else. I've got a sense for that sort of thing. With the women.

"Are you here for the festival?" she asks. Nice voice. Controlled and measured. A think-before-you-speak type. And rather posh, I'd say. She's not some rough old sort, that's for sure.

I nod, keep staring ahead; it's been ages since I've spoken to a proper woman. One that's not wearing rubber gloves anyway.

I feel 16 again, all tongue-tied. In fact, my tongue is sticking to the roof of my mouth. That shows I'm nervous, that does. It used to get like that at the reviews back in the big house.

I smile, can feel my lips pulling back over my teeth in a rictus grin.

I don't know what to say, don't want her to think I'm being rude, like. She's a tidy sort, after all.

I nod again, more firmly this time to make sure she can see.

Then I lean forward and touch the dog on its head as it turns towards me. For one horrible moment, I think it's going to pull back, bare its teeth and snarl at me.

That'd fuck me up with the woman, that's for sure.

But it doesn't. It cowers ever so slightly back as my hand comes towards its head – so as you'd hardly notice - and it sort of licks its lips nervously (if dogs have lips, that is). And then it lets me stroke its head. I do it for a minute, still not knowing what to say.

"She likes you," the woman says, "she doesn't like everyone." Then she smiles.

I nod, not sure what to say or do. I clear my throat. It makes it worse, harder to speak. I need to cough now. But I clear my throat again, a bit louder this time.

"What's her name?" I say.

"Mia," the woman replies.

"Nice name," I say (although, and I don't say this out loud mind, it's a stupid fucking name for a dog).

I stop stroking. Well you can't keep doing it over and over again. It makes you look odd, that does. Like you're simple or something.

They used to bring a golden retriever into the annexe and we all had to take turns petting and going "aah" over it as it stuck its big fat nose into your crotch. Personally, I'd have preferred to have wrung its fucking neck. But they've got big necks, retrievers. And you can't really get your hands round one. Not that I've tried, mind you. I've thought about it. But not tried. Not really, anyway. Not properly. It was only a joke. Just a bit of horseplay to impress Sprake and Ainsley. Got me into a bit of trouble actually. I never did it again.

"Would you like to feed her some biscuits?" says the woman, turning towards me now and offering up the brown paper bag.

I peer in the bag and then reach into it and take out a couple of small biscuits, one orange and one black (not that it really matters).

I lean forward and put out my hand, offering them to the dog. It moves forward, snuffles, and I can feel it taking the biscuits, its tongue licking the palm of my hand.

I lean back, trying to smile and resisting the urge to wipe the dog's slime off the palm of my hand. Dirty, filthy thing.

"My name's Julia," the woman says, smiling at me again. She has a nice face, actually. Very nice. Small and round. A bit like one of those monkeys at the zoo. I had one of them on my shoulder once, a monkey. And she has brown hair and lots of it. A nice smile if a bit lop-sided. I wonder, just for a second, whether she might have had some sort of stroke.

I think for a minute, smiling back. I give her one of my shy smiles and then look down again at the dog that's now snuffling by my feet.

"John," I say, after a moment or two. "My name's John" (well you can't be too careful can you?). I don't know what I look like really. Years ago at college, this girl I knew kept calling me Edgar, although that wasn't my proper name either.

So I must look like an Edgar.

But that's a shit name. Imagine being called that.

So I said John.

I'm not sure I like that either, even though it's my middle name, actually. It's an older man's name really. But it's better than Edgar. And I can't tell her my real name. She'd remember it, for sure. And later, maybe when she hears the news or reads the papers, she'll tell the police.

But does it matter?

I'll be long gone by then.

It doesn't matter at all. Not really.

By the time she hears it on the news or reads it in the papers, me and the little man will be well away. It really doesn't matter. For a moment, just for a few brief minutes, here and now, I can be myself for once.

"It's Raymond. My name. Raymond."

She turns and looks at me. She thinks I'm mad, I can tell. Our eyes meet and she's laughing. But it's a nice laugh. Not like one of Spink's sneering laughs. An amused, happy laugh, this one.

"So which is it? John or Raymond?"

"My friends call me John," I say quickly, because I can think fast, see, think on my feet, that's me. "It's a sort of nickname."

She smiles and nods thoughtfully and turns to look out at sea.

"I'll call you John then ... Honest John," she says, and again I catch the little smile she makes to herself.

We sit for a while just looking out to sea. Me and her and the little dog beneath our feet. Just like an old married couple, really. Nice it is. Real nice.

Out at sea we can see one or two little boats, their lights flickering, mirroring the fairy lights strung all the way along the seafront.

People pass by, going to and fro, back and forth to and from the main part of town.

It feels normal. You don't get a lot of normal, not where I've come from.

I can see her hands resting gently in her lap. It's all I can do to stop myself reaching across to take one of her hands in mine.

It's been years - years and years - since I did anything like this. Long time back it was. Back before, well, you know. I don't need to say, do I?

I want to hold her hand so very much. But it's too fast, too soon. You can't just reach out and take someone's hand like that. Not after four or five minutes. She'd pull back, recoil, think I was weird. And that would spoil it all. That would ruin the moment for sure.

So we just sit there, side by side. Alone with our thoughts and I get to wondering what she's thinking. And whether she's alone. Like me. Two ships in the night as they say, know what I mean?

And I wonder what it must be like to be, well, just as we are now - not just for a few minutes but all the time, day in and day out, week after week.

I look down and see she's not wearing a wedding ring on her left hand.

"You're not married," I say suddenly, almost before I'd even thought it. The question up and out of my mouth before I could stop myself.

That's done it.

That's fucked me up.

But then she speaks.

"No," she replies, as calm and relaxed as you like, or so it seems to me. "Divorced. And you?"

"I'm widowed."

"Oh," she says, and I can hear the surprise in that one single word. She says "oh" but what she really means is "how sad".

I just nod my head, not sure what else to say. I can sense her thinking as she sits there not moving, unsure how to respond. Perhaps she's feeling embarrassed now? Awkward, maybe? Wishing she hadn't started this conversation at all? She only sat down to feed her dog, after all.

Is she going to get up and walk off, not knowing what else to do?

She leans forward to stroke the dog and, despite that, she just seems so terribly still, almost as if she's holding her breath.

I'm not sure what to do. Should I start talking or hold on and see what she says? Or does?

I pause and then, finally, she speaks. Or, to be more accurate, she breathes out loudly and almost slumps back on the bench. It's not very lady-like, that's for sure. The dog jumps a little nervously, and then ducks under the bench out of sight.

"I've just lost my mother," she says. "She was only 62. Cancer. That's why I'm here. To sort her things out."

"Dear me." (Fuck, is that the best I can do? It makes me sound like a vicar or a maiden aunt.)

"It's so hard to know where to start. The house is just full of her stuff. Everywhere I turn I see her. It's heartbreaking, really."

Now what?

I think for a minute.

Not sure what to say.

It occurs to me that maybe I should put my arm around her

and say, "There, there." I saw one of the assistants in the annexe do that to Ainsley once when he was stuttering and sobbing over something and nothing about his watery cabbage and it worked a treat with him.

Of course, she had to move on eventually because he wouldn't leave her alone after that, if you know what I mean. But Julia's back and shoulders are right up against the back of the bench and I think that to put my arm around her I'd have to push my arm in there quite hard and that might seem a little bit odd.

So I sit there for a moment or two not really knowing what to do or say.

"What about you?" she then says. "What happened to your wife?"

"She died," I answer. "She was killed in a road accident. Run over, right in front of me, she was."

(I can say that matter-of-factly, you know, because it's how I always start talking at the annual review – to show I am calm and in control and all of that politically correct shit. I never say about me chasing Katie or anything else that happened just before that, obviously. None of that.)

I can see her sitting there motionless now, not knowing what to say either. I can sense, without even turning towards her, that she has a look of shock and horror on her face.

"She was only 32, no age at all."

And still she sits there, just looking at me. What's she thinking? How does she feel? Is she horrified to the point she wants to get up and walk? Or is she wavering, feeling sorry for me?

"She was coming up to three months pregnant at the time. She ..." And then, incredibly, the emotion cuts in and I really, truly can't finish the sentence properly. "...lost..."

I drop my head down into my hands as the feelings well up inside of me. I can't believe it, can't believe it still gets to me after all this time. It's the tablets, you see. The ones they give me – gave me – back in the annexe. I think they kept me steady. On an even keel. Steadier than this anyhow. I'm all over the place.

I sit there, bent over with my head in my hands, for what seems like minutes, sniffing and twitching and breathing heavily. I'm desperately trying to catch hold of my breath, stop myself crying, start talking normally again. I just need to calm down, breathe slowly and deeply, like they taught us in those classes back in the big house. I daren't even turn to look at her in case she gets up to go.

And then I feel it. Her hand, soft and gentle, just touching me ever so lightly on my back between my shoulder blades.

And that's just about going to tip me over the edge, I can tell you.

It's a kind touch and I've not had many of these recently. Fact is, I've not had any at all. It's all I can do to stop myself breaking down and sobbing my heart out. How I've lost everything. My wife. The baby. My freedom. All I have left now is little William. He's all I've got in the world.

And I've got to be strong for him, haven't I? I have to pull myself together and sit up straight and – hard though it is – I've got to get away from this woman and find another quiet place to wait for the Veitchs to go by with the little 'un. It's got to be done.

I'll be alright. Just give me a minute. It's not like me, all this. Not like me at all.

I have to be tough. And hard. For William's sake, because that's what's important. That's what matters. Really matters.

William. My little boy.

That's all.

Nothing else.

"Would you like to come back with us and have a cup of tea?" is what she says next.

And I look up at her, my eyes still full of tears. And she smiles at me. And I smile at her. And, unexpectedly, I find myself nodding and saying, "Yes, yes please, that would be really nice."

And you know what? As we get up together, it suddenly occurs to me straight out of the blue that she – Julia – almost certainly has a car and money and just about anything else I could want to get William away from here nice and safely.

Perfect. Just fucking perfect.

Safe? Of course she's safe. What do you mean, safe?

What the fuck do you think I'm going to do next?

5.00PM SATURDAY 31 OCTOBER

"How long do you let him sleep for?" asked the old man, sipping his cup of tea.

"Usually for about an hour or so after his lunch. It's a bit hit and miss today, though," the younger woman replied from across the room. "But if he doesn't have a nap now, he'll get tired and edgy at the fair and we'll pay for it later. He'll fight going to sleep tonight."

"It can't be an easy life," replied the man. He turned and listened for the old woman and the younger man who had gone through the kitchen into the back garden. In a quieter voice, he added, "She doesn't mean it ... what she says ... Will was too young to understand how to play anyway. That's all. It's just the way it comes out."

The younger woman thought for a few moments as she packed the snakes and ladders game away for him. She had always liked the old man, thinking he had a softness about him that balanced the sharpness of the old woman. She could talk to him. She debated whether she should share some of her thoughts.

"Are you coming to the funfair with us?" she asked eventually.

"We'll see," he answered. "We'll see what she wants to do. I struggle after a while, what with the standing about. I had to sit down for ages this morning when I went to the shops. Old age, I'm afraid. I'd hold everyone up. And the crowds..." He sighed.

"You're not so old," she smiled at him. "And you could walk with Will. See who's quickest."

He smiled back. "She changed so much when Roger died and then his Laura took the girlies back to her parents. New Zealand. We've not seen them since. Just cards. It's made her ..." He searched for the right word.

"Demanding? Controlling?"

"No, no ... not intentionally anyway ... losing Roger nearly destroyed her. And she thinks the two girls were taken away from her and it has made her rather bitter. She wants everything to be just so. Perfect. She can't handle toddler tantrums. We never had any of that when ours were small."

He paused, looking at the younger woman for her encouragement to say more. "It's the way it comes out. She doesn't mean to be nasty. It's not so much demanding as ... disappointed. Everything just seems to disappoint her these days. Everyone ... it's not about you or Will."

"And Rick disappoints her? Because he's not as perfect as Roger was?" she answered back.

"No, I didn't mean that either, Natalie, not like that. I meant losing her son. Either son. She'd have been the same if it had been Richard. That's what I meant."

The younger woman shook her head, "She wanted a perfect grandson. Rick's son."

He shrugged. "No, not exactly. I mean, you know ... we know things haven't been easy for you ... for you both. What you did was wonderful, really. Marvellous. The poor lamb. He's a good little lad really. She just doesn't cope well with anything that's not just so. And this diabetes thing and all that goes with it unsettles her. Hypo-this and hyper-that. She doesn't know what to say or do. She doesn't know what to talk to you about. She feels helpless."

The younger woman looked sceptical. She remembered glances and looks and the casual words of hurt from the old woman over the years. From way back, well before Roger had died. It was true, she thought, that the old woman had got worse since then, but the sense of superiority, the controlling nature and the nastiness when everyone and everything wasn't as she wanted, had always been there, she thought.

"Rick doesn't stand up to her, that's the problem," she responded at last.

"No, well no. That's not it really. No, that's not fair. It's not a matter of being hard with her, she needs sympathy. That's the thing to do. It's not always easy, I know. I find it … a challenge at times. There are moments when I could just … but she needs to be jollied along, not have some sort of confrontation." He shook his head, not sure whether this conversation had gone as he had hoped; to calm a tense atmosphere, to soothe things over. He hesitated for a moment or two.

"If you don't mind me saying, Natalie, I don't think you …" the old man started to say something else and then stopped as the back door was opened and he heard the old woman and the younger man coming back into the kitchen.

The little boy called out from upstairs, "Mama?"

"Here we go again," said the younger woman brushing past the older one on her way to the staircase.

5.12PM SATURDAY 31 OCTOBER

You know what I've got? Right now?

Options, that's what.

Big fat fucking options.

They told us all about options in the annexe, those of us with a chance of getting out of there, that is. How option one could take us one way (and not a very nice way if I remember) and how option two could take us to happy ever after.

Mind you, working in a supermarket and living in a bedsit for the rest of your life seemed to be the basis of option two, which isn't my idea of happy ever after, I can tell you.

They wouldn't tell me what option three was and got quite pissy when I began asking about it, but there you go – that's counsellors for you. Mad as bollocks the lot of them.

Of course, the nutters – the Sprakes and the Ainsleys of this world – don't have options. No fucking options at all; neither one, two or a non-existent three. They'll just spend the rest of their lives in the annexe, twitching and jerking and biting each other when Spink isn't looking.

But the rest of us – the normal, ordinary Joes who shouldn't really be there – do have options. And I am making the most of mine right now. I'm about to start exercising my very own option three – having a fucking good rest of my life.

I'm sitting here in the mother's house – Julia's house now, I guess – like a pig in shit. Well, in one of those fold-back recliner chairs, as a matter of fact. (Not that I have reclined it, that would be rather rude, wouldn't it?) I've a cup of tea in one hand and a shortbread finger in the other.

She's now doing something in the kitchen, feeding the dog and tidying around by the sound of it. I think she's got herself all embarrassed. She was alright on the seafront - rather nice actually – but walking back she went quiet as it got darker, like she might just be regretting inviting me. As though she were having second thoughts. Can't blame her, really. I'm a normal guy, your regular man about town, but I'm still a stranger to her, aren't I?

So I started talking, to cover her embarrassment. I said I'd come up for the day (I didn't say where from, well you can't, can you?) and that I was seeing my little boy William later (that took a bit of explaining because she thought I didn't have any children, but I managed to talk myself around that alright).

I talked on and on, much more than I'd normally do, quite chatty really, and she smiled and nodded and made the right comments at the right times and I said – to reassure her, like – how I'd just stop for a cup of tea and be on my way as I had to go to fetch William from his auntie's at 6 o'clock.

And that seemed to make her feel easier, but she's still given me tea and a biscuit and then shut herself away in the kitchen with the dog, tidying and straightening up and I don't know what to do now.

So I've been sitting here, nice and calm (as I always am), just thinking about my options and what I'm going to do next. I was going to snatch the little man from the seafront when it was really dark and crowded, make a dash for the car at the other end of the beach and then drive to Thurrock and blag my way on to a family coach trip to Disneyland in Paris.

I told you that, didn't I?

Remember?

Easy peasy.

But I'd be driving that woman's car, wouldn't I? The one in the kitchen back in that house in Nottingham? And maybe, just maybe, the cops would be on to it by now.

And possibly, just possibly, I might not actually get very far.

If I'm honest, really honest, it might all turn a bit nasty, with me and the little chap being chased across fields.

I can't have that, can I?

It's all a bit chancy, isn't it?

Not so pissing easy, in fact, when I really give it some thought.

And I haven't got any money. Not much anyway, only the loose change I snatched from that woman's house. It would probably be enough to get me and the little one on the train from Ipswich station, but it would hardly get us far or give us enough to go all the way to a new life in the south of France. And I can't really be doing with hanging about a railway station, not with CCTV and all they have nowadays.

You can't get far without proper folding money in your back pocket and that's a fact.

So this is where my option three comes in, see? This woman, Julia, has a car – one of those Japanese cars - parked out front. I can see it now, from where I'm sitting. A nice little car – nondescript you'd call it. No one would know I'd be driving that, now would they? No one would look twice or think of stopping me. And she'd not be too out of sorts if I took it – she'd have insurance and stuff like that, for sure.

And money – I reckon Julia wouldn't be short of a bob or two. Not if her mother has just died. So she'd have a purse full of cash. And if there wasn't enough in that, well, she'd have a card. Put one of them in a machine, with the right number, of course, and I could be looking at maybe £250 in tenners; even more depending on the limit she has on it. £500 would see me off to a good start, very nice indeed.

I'd probably have enough money to get to the south of France and maybe rent a place while I got myself a job. In fact, maybe she'd have a lot of money in the account and I could just keep dipping into it as and when we needed it. Maybe, if she is really shitbag rich, she'd not notice it and even if she did, well, the bank would probably repay her anyway. All in all, I don't think it would be a big deal for her at all, any of this car and money malarkey.

But it would make a massive difference to me.

And William.

And little William is all that matters to me.

But I've been thinking. Because she's a very nice lady and I don't want to let her down, I've been thinking of different ways of doing this. It's not easy, is it? After all, you can't just take someone's car and their cash card and all that without them noticing and you can't really say I'm on the run with my little boy, so do you mind awfully but can I borrow your car to make a getaway? And by the way, can I have your cash card at the same time?

No, you can't say that.

You can't say that at all, nor anything like it.

No way.

I can't just take them. It's not right, especially as she's been so kind to me. The thought has occurred to me, if I'm honest with you. A half-hour or so's chat and then, just as I'm leaving, I say excuse me while I pop to the loo. That's alright in someone's house, so long as you're just in there for a few moments. You can't go in for the other, obviously. That wouldn't be nice. Not when you're a guest.

And then, let's say, I simply find her handbag in the bedroom while she's standing there waiting for me in the hall. I lift out her keys and her purse and I'm away. But I reckon maybe you're up to speed with me here. Say she goes to her bag for something or other the moment after I've gone, notices, and reports it to the police straightaway. I might be stopped in the car before I got 500 yards out of town.

But I need another car to get away safely – and one that's not been reported as stolen.

And I need money, proper money, to help me and the little man to start over. And I can't have that reported either.

So, unless you have a better idea and you won't because I've been sitting here thinking it all through like Albert fucking Einstein, I don't know what I'm going to do – I need Julia's car and I need Julia's money, and I can't have Julia running to the cops two minutes later. That would fuck me and the little fellow straight off.

So you tell me – what do I do?

Can you think?

Are you thinking of something I might do?

5.20PM SATURDAY 31 OCTOBER

"We need to leave, Rick, this is too much," the young woman hissed under her breath.

"We can't," he whispered back. "It'll upset them, my mother especially."

She raised her eyebrows.

The little boy, sat between them, pulled away from his mama every time she tried to take a prick of blood from a finger.

"No, Mama, no."

She stopped, feeling increasingly flustered as she could hear the old woman and the man in the kitchen, preparing tea, neither of them speaking and making hardly any noise. She knew they were standing there listening to what was happening, and could hear the boy.

"Let me try ... William, look at me ... listen to me, listen to Papa."

The little boy turned away from the man and tried to hug his mama. She pushed him back upright, holding his hand firmly and offering it up to his papa. The boy clenched his fist and opened it flat, fingers splayed, and then clenched it again, this time harder, an intense look of concentration on his face.

Once more and his mama and papa both burst out laughing. The young man said, "That's just how he used to look when he was doing a poo when he was a baby." She nodded back as the little boy stopped and looked curiously from one to the other.

They both wiped their eyes. He smiled at them, now turning from one to the other, suddenly peaceful.

"Will," said the man. "We need to do the tickle on your finger. Be a good boy now and we can go to the funfair. Come on, sit up straight."

The little boy sat up. "Fair?" he asked, as his papa pricked the side of one of his fingers.

"Yes, we'll go to the funfair and you can go on all of the rides and we'll watch the procession and do everything. If you're really good, we can get a balloon and you can let it go over the sea."

The little boy turned to his mama, "Mama? Balloon?"

"Yes," she replied, "later, after tea. If you're good. We can get you a red balloon if you like ... or blue ... or a bright yellow one. What would you like?"

The boy thought for a moment as his papa busied about with the blood-testing equipment. "Tea?" he asked.

She laughed, lifting him up and moving towards the kitchen. "Rick?"

He frowned, "Not so good. Still too high. Higher actually. We need to get this under control as soon as we can."

5.21PM SATURDAY 31 OCTOBER

She comes back into the room, all calm and mannered, and sits down over by the window. She smiles tightly – nervously, I reckon – as she rests her cup of tea on the table at her side.

The table is unsteady and she spills the tea into the saucer but doesn't seem to notice.

I smile that big reassuring smile I've told you about. The one I give at the annual review. She doesn't look at me.

She leans back into her chair, moving to get comfortable among the propped-up cushions to either side.

I smile again. I'm not really sure what to say. This is all new to me, this is.

She looks at me at last and our eyes meet. She has a distant, way-off look about her as though she is thinking.

"That was my mother's favourite chair," she says eventually. "She liked to sit there and do her needlework."

I smile once more, ready to make polite conversation while I'm thinking what to do next. "It's nice," I say. "Comfy."

Now what?

She reaches into a pocket, takes out a lighter and packet of cigarettes, gesturing them towards me. I shake my head, no, I've never smoked. She takes a cigarette, struggling to get it out of the packet. I go to help her, but she waves me back down and I watch as she lights the cigarette, slipping the lighter and packet back into her pocket.

She leans back again, her head turned to her left as she looks out of the window. She pulls on the cigarette. I can see she is thinking. After a moment or two, she turns to look at me again.

"So, what are you here for?"

I go to tell her about William, and how he's been staying with his auntie for a little holiday and how I've come up to get him at six o'clock but she waves her hand to silence me.

"No," she says, her voice with a sharper edge to it. "What are you here for?" and she points to the floor; here, this cottage, this room, this chair. What am I doing here right now, here in this cottage?

I smile at her, not sure what to say.

"I'll tell you what you're here for," she says. "I'll tell you why you're here." And she looks at me, nodding, with a knowing look on her face.

I wait for her to go on. To say, or maybe mouth, the words she's thinking. But she doesn't. She just sits there looking at me.

I smile back. Can feel myself blushing. And stirring again. I know what she means. And she knows I know what she means. Is this how it happens? How people do things these days? It's all unfamiliar to me. I'm not sure what to say.

All I want, all I really want right now is to be gone from here, to get away and go for William. But I need those keys and some money. And maybe, just maybe, I need something else from her too.

But not that.

Not just the physical act.

I don't know what to do.

She struggles, slightly unsteadily, out of the chair and onto her feet. I think she is going to slump back down, but she moves away, cigarette still in hand, towards the kitchen.

What do I do? You tell me. This has never happened to me before. I've imagined something like it, God knows. I've thought about it often, something like this, back in the big house. But it's never been offered to me before, not like this. Not on a plate.

She comes back in. This time, she has an opened and half-empty bottle of gin in one hand and two glasses clinking together in the other.

"We're going to have a little drink," she says, sitting herself back down.

And we do, sitting there opposite each other, sipping at the gin and looking at each other.

She goes to pour me a second one, but I shake my head, putting my hand over the top of the glass.

"Not for me, thank you. I've got to be driving later."

She shrugs to herself, almost as if I'm not there, sits back and refills her own glass.

This time, she stops looking at me, sitting back in the chair and gazing out of the window.

Silence.

Utter fucking silence.

I still don't know what to say.

At some point, I've got to be going. But I need her car and some money. And I don't want to have to hurt her, really I don't.

She tips her head back as she takes a long drag on her cigarette. Blows the smoke up in the air.

"I used to be able to blow rings," she says, "when I was younger. My husband showed me how. Years ago. But I've lost the knack now."

Really? Well fuck diddly me.

I mean, what do you say to that?

Silence again. Complete fucking silence.

So what next? I can't just get up and go and ask for her car keys and some cash at the same time.

Can I?

What do you think?

I may just have to.

"You and me," she says at last, stubbing out the cigarette in the saucer. "You and me are the same. We've both lost everything." And she nods sadly, as though she is talking to herself now.

"I've lost my mother. My husband left me. Some girl at the office. Ver-on-ic-a. We couldn't ..." And she stops, as if she is about to cry. And she looks at me, her eyes full of tears. "At least, you've got your son."

She leans forward in her chair with her body shaking. I suddenly find myself with my arms around her, encircling first her shoulders and then her body and my hands are at her breasts, pulling down her dress at the front.

For a moment, I think she's going to struggle, put up a fight, but she seems to respond to me as I push her back against the chair. As I kiss her, I can taste the alcohol and smoke on her breath.

I'm scrambling and tugging at her clothes until I eventually start moving back and forth, steadily at first and then with ever-increasing urgency, the chair banging harder and quicker again and again against the wall.

And for a few, brief, desperate and beautiful moments I forget everything.

My wife.

The baby.

The trial.

The annexe.

Spink.

Even my dear, sweet, wonderful William.

As I come, thrusting up inside of her, I suddenly see how things could be.

For me and little William and also for Julia.

Julia's got the car and the money. I've got little William and the south of France.

A pretty cottage somewhere hidden away in the woods by the sea. We – me and Julia – sitting by a pool in a year or two watching William playing quietly in the shallow end.

What a happy little family we'd be. Her and me together with William and maybe another little sweetheart on the way some time soon.

As I look down at Julia now, aroused by the sight of her naked-ness, I smile at her. She looks up at me, trying to focus on my face.

And, as I wait for her to smile back, I find myself talking.

About my wife and the baby and the trial.

About the annexe and Spink and my dear, sweet, wonderful William.

About what really happened.

At last, as I finish my words, she focuses and suddenly seems to be concentrating and hearing what I am saying.

She's looking into my eyes.

She's wide awake now.

And the expression on her face changes.

6.26PM SATURDAY 31 OCTOBER

It's dark now, proper dark. And I'm sitting quietly, minding my own business, back on the bench on the seafront.

Have been for more than half an hour, I reckon.

Maybe more.

Just waiting, always fucking waiting.

I'm waiting for Veitch and the sister-in-law and the old fuckers to go strolling by with William, my little William, in tow.

Any time now, really.

I'll wait until they go by and give it a minute or two.

Keeping them within sight, of course.

I'll follow them and, when no one is noticing and it's all lights and noise and push and shove up by the funfair, I'll sweep in, lead sweet William away by the hand and there we are.

Sorted.

Yes, indeed.

I'll not be needing the old car now – the one I got from that woman back in Nottingham.

No, I don't need that now.

That's right. No, not any more. That's what I said.

It can stay just where it is.

Did I say? I've got myself one of those little Japanese cars. It's not something the police will be looking for and that's a fact.

And you can forget about a pocketful of loose change and how far that will take me (or not, as the case may be).

I've got one of those proper cash cards and I've even got myself a number for it too.

1.

1.

0.

6.

That's a birthday, that is.

Not mine, no.

11 June. 11 06, see? Took some doing actually, getting that.

1.

1.

0.

6.

I've been to a cashpoint already and got myself a pocketful of cash.

Plenty more where that came from, I can tell you.

No need to worry about money for a long, long time. Yes, that's a fact.

So I'm waiting. Just waiting to get my little boy and away to a new life.

But I've a cut on my hand. Did I tell you? It's cut rather badly actually. Quite close to my wrist.

It could be nasty, you know.

Dangerous it is, by the wrist.

Tosser Gibson cut his wrists once. Somehow, he'd got hold of a metal fork, no one knows how, and he started hacking away at himself in front of everyone.

He did it when some busy-body local officials came round as part of some inspection trip.

Sprake and Ainsley, snorting and giggling to themselves as ever, said afterwards that it was all done for show and that if he'd been serious, he'd have done it later, after lights out.

Maybe so, but it took four of them – Spink and her cronies - to bring him down and he ended up in the proper hospital for the rest of the month. And it was the better part of another month before we saw him in the annexe again.

I've wrapped some cloth around the cut. The first piece I used got soaked through. The next one seemed to slow it down and the one I've got on now, well you'd hardly notice the blood on it. I'll keep it nice and tight, though, just in case.

And I've a bruise too. Just to the side of my left eye. It's the sort of bruise you'd get if you turned round fast and caught it on the side of a door. Maybe you weren't quite paying attention to what you were doing. And a scratch, three or four of them to be honest, down my right cheek.

Yes.

Not so good.

I had a bit of trouble.

I've covered them all up, mind, as best I can anyway. Can't have little William scared, can we? No, I've just touched everything over with a little face powder. I'm not sure it was quite my skin type – I didn't really have time to check, okay? – but it will do the job for now for sure. I look fine, all things considered. No one would think anything was out of the ordinary. I'm just a regular guy having a little sitdown.

It's busy now.

Really busy.

Here on the seafront.

People are going by in both directions, mostly towards the funfair, and the promenade is packed full of them. Five, six, seven people spreading out right across its full width.

I've got to stay sharp. I've got to keep my wits about me.

I have to spot William and then duck back out of sight before any of them see me.

If they do, I'm fucked, plain and simple.

Veitch and the sister-in-law would turn on me, for sure. They'd not give me a chance to say anything.

And the grandparents, the old woman most likely, would sweep up little William and, well, there'd be a scene.

I'd have no choice.

No other choice.

What else could I do?

I'd never get another chance to get hold of little William and get away. I'd have to, well, I'd have to somehow see to Veitch and the sister-in-law.

And to the grandparents.

But there are the crowds. Dozens and dozens of people moving about. Hundreds of them. Someone would intervene. They'd have to, pinning me down, taking William away. Holding me until the police arrived in their cars, sirens wailing. And then it would be all over.

So I've got to do this carefully.

And cleverly.

Got to take him when it's crowded, when they've split up and I can get away with William in the confusion.

Christ almighty.

I see him.

William.

He just goes trotting by. I don't react as quickly as I'd expected. The little chap took me by surprise. I pull back, dropping my head down as though fixing my shoelaces.

I sit, holding my breath.

Waiting for them to see me.

But they don't; they just keep on walking, no more than two or three feet from my bowed head. William out in front, a yard or two ahead of Veitch and his wife. I daren't look up but I can just see – sense almost – the two of them walking by.

Still I keep my head down, making a pretence of tightening my laces, because I know the old folks will be a little way behind.

I'm clever, see? Anyone else would sit up at this point and watch their little boy walking away, all full of himself and excited about the funfair (it's a big night out at that age, after all).

Not me, though – I stay cool – I'm not going to sit up straight until the grandparents have walked on by.

30 seconds.

One minute.

90 seconds.

At 120, I move my head slowly to the left, still keeping it down, but turning it enough to see Veitch and the sister-in-law moving away into the distance and disappearing back into the crowds.

They don't stop and wait or even slow down – they don't even glance back.

Then I do the same the other way, slowly moving my head to the right, keeping it down, but turning it just enough to see back down where they'd come from. To see where the old folks are.

No sign of them. No sign at all.

They're not coming. The old folks are not coming.

That's not good, not good at all.

I was going to take the little chick-a-dee when the four of them wandered apart.

I've no chance now.

No chance at all.

There's no way that Veitch and the sister-in-law are going to split up and let my William out of their sight.

I'm fucked.

Well and truly.

Unless.

Unless.

I've one chance. One chance only. But I'll need to be quick.

And lucky.

Very, very lucky.

I'm up, on my feet, following them now, weaving in and out of the crowds to keep them in sight.

Come on, hurry up, we've a little man to catch before the night is through.

6.32PM SATURDAY 31 OCTOBER

It had taken ages and ages before the excited little boy could set off down the prom towards the funfair with his mama and papa.

First the old man and woman were coming.

Then they weren't.

His mama was cross with them.

Then his papa had wanted him to have a cycle along the prom.

He had put his helmet on and was all ready to go.

Then his mama had said it was too crowded.

Now his papa was cross as well.

Eventually, the three of them started walking along the prom and the little boy was trying very hard not to wet himself as he trotted along as quickly as he could.

He could see the lights in the distance and he could hear the jingly-jangly music from the fairground.

He had been to a funfair before and had won a bright yellow duck.

He remembered waving a long stick around as he tried to hook the duck in the water.

People were smiling and laughing – even the man with the funny eye who gave him the stick and looked a little scary.

But then, as he struggled to work out what he was meant to do, his papa had taken the stick and had won the duck for him.

He loved that duck, but he did not know where it was. Duckie. He tried hard to think where it might be.

He would get another one now, he thought.

He would do it all by himself too.

He was a big boy after all, his mama had said.

But he knew he must not wet himself. If he did, his mama and papa would take him back to the cottage and make him change his pants and trousers.

If they did that, he might miss the funfair altogether.

And that made him more anxious.

Even though mama had told him to have a wee before they came out, and he had done so in the toilet with the chain that was too high for him to reach, he still needed to go again now. It was always like this when he felt excited.

The closer he got to the funfair, the more he wanted to wee.

The faster he walked, the more he needed to go to the toilet.

When he walked slower, as slow as he could, he thought he might not get there in time to get his duck and that made him want to have a wee even more.

The little boy broke into a skip, moving in and out of the crowds, and that seemed to help a little.

If he concentrated on skipping between the people in front, he would not think about the funfair or the duck or needing to have a wee so badly.

"Will!" cried out his papa behind him, "Will, stay in sight."

The little boy giggled.

He knew his papa would run to catch him if he disappeared and he thought that would be fun.

So he skipped a little faster towards the funfair, moving into the crowd.

He didn't think about needing a wee any more.

6.34PM SATURDAY 31 OCTOBER

Half a mile to the funfair at most, I reckon. Maybe seven or so minutes and I'll have my little William back.

It's dark and busy now, as the carnival gets underway.

Noisy too, as we move ever closer to the funfair. And rougher, with lots of teenagers all rushing along and laughing and joking and pushing their way through the crowds.

They're about 10 yards ahead of me. Veitch, the sister-in-law and little William.

They bob and duck out of sight and then reappear as I keep up a steady pace behind them, near enough to see them but not so close as to be noticed.

Just walking along, I am, as if I'm enjoying the atmosphere.

Walking and watching.

Waiting for my moment.

Just ready for my opportunity – I only need the one.

Until then, anyone who looks at me will just assume I'm your Mr Average, out for a nice time, no more, no less.

Six, seven minutes to go now.

You know what? They don't have a clue they're being followed. Not a fucking clue.

Told you, didn't I? About the police not knowing about how they came to the grandparents at Aldeburgh every Halloween.

There's no one going to stop me now.

Nobody out there to help them.

Little William's mine for the taking.

Whenever and wherever I want.

I just need to wait for my chance.

They don't even know I'm there. They've no idea they're being followed at all.

Why should they?

Who turns and looks back when you're on the way to fun, fun, fun?

Hurrying along, keen to get to the funfair farther up the promenade.

It's where it's all at.

A half-hour or so there, then fish and chips, followed by the Halloween procession.

That's what they do every year, did I tell you?

I know. Been there. Done that.

It's what they think they're going to do this year.

The procession's where the whole town crowds into the high street, half of them, families with kids, carrying lanterns and the other half watching.

They make their way down to the green by the seafront where they let off the fireworks at 7.30pm.

Be a bit different for them this year, won't it? They won't have William for the fish and chips, that's for sure. Nor anything else for that matter.

Five minutes, that's all, and he'll be mine.

It's easy to follow them, dead easy.

I'm just waiting for my chance. I said, didn't I?

Only need the one and it's all over for Veitch and the sister-in-law. They'll be fucked.

They're not moving that fast, I can tell you – the sister-in-law is holding William's hand now, very tightly, by the look of it, holding him back, stopping him from running away, I reckon. And Veitch, the stupid bastard, is in front of them, leading the way through the crowds.

Makes it easy for me, this does.

That'll be his downfall, that will. Veitch's. Mark my words. Marching ahead and not paying attention to the wife and child just behind. Anything could happen to them and he's too far ahead to notice if anything did.

I can see her, evil cow, trying to keep up with Veitch. She's holding William's hand and every time he stumbles, because she's going way too fast for his little legs, she pulls him to his feet and keeps walking.

Poor little mite.

I'd like to push on up behind her and jostle her to the ground next time she does that and then, as she stumbles and falls, I'd take little William by the hand and be away into the crowd.

He'd look up at me in surprise and I'd look down at him and smile and say something sweet and kind and he'd smile back as we disappeared away together forever.

You know what, I might even kiss him on the forehead. That's what you do, that is.

Kiss little children.

I can't move in and snatch the little fellow, though, not really. Wishful thinking, that is. No more than that.

Well, I can't, can I? Not with all these people about.

I just have to wait for my chance, don't I?

Sometime in the next four minutes.

Mind you, it's heaving. Most people are sweeping along towards the funfair, although there's a steady stream of other people going back along the prom back out of town. They're all bumping into each other and saying "Excuse me" over and over again.

Utter confusion.

Complete madness.

Confused as fuck.

Not me, mind. I'm concentrating. I'm just being oh-so-careful and keeping 10 yards back and out of sight, tucked in behind some woman and her three gormless-looking children. Anyone who looks my way will think I'm with them, God help me. They're like the Addams Family.

I keep it all nice and steady as I move by them. I've not said "Excuse me" once, don't need to. I'm careful, me. Just your Average Joe, out for a stroll.

No one can hear anything anyway, other than the din of the

fairground rides over the hubbub of excited children's voices. You can't even hear yourself think.

It'd be easy to do it right now. Just take a second or two and then I'm away into the crowds.

But it's too risky. Way too risky. It only needs someone behind me to see what's happening and anything could happen. Maybe a group of teenage boys with some big-mouthed fucker wanting to impress his mates.

I can't have any of that.

No, I have to be patient, got to walk and watch, that's all. My chance will come.

And soon, very soon.

All I've got to do is to keep them in sight, and wait for my moment to pounce.

I walk a little quicker, I walk a little slower – I just keep on going, watching for that instant.

Just keep it going, on and on, in and out, waiting to make my move.

As I get to the funfair, they'll split up, did I say?

I think I did.

One will go and get some candy floss, while the other takes sweet William to the toilets there.

He's little, see? He'll need a tinkle before he gets to go on all the rides.

In about three minutes that'll be.

We're almost there, about to be reunited, a daddy and his much-loved son.

6.39PM SATURDAY 31 OCTOBER

The little boy stood behind the old fishermen's hut on the beach and tried to do a wee like his papa said he should. A drop or two came out, but not as much as he hoped. He had thought he would have done a really big wee the way he felt. He tried to do some more. He knew his papa would get cross if he said he needed to go again in a few minutes.

His papa stood next to him, waiting, and was telling him all the things they would do at the fair.

"There's a roundabout, Will, over by the boating lake, with different cars on it. If you're quick, when the ride stops and the other children get off, you may get on the police car."

The little boy looked up. "Police car?"

Papa nodded.

"With a light?"

"Well, yes, sort of." The man laughed. "It's on a ride and there will be a police car and a bus and ... I don't know ... maybe a pink car and ... all sorts really ... a frog and a dog and a cow. They're all rides you sit on."

The little boy looked back down again, puzzled.

He thought for a moment or two, about a pink car. He had never seen one. He had seen a red one and a yellow one but never a pink one. He thought it would look funny. He imagined himself in a pink car that looked like Peppa Pig.

"And floss?" he asked Papa. "We have floss?"

"Candy floss? Yes, that's pink too, clever boy," answered Papa, thinking for a minute before going on, " ...we'll have to see what Mama says about that. But there are lots of rides for you. Maybe some teacups? Like we did at Disney?"

The boy nodded. He remembered the teacups. They were scary but fun as he held on to his mama on one side and his papa on the other as they swung back and forth, slowly getting faster and faster. He thought he'd like to go on them again now he was all grown up.

"Come on, Will, hurry up and sort yourself out, Mama will be waiting for us."

The little boy struggled with his pull-up pants and trousers, grabbing at his pants but not his trousers and then pushing his pants back down again. He then pulled both pants and trousers up together, but it did not feel comfortable. Something somewhere seemed to be in a tangle.

"Papa?" he said, turning towards the man who smiled down at him.

"Ready? Come on, let's find Mama … see if she's on a ride already."

The boy looked back at his papa and then beyond him, down the pebbly beach to the sea. Something was coming towards them from out of the black and the wind and the spray. It was moving very fast. As it got closer, he could see it was a man, a very angry man with a torn face and wild glaring eyes that stared first at the boy and then, as he stopped, at his papa.

Seeing the expression on the little boy's face, his papa turned to see what had startled him.

6.41PM SATURDAY 31 OCTOBER

As Veitch turns, I hit him hard. On the side of the head.

I've no choice.

It's all gone wrong. Horribly wrong.

Veitch didn't expect it. Didn't see it coming. He staggers sideways, cracks his head on the wall. Falls forward onto his knees.

It all started just as I said it would. The sister-in-law queueing for food. Veitch taking little William off to the toilets down by the beach.

Dear William. Looking up at me now. His innocent little face.

The toilets were solid with people queueing outside. Just as I had thought. I'd planned to take William away in the confusion as Veitch saw to the little man and then stayed inside for a piss himself.

I hoped William would be standing outside for a moment or two while Veitch did his business. I'd have swept over, picked him up and been and gone in no time at all.

No harm done.

No trouble.

Nice and simple.

And I'd have had a good 10- to 15-minute head start while Veitch went looking for the sister-in-law. He'd assume little William had wandered off to look for her.

And then another 10 to 15 minutes while they searched for him along the beach, with ever-rising panic in case he'd stumbled into the water and been swept out to sea.

When they finally called for help, they'd never think of me. They'd not realise me and William were now together and on our way out of town.

The thing is, though, Veitch didn't go into the toilets and leave the little fellow outside for two minutes.

It wasn't nice and simple.

In fact, it's been trouble.

And plenty of harm done too.

When Veitch saw how full the toilets were, he kept on walking, taking William farther along the beach, behind one of the old fishermen's buildings. I thought I'd lost him for a moment, that he'd got away. I circled round and chased him down, though, all out of sight. That's when it all went wrong.

I had to hit him.

What else could I do?

It was my one and only chance.

"Papa?" says William, lifting his right hand. Towards Veitch, though. Not me.

Veitch shakes his head. Dazed, he is. Still on his knees. His head in his hands now.

I've got to be quick. This is it. My chance to take little William away.

I grab William's hand, pull him towards me, swinging him up into my arms.

"Daddy," I say, "I'm Daddy. I'm your Daddy." My voice breaks. I can't believe I've got him at last.

He looks at me blankly, not really taking it in. He doesn't know who I am, that's the thing. Then he turns to look down, watching Veitch, his head first in his hands, then gazing at the blood on his palms from where he'd struck his head.

Maybe Veitch didn't actually see me. Doesn't know it's me back to get my little boy. I'd rushed towards him as he stood there, little William to one side and slightly back. I was just going to snatch the little 'un and run. But Veitch turned as I approached so I panicked and hit him on the side of the face and down he went.

Well, wouldn't you?

Think about it.

Give me a fucking break for once, why don't you?

"Shhh," I say to William, "shhh."

Well, what else can I do?

I swing round, William in my arms, back towards the funfair.

As I do, two, three, four men come round the back of the building.

Christ, I'm done for.

Think quickly.

Got to be fast.

The first, already reaching for his flies, glances at me and then looks down at Veitch crouched over on his knees.

He can see what I've done.

I've had it now.

Well and truly fucked.

There are four of them. Army types. Cropped hair. And big fuckers. Huge they are. And they've been drinking. A lot. Fact is, they're pissed. I can tell.

"God," I say out loud, without thinking, instinctive-like. "That ... he tried to ... he touched ... my little boy."

My voice catches, almost like a sob.

Smart I am, really smart.

I told you I could think on my feet, didn't I?

They're swarming around menacingly. Staring aggressively at me and at William, who just gazes curiously, oh-so-passively, back at them.

It's William's calmness with me that fools them.

I help things along as I turn to Veitch, still crouching there on the ground.

"Pervert," I spit.

The first one, the one who led them round the corner, suddenly kicks out at Veitch, catching him just below the ribs. Must have hurt that, really hurt. Veitch cries out and rolls sideways and onto his back as the four of them circle around him.

I've got to move fast now, got to get little William away before he sees Veitch get a real kicking.

Can't have that.

What sort of daddy would let his little laddie watch someone take a good hiding?

"Come on," I say to William, "come on, time to go. Let's go. Come on now." I turn away, William in my arms, and take one final glance back at Veitch being kicked. I can't help smiling to myself.

"No," shouts little William. "Fair."

(So much for "Papa", Veitch!)

"Yes," I reply. "Funfair, we'll go to the funfair. But you've got to be quiet. Hush now and we'll go to the funfair."

We're hurrying along, moving away from the fishermen's building by the beach and back towards the funfair.

There's not much to it, really. A little children's Ferris wheel is the centrepiece on the green with three or four other rides all around it. Then, opposite, along the prom, there are stalls and caravans, all selling candy floss and burgers and bags of pick-and-mix sweets.

Got to keep away from the stalls – that's where the sister-in-law will be I think.

I have to cut across the green, turn left along the high street to the end, where I'll turn and go up the hill to get the Japanese car and then away with little William.

It's easy – just so long as I keep moving away from the sister-in-law on the seafront and Veitch and the army boys behind me.

No one's going to notice a daddy and his son moving quickly through the funfair. The rides are full, with queues of mums and dads and children for every one of them. There are big queues for the food too, teenagers mingling in with the mums and dads.

And, know what? Even if the little chap kicks up a fuss, it won't make any difference.

The noise now is furious – the laughter and shouts of the funfair drowned out by the music blaring from the different stalls and caravans. Kids yelling, people screaming and teenagers effing and blinding their heads off. You can hardly hear yourself think.

No one's going to notice a child crying. Or they'll just assume he wants one more go after Daddy's been on endless ride after ride and spent all his pennies.

We've just got to push our way through this little lot, go through the funfair and back up into the relative quiet of the high street and then up and through a dead-quiet side alley to get to that woman's house where the car is parked up on the hill.

To the car and money and away to France.

Our new life.

Me and my little love.

William is looking at me now, as we hurry along, just about reaching the crowds. He looks curious, so I smile at him.

(God, he's heavy in my arms; he's a solid little chap, I'll say that.)

"Fair?" he cries, his hands stretching up in the air as if he's just won the World Cup. He beams at me. "And floss?"

"Yes, candy floss, you can have candy floss but you've just got to be quiet for a few minutes, that's all. Just be quiet." We hurry on.

(You know what, I'm struggling to carry the little fellow, but if I make him walk it will slow us up. I've got to hold him, just got to keep going.)

"Papa? Papa coming?"

(For Christ's sake, stop talking, will you? I can't walk fast and talk at the same time.)

"He's not feeling very well," I puff. "So he's just having a sit down. We'll see him later. We're ... getting some toys from my car and then we'll meet him back at the funfair."

(I think quickly see, you've got to when you've a young child, you know.)

"Toys?" he says. "For Will?"

(God almighty, now he's talking in the third person.)

I smile, nod at him. We've really got to get going now, move as fast as we can.

Hell, it's so busy. It's going to be a nightmare pushing through all of these fat lardy fucks.

I stop for a second; now I'm on the prom again, and look right to see if it's quieter that way.

Just as busy.

That's no good.

No good at all.

I look left along the prom to see if it might be easier to go along that way. It's just as busy. But not so good.

In fact, it's worse.

The sister-in-law is three feet away.

And she's turning towards me ...

Part 2

THE HOUSE

6.46PM SATURDAY 31 OCTOBER

"Will! Will?"

I can hear her crying out as I push my way back through the crowds towards the funfair and beyond.

"Will?" Her voice, loud and querulous, almost cracking now with emotion. Above the noise and hubbub of the fair.

But she's not 100 per cent certain.

And she doesn't want to make a scene.

Yet she's calling out, frightened and unsure.

She must have seen him, must have. But she couldn't believe it was him. Couldn't credit what she was seeing. Could she be certain? I don't know. I can't take the chance.

She was turning, see? From the stall, holding bags of food. Turning towards the huts where Veitch and sweetpea had gone. Was going to go back and meet them halfway, I reckon.

As she turned, I saw her just in time, like I told you. I swung round, my back towards her. Instinct it was. Pure instinct.

Whoever's going to recognise someone when it's dark and they've got their back to you? No one, that's who. And they'd never expect to see you there anyway. Never even given you a thought for ages. Even thought you were dead, maybe.

"Will?"

Trouble is, I was holding little William. As I turned, he came face-to-face with her. Must have done.

She would have looked straight into his eyes.

I didn't hang about, I can tell you. Moved straight off and

away from her, pushing hard and fast into the crowds and out of sight.

I brushed by a young couple, struggling with a pushchair. He made a sarcastic comment as she was forced to stop to let us go through. Acting the big man for her.

I'd have given him a good slap if I'd time.

Then a group of teenagers, spiky-haired boys chatting up a couple of hard-faced girls. None of them took any notice of us.

And a couple of fairground workers, standing about with big mugs of coffee. They looked up as the sister-in-law called out again.

"Will! Will? Is that you?"

But they didn't even notice me.

Not a single glance.

Just hesitated for a second or two, then got right back down to their conversation.

I'm moving quickly now, ever so fast, getting farther away. Leaving her standing there. Not sure what she saw. Imagined it, surely, she'll be thinking. A child that looked like William. What you might call a body double.

A lot of them do look the same at this age, you know. Little boys. Blond hair, rosy-red cheeks. All dressed up nice and warm for the cold night air. Wrapped up tight so only their tiny faces are showing. She never saw his little face properly. Yes, easy to make a mistake. She'll have second thoughts in a moment or two. Will start to feel foolish.

She's called out four, five times now.

And no one's taken any notice of her.

Nobody's given me a second look, either way.

I just look like a daddy who's in a hurry, maybe going to meet Mummy on the other side of the green, ready for the procession.

About halfway across now. Still lots of pushing and shoving. It helps a bit – carrying a small fellow. They give you some leeway, leastways some of them do.

I was holding the little chap up high – easier that way – but I've dropped him down now, carrying him on my chest.

Just in case the sister-in-law is looking this way. I don't want his head up above my shoulders and looking back towards her. If she sees him again, she'll know for sure. Bound to, given a second chance to see his face.

Then she would come after me, wouldn't she? Yes, she'd have to.

I'm keeping going, nice and steady, with an "Excuse me" to the left and a "Sorry, in a hurry" to the right.

Little William doesn't speak, doesn't seem to have heard her, what with all the noise. But his head, pushed close to my chest now, twists first one way, then the other, trying to get a good look at the Ferris wheel lights.

He's wriggling.

Now he's struggling.

He's calling out.

"Fair? Fair?" He attempts to free an arm, wanting to point at the Ferris wheel where he wants to go.

"Sssshh," I say, "sssshh." (I'm trying to listen.) I think the woman's stopped now. I'm straining to hear as I'm moving along, hurrying away. Yes, she's stopped. Definitely. She's had second thoughts. Thought better of it.

Made a fool of herself and no mistake.

Stupid bitch.

Made a complete fool and now just wants to slink away, hoping nobody noticed.

She's stopped and is now walking, trying not to hurry, attempting not to panic, back towards the fishermen's huts, where she'll expect to see Veitch and little William.

Of course, when she gets there, she'll find Veitch lying unconscious in a pool of blood and no sign of William. Then she'll know. She'll realise then that she wasn't mistaken. She'll know that someone is running away with William – will she realise it's me, though?

How long have I got?

Before the police are called?

Five minutes, ten?

Thing is, there are coppers. Dotted here and there among the crowd. I've got to hurry. Once the word's got round, they'll all be on the lookout for a man with a little boy.

I've got no more than ten minutes to get to the car and away.

Have to hurry, no time to lose.

God be with me, please.

6.52PM SATURDAY 31 OCTOBER

The young man, helped by the St John Ambulance men, struggled to sit upright. He groaned and touched his forehead, looking at the smear of blood on his hand.

"Just stay still for a minute. Gather your thoughts," said the older of the two ambulance men. "We've called for help and someone's gone to find a policeman. Just sit quietly and get your breath back."

The young man felt on the ground around him, searching instinctively for something. He winced in pain, feeling as though part of him, at least on the left side, was broken.

One of the ambulance men handed the younger man his glasses. "Smashed, I'm afraid. Do you have a spare pair? Just hold on now, someone will be coming very soon."

The young man took the glasses and tried to focus on the broken lenses and twisted frame. One of the lenses had a small but perfectly formed blob of blood in the middle of it. He touched his forehead again, puzzled about the blood and how it had got on his head from the glasses.

He looked up at the crowd that was gathering around him, making sympathetic sounds and noises.

"They made off that way," said an elderly woman. She pointed. "Along the beach towards Thorpeness."

"I didn't see them," said a man, "...they've left him in a terrible state."

"It's what comes of letting them drink all day long," added a third voice from within the crowd.

The young man knew he had to think of something. It was important, but he did not know what it was. He knew it was a bad thing that he had to deal with straightaway. Something terribly urgent. He wondered for a moment if the thing was to do with the sharp pain in his side and up towards his chest when he moved suddenly.

"My heart?" He said suddenly, looking up at the two St John Ambulance men. "Is it my heart?"

"You just hold on, old son. The ambulance is coming. You've been in a fight. Came off the worse for wear. Just you wait."

A fight? Why would he fight? He had never fought, not since his school days anyway. Playground scraps, that's all. He tried to make sense of what they were saying to him. Needed to under-stand why people were standing around, looking at him with a mix of curiosity and pity. He had to remember.

"We've called for an ambulance, but it may take a while to get here through the crowds," echoed the younger of the St John Ambulance men. "So you just sit and wait until it does. And the police are coming as well. Someone's gone to fetch a policeman."

The men were talking to him, but slowly. As if he were ill or something. He struggled to remember what it was he needed to think about. What it was he had to do. There was definitely something that he must do, and urgently.

He tried to get to his feet and went as far as going onto his knees. He reached for the ambulance men's arms as they moved across to support him.

"Will you sit down please," asked one.

"Will you wait a minute," echoed the other.

Will.

Will.

Oh dear God, it was Will that he meant to remember. That madman coming out of the night and punching him. The other men kicking him on the ground. The madman – that old familiar crazed face – turning to laugh as he hurried away with Will in his arms.

The man pushed himself to his feet and screamed out, "Will…"

6.58PM SATURDAY 31 OCTOBER

"Sweeties?" he says suddenly, "sweeties for Will?"

The little devil kicked off when we were about halfway across the green, just as we went by the Ferris wheel. He started up as he realised he wasn't going to get a go on it.

(Well be sensible, how could I?)

We just kept on going, though, the little tinker getting more and more upset.

He began with a yell, almost indignant it was.

Still I kept moving, going faster and faster. I ended up barging my way through, pushing people aside in my haste to get away.

Then, God almighty, it turned into a high-pitched screech.

On and on it went, getting louder and louder the farther away we got from that fucking wheel.

Know what? He was causing a scene.

Something of a stink, you might say. People were turning and looking at us. Angry looks, from some of those I'd pushed aside. One or two shouted at us. One old man flailed his arms in our direction, gesticulating wildly because I'd banged into his stupid wife.

Still the little 'un kept wailing, with more and more people turning as we went on by. And not just looking but seeing and remembering us, that's the thing.

(Well you would, wouldn't you?)

"Ssshh," I kept saying, as loud as I could, "later, we'll do it later."

(Well I couldn't think what else to say.)

Almost there, almost there, almost there to the high street.

"Sweets," I tell him at last, pulling him up and bringing his head close towards mine so he can hear me clearly, "let's get some sweets. What sweets do you like?"

What sweets do children eat these days? In my day, it was all blackjacks and fruit salads and pink shrimps. Those are what I ate.

"Smarties?" he answers, his hands going up in the air again in triumph. "Smarties?"

"Yes," I say, "Smarties for William. I'll give you some money to buy Smarties."

Into the high street. It's busy, but not as manic because people are standing and waiting for the parade. It's where families march down the high street with lanterns and torches, down towards the funfair. I told you, didn't I? Remember? Seven, half seven, maybe? They're starting to move in now, away from the seafront and the funfair, lining the pavements to either side of the street, waiting expectantly.

"Here," I say, turning and looking at William, "hold on to this. For sweets."

His eyes light up, as he reaches and grabs the ten-pound note, squeezing it in his tightly closed fist.

"For sweeties? Sweeties for William?"

"Yes," I say, "Now come on, we've got to go to the car, then we'll get as many sweets as you can eat."

We've got to walk right along the high street almost to the other end to get to the road that takes us up towards the car. It's late now, although some of the shops on either side of the road are still open.

And the streets are lined maybe two or three deep in places with people waiting for the procession to come by. It's warming up, I can tell you. A definite buzz in the air, with lots of excitement for the coming procession.

I tuck my head down, hold William's hand and start moving; got to be quick, no time to waste. No time at all. Won't take us long, though, just to the end of the high street, cross over and up the hill to the car and away.

Keep my head down.

Moving along.

A dad in a hurry, on his way home for tea, that's me.

It's busy, but I'm moving along nicely. Except the little one doesn't walk in time with me; he isn't hurrying along. He's doing some sort of skipping routine. And pulling his hand in and out of mine as he shuffles back and forth. Two steps forward, one step back. We've not got time for this, really we haven't. Two steps forward, another one back. But he's quiet and happy and he's moving along. So we'll go with it. For now.

Not far, we're moving along well enough.

Two steps forward, one step back. Two steps forward, one step back.

And now he's humming. God knows what. In fact, he's singing to himself.

Along we go. Not so far until we are off the high street, across and up that quiet side street and at the car and off and away. No one is looking at us. Nobody is taking any notice.

Piece of cake, this.

Easy-peasy.

Done and dusted.

So then he stands stock-still, the little man. And he's staring ahead, with a look of concentration on his face. What the hell is he looking at? Is it her? I look up. The sister-in-law's not there. No coppers. Nothing. Nobody at all. Just people, mums and dads and kids, all waiting for the procession to begin.

"Come on," I say, chivvying him along. "Hurry up and we can get those sweets."

"We?" he says.

"Yes, we."

"We?" he says again.

We? We what?

"Come on," I repeat, pulling his arm now, "we've got to get going, come on William, hurry."

"We?" he says and then once more, this time more emphatically. "We!" And then I get it: not "we" but "wee". He wants a wee right here and now, halfway up the high street. No time to waste, I sweep him up into my arms.

"Come on," I say again, moving forward into some sort of shuffling run as best I can with so many people now moving back and forth across our path. "Nearly there, nearly there; we need to cross the road and then you can have a wee."

On we go.

On we go.

He's quiet for a moment, as I move as quickly as I can behind the gathering crowds.

On we go.

On we go.

"Excuse me," I say, dropping William to the ground and pushing my way through the crowd to cross the road. "Excuse me."

They move, reluctantly, to let us through, not wanting to lose their position at the front of the pavement, the best view of all. William's quiet, or at least I can't hear him, as his head is down and it looks as though he is trying to keep on his feet.

Then we're through the crowds and at the pavement and I can see, farther along and up to my left, ready to start, the long queue of the procession itself. A mix of mums and dads and children holding Chinese lanterns and torches that they're waving about, lighting up the night sky.

The police are all down that end too. I can see three or four at the front of the procession, ready to lead it. And more, so far as I can see, to either side and stretching back, ready to contain the procession and stop it spreading and spilling onto the pavements as it moves along the route.

All we need to do is cross the high street – now – and get along and into the darkness of the side road. I step to the edge of the pavement, pulling William along behind me. Got to make this nice and calm and peaceful because, the thing is, the whole of the fucking high street, three or four deep to either side, is looking down towards the procession. Each and every one of those fuckers is going to see me and William as I cross the street. So it needs to look dead natural and ordinary, doesn't it?

A normal dad just crossing the road with his lad, maybe nipping back home, just round the corner, so the tiddler can do his business. Then back out again to the procession and the fireworks.

Perfect. Who'd think anything else?

I pull William to his feet; don't want to snatch him up in my arms again as we cross just in case he cries or struggles and people look at us, and remember.

I take his hand in mine and he looks up at me and smiles. I look down at him and smile back. We're okay, him and me. Big Dad and little lad, that's us.

We step out into the open.

I turn my head to the left towards the procession, almost automatically, even though I know there's no traffic there.

I turn my head to the right for a split-second, no traffic there either, of course.

I turn my head back automatically once more, look left again.

And then, above the chattering of the procession, the hubbub of the crowds and the noise of the funfair in the distance, I hear her again.

"Wiiilllliammm!"

That fucking woman.

Dear God.

I turn back to my right, I know she's there, that she's seen us, been following us, hunting us down, but I need to see how close she is to us. I need to know how long I've got.

100, 150 yards away, that's all.

And waving her arms in the air. The crowds turn to look at her.

"Wiiilllliammm!"

7.06PM SATURDAY 31 OCTOBER

A small crowd stood watching as the young man, unsteady on his feet, was supported by the St John Ambulance men. The young man faced the policeman who had come forward as the crowd shuffled to either side.

"No, officer," said the young man, his voice rising. "You're not listening. My son, my adopted son, Will, has been taken by his biological father. Just now. He's snatched him. You have to do something about it. He's in great danger."

"If you'll just wait a moment, sir, I can take a statement."

"There isn't time for that, really there isn't. My wife and I, his aunt, adopted Will after his mother died ... was killed by his father, actually. You see, his biological father, he's dangerous. He's been certified and sectioned because he's a menace to the public. He's just got him, Will, and he's run away with him."

The young man could hear the panic in his voice and knew what he was saying sounded nonsensical. He tried to appear calmer and more rational, talking steadily, explaining himself.

"So this man – the biological father, you say – is he the one you've been fighting with?"

"No, I've not been fighting with anyone. I was behind the hut so my son could go to the toilet when his father came and knocked me down and these squaddies then started kicking me. It was only when these ladies here saw what was happening that they stopped and ran away."

"And why would they do that, sir? These squaddies. Why would they set upon you?"

"Listen ... because ... his father told them I was, look, he said I was a paedophile and they believed him. My son's a type one diabetic so we need to find him quickly. He needs help, constant checks ... injections."

"I'll report it to the duty inspector now sir and he'll pass it straight on to the CID team on duty. Meantime, we need to get you down the station and take a proper statement from you. Get those cuts and bruises seen to as well."

The young man lunged forward, his arms pushing at the policeman's shoulders. The policeman stepped back as the two St John Ambulance men held on to the young man's arms, pulling him away.

"You're still not listening to me," shouted the young man. "Will's in terrible danger. You need to alert all the police round here, right here and now on the streets. Not some duty inspector sitting miles away in some office. His father's mad ... and dangerous. I'm telling you. And Will could go into a coma if he's not looked after. Why won't you just do something to help?"

The policeman reached for his radio and turned away as he started talking. The young man caught snatches of what he was saying, "...send a car...paedophile...seafront toilets."

The young man let out a cry of anguish.

7.07PM SATURDAY 31 OCTOBER

I drag William up into my arms, high against my shoulder. I swing him round to my left, so I'm between him and the woman down the high street.

I smile at him, pretend to be talking, acting natural.

All the time, I'm thinking, be calm. I can't lose control, see? I can't rush, break into a run, making it look like I'm trying to run from that screaming fucking woman. Someone will grab me, pull me to the ground, stop me getting away. I couldn't bear it, not now. Not now I've got him.

"Wiiilllliammm!"

Christ, there she goes again. What's she doing? Is she standing there pointing at me? Is she running? Is she racing towards me?

I daren't look. Mustn't turn around. I've got to act natural. Make it seem as though I haven't heard her. That she's nothing to do with me. A nut, that's what she is. A drunk, maybe. Someone who's not worth a second glance. Not by me anyhow. I'm just a normal dad out and about with his little fellow-me-lad.

I'm out now, off the pavement, away from the crowds behind me, almost halfway across the high street.

"Wiiilllliammm!"

She's done it again.

Mustn't look to my right.

I just mustn't.

I can't lose him now, I really can't.

Got to focus on the crowds in front of me, lining the other side of the street.

They're now looking to my left, towards the procession.

They're not looking the other way, down towards the sister-in-law.

They must all think she's some sort of drunken slapper, I'm sure of it.

Wiiilllliammm?

Wiiilllliammm?

It's an echo, my imagination playing tricks. I'm waiting for it. Waiting for the next cry. But I can't hear her, nothing at all, she's gone quiet.

Wiiillllliammm?

Wiiilllliammm?

Imagination again.

I mustn't turn.

I just mustn't.

Really, I can't.

What's she doing? Right now? Is she coming ever closer, 100, 50 yards away now?

Is she about to run at me?

Is this how it's going to end?

Sprawled in the street, fighting for the little lad?

Suddenly, making me jump, the noise of the procession starts. A band, some sort of fanfare. Oompah. Oompah.

A great roar goes up from the crowd. They've all turned now, each and every one of them, to my left, watching the procession.

They've forgotten about the woman.

They're taking no notice of me either. No fucking notice at all.

Something and nothing, that's what they're thinking.

Even so, I can hardly breathe. I daren't look. Every nerve in my body is tensed, waiting for her to throw herself at me, bringing me down, wrestling with me for William, fighting for his life.

"Excuse me, excuse me," I cry out (I can't help myself), pushing my way through the crowd on the other side of the street. People move, irritated and slow, far too slow, out of my way, their eyes fixed on the procession coming towards them.

I'm in the crowd.

I'm moving through.

I'm out the other side.

I'm walking quickly, half running, by the back of the crowd, along the pavement, up to the road that takes me – us, me and William – to the car and away.

I know she's behind me.

Somewhere.

That she's coming and she won't give up.

But I'm ahead of her. Well ahead of her really.

And getting farther away every second.

I'm moving along at a fair old pace (William's weight permitting).

And think about it.

Just think for a moment.

Work it through in your head, like I'm doing.

She's got to run down that high street, just as the procession is coming up it.

What's she going to do?

She can't exactly run headlong through the police, the oompah fucking band and three hundred or so mums and dads and kids, can she?

She'll have to cut through to the side, come along the back of the pavement, like me.

But the crowds turn and follow behind the procession. I know, I've been here before. I've seen it happen.

So she's going to have to fight her way through the oncoming crowd of hundreds; swimming against the tide, as it were. And a strong one at that. A tsunami, you might say.

Not easy at all.

Not when you're panicking.

Not when half the town is lined up and moving against you.

And, I'll tell you something else. (Christ, I'm slowing, this boy is heavier than he looks.)

She won't know which way I've gone.

She saw me cross, I'll give you that.

She probably saw glimpses of me moving behind the crowds.

(I can't keep up this pace, can't carry him for too long.)

But she won't know for sure which way I've gone off the high street. There are two alleyways along the high street, one at the start, another farther down, and these lead upwards to steps that take you to the road behind. And then there's the little road I'm heading for at the far end of the high street, down near the town's other fish and chip shop.

Perfect.

Just keep going.

Absolutely perfect.

I'm now in that little road at the end of the high street. 200, 300 yards away, and going up the hill where we'll get the car and we're away.

You know what? We're safe. At last. I can feel it. Freedom. I can feel it in my bones.

I drop William down onto his feet, taking his hand, and we start walking along together.

Briskly, mind. Just in case.

(And as briskly as you can when a cheeky chappie is doing that skipping-shuffling thing again.)

But walking, definitely walking fast.

(And now he's humming and singing to himself as well, watching his shoes and making some sort of whooping noise in time with his footsteps.)

Still, he's moving.

And he's forgotten about his sweets.

And somehow, he doesn't seem to need a wee any more.

Magic, just magic.

It's quieter now as we move steadily up the hill. It's a different place, away from the mayhem of the high street and the seafront.

Me and Charlie Chuckles, we're now walking in step and in time with each other. By one terraced house. Then another. Up the hill and away we go.

He's humming and singing still and I'm trying to catch what it is, see if I know it, see if I can join in.

Wheels on the bus?

Round and round?

I know it. Bet you do too.

I join in, softly at first, shyly even – I don't sing much, well, you don't get much chance in the annexe, that's for sure (and when we do, Sprake starts bellowing at the top of his tuneless fucking voice, which puts paid to it all almost straightaway). But, as we keep on walking, we're singing together. Me and the little fellow. I keep trying to catch his eye, so I can smile at him encouragingly, but he's in a world of his own, bless him, singing and skipping and shuffling along.

But we're alright we are, proper alright. A real dad and his real son. That's us.

Not far now.

We're getting close and I stop walking, letting go of William's hand to reach for the car keys in my pocket.

He stops too, still singing, then looks up at me and smiles.

A real butter-wouldn't-melt smile, that's what it is.

It certainly melts my heart, I can tell you.

"Disneyland," I say, "how would you like to go to Disneyland? See Mickey Mouse and Donald Duck. And ... (what the fuck's the dog called?) ... Goofy." (Or is it Pluto?)

"Now?" he replies. "Now?"

"Yes," I say, "come on, let's go to Disneyland Paris right now. We'll drive through the night."

I sweep him back up into my arms, kiss him and pull him towards me, our faces brushing together. He struggles a little, pulls back, away from my face. Must be my beard, I reckon, maybe it tickles him.

I laugh, a little more loudly than I need to, just to reassure him. He looks alarmed, so I drop him back down to the ground. I'm not sure what to do next (well, I'm out of practice as a dad, aren't I, be fair).

"Come on," I say, finally, "let's hold hands." He seems happy enough to do that, so, with his little hand wrapped inside mine again, we approach the side road.

It's quiet and there's no one around.

And we – wait for it – come to the corner, almost skipping!

Well, I just start doing it on the spur of the moment really, knowing the little laddie won't be far behind me when he realises what I'm up to.

But William stumbles and falls forward. I bend over, pulling him back onto his feet.

"There, there," I go. "Come on, let's skip to the car and go to Disneyland. We'll be there by morning."

He looks up at me again and smiles and I smile down at him. Then we turn and start skipping.

On we go.

On we go.

We're laughing now, the two of us, him and me.

Round the corner, we go.

Round the corner, we go.

It's like a song, isn't it, 'Round the Corner, We Go'.

Round the corner, we go.

Round the corner, we go.

I stop, gripping William's hand ever so tight.

I see up the length of the road stretched out ahead of me.

A police car at the far end.

And another police car closer to us.

Coppers on guard.

People in white suits and masks and white shoes going in and out.

The whole fucking shebang.

I knew I should have killed that nasty barking dog.

The woman's house, our getaway car, everything, absolutely everything everywhere, is ablaze with lights.

It's Wembley fucking Stadium on Cup Final day.

And we've just walked out of the tunnel.

7.19PM SATURDAY 31 OCTOBER

I turn instinctively, grabbing William as I do, ready to move back down the way we came, as fast as we can, before any copper or nosy neighbour looks round and sees us.

He struggles, not liking it, so I have to hold him firm and tight.

He has to be quiet. Dead quiet.

Else we're fucked.

I put my hand over his mouth, pressing it as hard as I can against his lips.

God knows I don't want to hurt him, he's my little boy.

But he has to be quiet.

And he has to know he has to be quiet.

He looks at me, with tears in his eyes.

Or am I imagining it?

I can't bear it.

I'm not imagining that.

"Shhh, shhh," I go.

We have to be quick, making our way back down from where we came, hoping we can somehow cut our way through, away from the sister-in-law, and along towards the car park where I left that car from Nottingham. I have to hope no one's put two and two together yet and I can use that to get away from here.

Fact is, it could work.

We still have a chance.

A good chance, I'd say.

I reckon they'd have found that Nottingham woman by now. They must have done. But maybe they've not yet joined up all the dots, so to speak, connecting me and her car with here and what's happening now.

It's quite a long line of dots, wouldn't you say?

If we can get to that car and away, we can still make it to Disneyland, where dreams come true. I've got cash and I can get some petrol in an off-the-beaten-track petrol station. I reckon we can be at the Disney coaches in less than two hours from here, can lose the car by tucking it away at the back of the massive car parks there and be on a coach and off before the police have even pieced it all together.

We could do it.

For sure we could.

But we need to be fast.

And we need to act normal; that's important, that is. You see, I don't reckon the police and everyone around the house behind me will have worked any of it out yet. Not really. I think a neighbour must have heard the dog barking relentlessly, would have knocked on the woman's door, then looked through the window and called an ambulance. I should have moved her out of sight, I know that now. I didn't think. A rare mistake.

So what?

So fucking what?

After all, what have they got?

They've the woman, that's all. But she's not talking, that's for sure. I made certain of that. (Well, I had to, I had no choice. It wasn't what I wanted.) There's still nothing at this stage to link her with me and absolutely fuck all reason to think that a dad and his little 'un coming round the corner are anything but what they seem to be.

Out for some fun.

Just having a good time.

Enjoying a little chuckle together, as it were.

I've nothing to fear from this lot behind me. Police, forensics, neighbours? The whole fucking bunch of them wouldn't even give us a second glance tonight. All we've got to do is just keep moving back down where we came from and start all over again.

It's quiet.

It's easy.

No trouble at all.

I slip William gently onto his feet and his head drops down. Okay, I know I hurt him. I know that better than anyone and maybe I was too hard. I have a heavy hand, everyone knows that. It's common knowledge back in the annexe. "Issues", that's what that Fat-Arsed Eileen says I've got.

But I did what I did with William and I had no choice; you know why? You can't have a child shouting and yelling, no matter what the reason, not when the police are around. The coppers will look up and, well, you can't be too careful, can you? And, after all, that's how I've got this far isn't it – by being oh-so-very-careful.

Still, it gives me a moment or two to myself. You don't get too much time to think when you've got children and that's a fact. Any mum or dad knows that. I stop for a second, thinking. Coming down the hill, I now have several choices. Want to know what they are?

Think it through for yourself.

Go on.

Have a go for once, why don't you?

There are three options. One, I can go back into the high street and along. That will be quiet now the procession has gone by and we can make our way quickly to the car; then again, the woman may be there. That could get very nasty. She's not getting William back, I'll tell you that for nothing. No matter what, he's mine now. No one else will ever have him, I promise you that.

Two, we can push back on to the seafront and along by the Ferris wheel and funfair; that will be busier as everyone will be waiting for the fireworks to begin. We've less chance of being seen, but being so busy it will take us ages to get through.

And three? Our best bet is to cut down the alleyways behind the high street and near enough towards the car park; chances are, no one will see us along there and, if they do, we could say the little chap needed a wee. People don't mind little boys doing that, do they? Down an alleyway?

The sister-in-law's the thing, though. I can't risk being seen by her. So the key question is this – where is she now?

Think it through again.

It's not difficult.

Just apply some cold, hard logic.

Did she turn back when she lost me, making her way back through the crowds and back down to Veitch? Has she found him yet? All hell will break out when she does.

No.

Is she maybe wandering round the high street now that it's empty, going from shop to shop asking if any of the shopkeepers have seen a sweet-faced, fair-haired little boy?

No.

Did she turn left off the high street, back towards the prom and the old fuckers' cottage?

No.

She did none of those.

I'll fucking well tell you what she did.

When she lost sight of me, she went as quickly as she could to the nearest policeman. She explained what had happened. The copper then radioed for help. Two coppers in a police car, when the crowds had parted, drove down the high street to where she was waiting for them. She got in the police car and they drove into these back streets behind the town.

How do I know this?

Easy. I just put two and two together. Two and two makes four.

And the proof of all this?

As I come down the hill I see the police car further down turning in and coming up from the bottom. Any second now, the police car, with the woman and two fit young coppers in it, is about to come fully into view.

I am just standing here.

They will spot me.

And then I'm done for.

7.21PM SATURDAY 31 OCTOBER

The young woman peered out of the windows in the back of the police car as it drove up into the maze of back streets. She moved quickly from one side to the other, leaning forward and wiping the steamed-up windows for a clearer view of the street.

"He snatched my boy," she said frantically, almost to herself, over and again. "He snatched my boy."

"Keep looking to your right, please," responded the policewoman in the front passenger seat. "I'll look for a man and a boy to the left. PC Wilson will look ahead."

"He won't be far," replied the young woman. "Will can't walk fast. Even if he carries him, he won't have got much farther than here ... what's that?"

She cried out in alarm as she saw the police cars and the forensics team coming in and out of the terraced house.

"Oh God," she said, "what's happened? Pull over, please. Pull over."

The police car stopped and the policewoman turned to face the young woman. "It's a domestic incident involving a middle-aged woman. It's not your son. We don't think there's any connection."

"He won't have gone up here with Will. He'd have turned back or gone into one of the private roads – the alleys - when he saw all this." The young woman looked out of the windows again, first to the left and then to the right. "It's too late. We've missed him. He must have gone another way."

"We'll get out of the car and walk up and down with you. Let's see what we can see."

"I need to get hold of Rick, my husband," she answered, opening the car door and stepping out. "He's down at the seafront waiting for us. He'll be worried; he'll think Will has wandered off."

In the car, the radio crackled and the policeman leaned forward to listen. A report of a child taken away from foster parents by his biological father and a man taken into custody. He got out of the car, looking at the policewoman and the frightened young mother walking up the hill. He whistled at his colleague but she did not hear. He walked briskly towards them.

"It's okay," he said quietly, as he caught up with them. "From what I can make out, and it's a little confused, they've made an arrest down on the seafront. Come back to the car and we'll get you to the police station. You can ID the man and collect your son."

The woman sighed with relief. "Thank God. Is Will safe? Are you sure he's okay?"

7.23PM SATURDAY 31 OCTOBER

Did they see me?

Did they fuck.

It was close, mind.

The second I saw the front of the police car turning, I snatched up William without thinking, swung open the front gate of the terraced house next to us, slipped inside, and crouched down low behind the brick wall.

That's where we are now.

I've got him in a grip, I can tell you.

Daren't take any chances. He has to be quiet.

I'm kneeling, crouched over, sideways on to a waist-high brick wall that separates us from the pavement.

The little fellow's jammed tight between my legs, my hand clamped hard on his mouth.

He's struggling and he's a determined little chap.

I have to hold him tighter.

Not a sound, little William, not a sound.

The police car's come to a halt and is parked in a space a little way down from me, I reckon. May be uphill, to my left, though. I can't quite tell. I think we've got coppers up to the left of us, up by that woman's house, and the sister-in-law and the coppers down to the right.

I daren't sit up and even look over the wall. They might see me.

From the left?

To the right?

I can't even look up and over at the terraced houses on the opposite side of the street.

Know what? The whole street, from top to bottom, is soon going to be lit up brightly.

I can hear the sister-in-law's voice; she's just yards away from us now. From the left, hurrying along.

Now going past.

Now gone.

She's normally loud and strident, though this time she sounds scared and whiny. I can't make out the words, but she's obviously telling the coppers what happened again. I can hear them talking, moving quickly away.

A whistle.

Someone running.

A flurry of voices. It sounds like they've stopped, are turning, are coming back up, this time more slowly.

I guess these coppers have put two and two together. She's told them about me and sweet William. They've probably had a report about Veitch being beaten up by the toilets. Then there's this business with the woman up at the top. Never mind what happened in Nottingham – those three things occurring in a town of this size, on the same night, all within an hour or so of each other. Well, it's too much of a coincidence, isn't it?

I crouch down low, still holding William tight.

I can't breathe, daren't. William's the same, I can sense it.

I hold him tight, so tight, I imagine my fingers turning stiff and white.

They're almost upon us again, walking up towards that woman's house where all the police are gathered; that's where the coppers, constables, most probably, will hand the woman over to whichever CID man-in-a-suit is coordinating everything.

From there, once they've heard her story, know who it is they're looking for, they'll flood the town with coppers, roadblocks on the way in and out, helicopters, dogs, the whole fucking lot.

I feel the little 'un twitch and jerk violently in my arms.

Have I held him too tight? My hand clamped over his mouth and his nose together?

Or is it some sort of fit? He twitches again suddenly as I hold him down; we daren't make a noise. It's for his own good. Really it is.

Then they're alongside us, no more than a foot or two away, moving ever so slowly it seems. If they turned, maybe heard a noise, looked over the wall, we'd be done for. I can hear one of the coppers clearly now, just a snatch of conversation, " ...tor Hudson will know".

What's that? Hudson will know? Was it Inspector Hudson will know? Know what? What's happening?

My guess is that Inspector Hudson – whoever he is – is up at that woman's house. He's CID and coordinating it all.

He's the copper in charge I reckon; he's getting everyone together at the house to compare notes. The neighbour who raised the alarm – what did she hear or see? Veitch? Maybe the coppers who attended to him have reported back. The sister-in-law? She's the final piece of the jigsaw for sure. The coppers will know I'm in town and I've got little William. That's all they need to know to trigger the full-scale, bells and trumpets, whistle and drums alert.

If only they knew where I was.

Just a stride away, hidden behind a garden wall.

I hold William ever tighter, willing him now to be quiet.

And then, as quickly as they came, they're gone. The coppers and the sister-in-law. They're up and by us and on the way to the woman's house, their voices drifting into the distance. Simple as that.

It's okay, William, it's okay.

I loosen my grip, remove my hands, turn him over.

He's lifeless in my arms.

I've killed William.

7.31PM SATURDAY 31 OCTOBER

The young woman stepped back when she saw him, his face bruised and battered.

"Rick, Rick, where the hell is he? Where's Will?"

The young man stepped forward, moving to put his arms around his wife.

She shrugged him off, twisting towards the policewoman and men standing close by them in the police station reception.

"You said you had Will, that you'd made an arrest. Where is he? Where's Will?"

The police officers looked at each other, waiting for one of them to speak.

"He took him off me, Nat, took Will away," answered the young man, his voice shaking. "Down at the beach. He hit me, look, here ... took me by surprise. I couldn't stop him. He's out there somewhere. I keep telling them but they won't listen."

She spun back towards the police, focusing on the police-woman who seemed to be in charge.

"I saw him, running away with Will. Along the parade. I chased him, but it was too crowded. I told you this. I thought he'd gone up the hill down by the bakers, out of town. You said ..." She turned towards the policeman next to her, "...he'd been arrested.

This is Rick, my husband, Will's dad ... You've not got him, have you? He's still out there somewhere with Will."

The young woman and the young man looked at each other in despair.

They embraced.

"He won't hurt him, whatever he does," murmured the young man. "He's his son ... and he won't do anything else. He's never been that way."

She pushed him back. "So far as we know. He's mad, Rick. And nasty. You don't know what he's going to do or when. Look what he did to Katie. She said he never knew what he was doing himself from one minute to the next."

"You have to find him ... quickly," said the young man, turning back towards the police. "Nat, where did you last see him with Will?"

The police looked at the young woman, seeming now, so the woman thought, to realise exactly what had happened.

"He was running along the high street, the other side of the parade. I thought he'd turned and gone up the hill but I think he must have kept going back towards ..."

The young woman and the young man looked at each other.

"Shit," said the woman, "he knows we were down this end of town. He's gone to the cottage to get our car – he'll use that as a getaway."

"He's going to need my keys," added the man. "And my parents will be in the cottage when he arrives." He gulped in air. "Seriously ... please ... you have to be quick. You have to get there before he does. It may be too late ..."

7.33PM SATURDAY 31 OCTOBER

I turn, oh-so-slowly, and look up at the terraced house behind me, then, ever so carefully, along the row of terraces, both up and down the street.

I've got lucky.

All I can see are lights on two or three doors down and lights on, farther up, towards the woman's house. It's a blaze of lights up there and all eyes, anyone looking out of any window, will be towards that, not me.

In between, nothing.

This house, the one I'm in front of, and the ones to either side of it, are dark.

I reckon the owners are at the seafront or maybe, just maybe, like that woman, they're from London and these are their holiday homes left empty most times.

I've got lucky again.

Told you I'm a lucky fellow, didn't I? Remember?

It gets better.

The house I'm crouched in front of has a pathway between it and next door. The pathway goes between the two houses and into an alley with what look like back gates to either side. All I have to do is step over the knee-high wall to the side and onto the pathway, take a dozen steps into the alleyway, open the back gate and I'm out of sight in the back garden.

Know what I'll do? I'll break in.

Lie low as the coppers flood the streets in the next half-hour. Stay still as the helicopters fly over.

Put my head down as the storm rages around me for the next 24 to 48 hours at most.

Then, on Monday evening, nice, quiet Monday evening when the storm has subsided and everyone assumes I'm long gone, I'll slip out in the dead of night, make my way along to the car from Nottingham that's parked at the far end of the seafront and away I go.

What's to link me to that car from Nottingham? Nothing.

Who's to know it's there? Nobody.

What's to stop me simply driving away? Nothing at all.

It's all going to go just as I planned. Down to Thurrock, onto a coach to Disneyland, over into Paris and away down to the south of France. A new life.

But not with little William.

Not my little man.

God help me, what have I done?

I have to hold myself together, not break down and sob; I have to do this quickly but oh-so-carefully. I have to concentrate on the task in hand. I have to put everything else – awful though it is – out of my mind.

I look up and, ever so slowly, peer over the wall that faces the pavement and the houses opposite. If anyone looks out and sees me, a man kneeling in someone's front garden, I'm done for.

The houses opposite all look quiet, some dark, some lit, but all, so far as I can see, with blinds down and curtains drawn.

No time to waste.

My only chance.

Have to do it now.

I scoop up William's lifeless body – I know, I know, what can I do? – and turn and step over the brick wall to the side.

I glance backwards, can't help myself, to check the houses and the street are still quiet.

They are.

Thank God.

My luck holds.

I walk swiftly down the pathway, William's body held upright against mine, his head lolling. It breaks my heart, but, from behind, from the houses opposite and the street to the left and right, no one would see William. They'd just see a man walking, between the two terraced houses, along the alleyway and out of sight.

I have to be strong; it was an accident, after all.

I have to be practical. I can't break down and cry, not here, not now.

I can't think about what I've done, I still have to get away. It's what William would want with all of his little heart. I know it is.

I'm at the back gate now. On a latch or bolted? I can't put William down in the mud; no matter what, I can't do that.

Supporting William with my right arm, I push the gate handle down with my left hand. The gate swings open, we're inside, the gate's shut, we're safe, at least for now.

Moving quickly, no time to waste, I lay William on the patio, and peer up at the house. It's hard to see much inside, everything's so dark.

For the next hour?

For the winter?

Who's to tell?

I'll worry about that later. First things first, I need to get into this house with as little noise and damage as possible. If not, someone may hear me break in, maybe a copper will see a broken window when they make house-to-house enquiries – I'd guess, in the morning.

I try the handle of the back door, which opens on to the kitchen. It's locked.

I'm not bothered. Want to know why?

Most people leave a spare key outside their back door some-where – it's a proven fact: something like eight out of ten home-owners do it. Holiday home or not – it's just in case they lose their keys or maybe, with a place like this, they have a cleaner come in the day before they travel, just to give everything a going over. That spare key is somewhere close to me. I know it.

Doormat? No luck.

Beneath the plant pot by the door? No.

Round the soil of the pot. No.

There's a ledge above the door. I run my fingers along it. No, nothing there.

I stop, turn round. Not much of a garden really. 15 feet wide maybe, 20 feet long.

So where's the fucking key?

There's a tiny shed at the end of the garden. That's where it will be, for sure.

I glance up at the windows of the houses to either side. Dark, all quiet.

Four, five, six strides is all it takes.

It's locked.

Not there then. Where next?

I look down. There are rows of different-sized pots to either side of the shed; full of straggly, half-dead plants by the look of it.

That's good – it tells me that this is a holiday home that's not used that much.

If it's not used for the next 48 hours while I lie low, I'm in luck.

Even better, I'm lifting up one pot after another and, under the fourth one, at the back to the right of the shed and well out of sight to the casual eye, I find it.

The key.

All I need to do now is let myself into the house and we – I still think of 'we' rather than 'me' because that's the kind of daddy I am – can lie out of sight for a day or two.

Easy to do.

Nice and simple.

Behind me, I hear a cough.

7.39PM SATURDAY 31 OCTOBER

"I'm not going to come here again," said the old woman finally, looking at the old man opposite, reading a book by the fire.

"I've had enough of this. It's my last visit. It's too ... much."

He sighed, seeing that she had worked her way slowly through more than half a bottle since he'd come in from chopping wood at half past five or six. No mixers either, he noted.

Lifting himself slowly up and out of the armchair, he reached for the axe resting by his chair and used the head of it to prod the fire in the grate back into life. "I'll need to get some more wood," he answered, ignoring her comment. "I didn't do enough ... some of it may be damp."

He smiled grimly to himself, realising that, for all the household DIY and chores he did, he had never really got to grips with chopping wood and lighting fires. Even now, he wondered what he'd do without a firelighter and newspapers. He wasn't very good at handyman jobs, he thought. The place was too old-fashioned and had never really been updated since the 1970s, maybe earlier. There was simply too much to do. He didn't know where he'd start.

It occurred to him suddenly, for the first time, that the place really was a dump. She had said it was, one way or the other, several times that day in an increasingly tetchy voice that got on his nerves. He had never really seen it until now. And that, for some reason, angered him. He wondered how it could have got into such a state. How everything, his whole life really, had got as bad as it had. He wondered why he had not realised it until now.

"We'll need to get the place warmed through a bit more by the time Richard gets back," he added, trying to ignore his sudden surge of anger. "You can't let a kiddie sleep somewhere damp. The cold's not so bad that you can't wrap up against it, but the damp will get on his chest. You can't have that if he's a diabetic, it could kill him. The damp."

She looked at him scornfully.

"He's diabetic because she's not fed him properly. You only

have to look at him to see how thin and scrawny he is. All this modern food and fuss and nonsense with injections. It's all self-indulgence. Like all parents these days. They wrap them in cotton wool. She just likes the attention. They should throw that lot on the fire and start looking after him properly. Three square meals a day. Proper meat and vegetables. That's what he needs."

He shook his head, exasperated.

"It's nothing to do with that at all," he answered, his voice rising with anger. "Richard told you that, not her. He said it was just pot luck. Nothing to do with what they feed him or don't feed him. It's to do with insulin and blood sugar levels and all of that."

He got to his feet, swinging the axe in his left hand. "I've had enough of this. I'm going to chop some more wood."

"If you can manage it," she shouted, struggling to her feet to confront him. "I've a good mind to do it myself."

"Do what?" He replied. "Chop some wood? That would be a first, wouldn't it, you doing something useful for once? Sit down and drink yourself silly, leave me to sort things out for them."

He hesitated for a moment.

"Why don't you take the bottle upstairs with you? Get out of the way before they come back. Richard said they'd be back by eight, for William's checks. Go up now; I'll say you have a migraine."

"Not the wood," she spat at him. "You chop wood and you don't even do that properly, do you? The diabetic things. I've a good mind to throw them on the fire myself. It's about time someone stood up to her, made her sort herself out."

She looked across the room at the hold-all in the corner. She had seen the young woman take testing equipment from there and putting it back.

"Don't you dare. Leave it alone. It's nothing to do with us. Type one is a serious condition, that's what Richard told us."

She moved towards it, unsteady on her feet.

He switched the axe from his left hand to his right one.

"I said leave it."

As he moved towards her, he heard the sound of a car, approaching the cottage at what seemed like high speed, spraying up gravel as it came to a halt close to the front door.

7.40PM SATURDAY 31 OCTOBER

Neighbour?

Copper?

William!

It's the little fellow himself – he's sitting up and twitching and spluttering back to life.

Know what?

He blacked out.

That's all.

His hands go up to his face and he rubs at his eyes like he's coming round.

I race across, sweeping him up in my arms and smothering him with kisses. I can't help myself. I make lots and lots of "mwah mwah" noises each time I kiss him just like an ever-loving daddy would do.

He pulls his face back, focusing on me, uncertain, not sure where he is.

He's just woken up, after all!

Most children would cry; but not my fine little lad.

"Hello, William, hello," I whisper softly, and as lovingly as I can. "Do you want some sweets? Some really nice sweets?"

He takes a minute or two but then seems to know what I'm saying, nodding and smiling slowly as he comes to. It's that magic word, 'sweets', you see. The hands go up in the air again, his little fingers closing triumphantly into fists like he's won that World Cup.

That's my boy!

"Come on, William," I say quietly (I daren't shout, after all). "Come on!" We move to the kitchen door, me ready with the key.

Opening it.

Moving inside.

Shutting it.

We're safe, at last – at least for the time being. I need to look over these kitchen shelves and the fridge – I'll open that for a little light - and the cupboards. There's a larder too. I must find something to feed William. Keep him quiet and happy. I can't risk him crying out with hunger – he might be heard. There's a gap, thanks to the alleyway, between us and the house to one side, but the house to the other side may be occupied.

The next-door house is dark and there were no signs of life when I looked up at it when I was outside. But who's to say there's not an old dear lying in bed who'd hear the little fellow crying? She'd soon be up against the wall, straining to hear if she'd imagined it or not. How are we going to spend the next 48 hours in this tiny terraced house without making any noise at all?

Not easy. No, not easy at all.

And then it hits me. What if there isn't an old dear lying in the dark next door?

But what if there is in this one?

What if she's here, in this house, upstairs right now?

Say she looked out and saw me in the garden, heard me opening the back door and, while I am standing here deciding what to do, she is pressing 9 ... 9 ... 9 on the mobile phone her son bought her, which she keeps by the side of the bed at night just in case?

I've no more than seconds.

Dropping William onto the floor, I'm racing out along the

narrow hallway, turning back and up the stairs, onto the landing.
I open one door. A tiny bathroom. Another, a spare room stacked
full of boxes and half-open bags of household items. Third and
final door, the front bedroom.

A double bed.

No one here, thank Christ.

I sit down on it.

Fuck, he's yelled out. William, the little'un, back downstairs. A
sudden yelp of pain. Something's happening and if there's anyone
next door, awake or asleep, or anyone passing by on the street,
they'll hear him. Sure to if he does it again.

I'm up off the bed and back down the stairs.

Doubling back into the kitchen.

Hands over his mouth, he has to be quiet, no matter what.

Somehow, he's opened the fridge and the door's swung back
and trapped his hand. He's struggling, determined to free himself.
I pull his hand out, holding him tight, one hand over his mouth
again as I stand there, straining to listen for sounds next door or
outside on the street.

"Be quiet," I whisper urgently as he wriggles in my arms. "Stop
it, William."

He wriggles harder now as if he's fighting me, desperate to
be free; if I let go, I know he will shout out long and hard and
everyone, next door and outdoors, the whole fucking world, will
hear. Then we're well and truly shafted. That will be the end of it.
I'll go down all guns blazing, though, I'll tell you that now. Listen
to me.

Holding William as tightly as I dare with my right arm, hand
over his mouth, I pull the fridge door open again with my left.
Sweet F.A. in it; no one's living here at the moment. At least, not
on a day-to-day basis. There are just leftover bits and pieces in
the fridge.

A tub of margarine and yoghurts.

"Look, William," I say, "Yoghurt, strawberry yoghurt!" I reach for a tub, pushing it in front of his face so he can see. He focuses, thank God, and smiles. I loosen my grip on him, ever so gently at first, ready to clamp my hand back tight again if he makes the slightest sign of calling out.

"Spoon?" he says. "Spoon, please."

I fumble around as fast as I can, find one in a drawer and sit down next to him. Handing the spoon to him, I get a chance to listen.

No sound from next door.

Nothing from the back.

Will check the front in a minute, just need to get my breath.

Know what this is? I reckon it's a second home and a couple from London has bought it recently and is now starting to move some bits and pieces in. That would account for the bed – it's got pillows, a sheet and a duvet on it – and the snacks and stuff in the kitchen. And the boxes and bags in the spare room; those might be full of bric-a-brac and household knick-knacks but could be useful for spare clothes, maybe a shaver and even some things I can change William into.

William stretches up, holding the pot towards me. He has a puzzled look on his face. What's the fucking matter, William? (I think this, of course, I don't say it – nice dads like me don't say that sort of thing, not to little ones anyway.)

"What?" I say, nicely. "What's the matter?" I try one of my cheeky grins; that should do the trick. Is it sweets he wants, is that it? I'm not going to say "sweets" and that's a fact. If I say that word and there aren't any in the house – and there won't be, I don't reckon – it might make things tricky. He might get restless and noisy.

And then what will I do?

You tell me.

He has to be quiet. No matter what.

It's the lid, stupid. The yoghurt pot still has the lid on it. I didn't peel it back and he can't do it himself with his little fingers. Clever boy though he is – like father, like son – I guess he doesn't know the word 'lid' yet either.

I open his yoghurt for him, make some soothing noises and then start rummaging through the cupboards, just to see what's in them. I'm feeling rather hungry myself now and, if we can find sweets, or anything like them, maybe a banana or something, that will come in handy later for keeping William quiet.

What we need to do, thinking about it carefully – rationally, if you like – is very simple. We gather up whatever we can find to eat, take it upstairs to the front bedroom, and sit quietly in bed together and eat it all up. Once we've done that – and I know the little fellow will probably need a wee and a wotsit too – we settle down for the night and have a good sleep.

Tomorrow?

We'll worry about that in the morning.

I'll think of something for sure.

Two nights here should do it, to let things blow over, with us leaving when it gets dark on Monday evening.

William has finished eating and has what looks like a big fat blob of strawberry yoghurt on his chin.

I crouch down, "William, you've missed a bit", and I point to my chin and then to his. He touches his face, somehow smearing the blob all over his cheek. He then pulls his hand away and looks at it.

Little tinker.

It's all over his chin, his face and his hand now.

Messy devil.

"Wait, William, wait," I say, turning to the larder that's behind me, just by the back door. I open that – nothing to drink, not even orange squash, so we'll have to have tap water when we get thirsty. Not much to eat either. Two packets of biscuits, a big bag of crisps and a pack of cream crackers won't keep us going for long. Down below, there are some cleaning items, including a roll of kitchen paper, in a bucket.

"Fingers," I say, pulling him up and onto his feet, "give us your fingers, William, I'll wipe them." Again, I make soothing noises. That's what you have to do with little people, you know – the 'kiss it better' routine as you clean them up.

Suddenly, I hear the sudden revving of a car out in the street; sounds like it's down to the right and coming up the hill, towards the woman's house. Another police car? More CID? Beat bobbies? I can't help thinking that the police are starting to pull things together at last.

No time to waste.

"Here, hold these," I say to William, tearing open a packet of biscuits and handing it to him with the crackers from the cupboard. He drops one packet, reaches for it and then drops the other as well.

Do I have to do everything myself?

I pick up the biscuits, pulling two out and pushing them into his hands, then turn and shut the larder door.

"This way," I whisper to William, "follow me." I shuffle to the door and out into the hall.

"Come on, William, hurry up."

He's not followed me. He's still in the kitchen.

I turn back, standing in the doorway.

He's sat back down on the floor, cross-legged, with the biscuits in his lap. He looks up at me and smiles a big beaming smile, his mouth full of chewed-up, mushy biscuit. He's pushing the mush through his teeth with his tongue, like he knows he's being cute.

It's hard not to laugh, despite everything.

What a sweetheart.

As cute as a button, he is.

I put what I'm carrying down on the floor, neatly as I can, just outside the kitchen door – I'll come back downstairs for them later, when William is settled. I take a step forward and pick William up in my arms. He holds on tight to the biscuits.

Letting go of those, little William?

No fear!

I'll have trouble getting one of them for myself, and that's a fact.

We step into the hall. It's long and narrow, with the stairs in front of me to my left, doubling back above my head towards the bathroom.

Living room door to my right – we'll leave that for now as the front window will overlook the street. Too risky. Too dangerous by far.

The front door is at the other end of the hallway. Wooden, old-fashioned and with two strips of coloured glass at either side. You can make out all sorts of patterns in it. When I was small, we had something similar, but religious-looking. Fire and brimstone it was. Mother said the devil was moving about in it and watching me.

This glass is exactly the same. Like it has a life of its own. As I turn my head to one side, it kind of changes shape, shifts a little. As if it mirrors my movements. I bring my head up straight. The glass stays the same. I move my head to the right this time. Again, the glass stays as it was. Odd. I must have imagined it. I bring my head back up straight again. This time, the glass moves on its own, to the left and back up.

I realise what it is.

A man on the doorstep, shuffling about. A copper. I can see

the dark outline of his helmet. He's 10 feet away from me and William.

He moves again.

Rings the doorbell.

"Anyone in?"

7.49PM SATURDAY 31 OCTOBER

I freeze, facing the front door, little William in my arms, his back to it.

Whatever I do, I cannot move. If I can see the copper's outline swaying from side to side, he will see me and little William if we make the slightest movement.

There's a second or two of silence.

The copper waits for a reply.

Nothing. Well, what do you expect?

William has his head down, is focusing on chewing his biscuit. He has both hands holding tightly onto the packet. I look at him, willing him not to move.

He's humming happily.

William.

Wheels on the bus.

He starts to move, ever so slightly. He's sitting on my crossed arms, rocking his bottom back and forth in time with what he's humming.

Can the copper see William moving?

Hear him?

I can't move a muscle.

I have to just stand here and hope. If I were religious, this is the moment I'd start praying.

Another second or two's silence.

Other than William's gentle rocking and humming.

If the copper pushes his face up against the glass, peering through, we're certainly fucked.

If he crouches down and opens the letterbox to look in, we're definitely fucked.

If the copper does anything but move away, now, right now, we're well and truly fucked.

You see, William's finished his biscuit. He lifts his head. Looks at me. Opens his mouth to show me. The mush, leastways most of it, seems to have gone.

William makes an "urr" noise, at the back of his throat. Like he's just realised he's finished it and really, really wants another.

I daren't say anything.

Can't even nod.

What do I do?

All I can do is look at him eye-to-eye, then drop my gaze down to the packet of biscuits in his hands. I do it again. Eye-to-eye. Drop gaze to biscuits. Once more. Eye-to-eye. Drop gaze to biscuits. Got it, William? (Take another fucking biscuit for yourself, why don't you?)

No use. He makes another noise now at the back of his throat, wiggling his bottom.

He's about to make a louder noise now, one that will be heard.

And all I can do is stand here.

Just like the copper is doing on the doorstep.

A second passes.

William stops moving, looking at me as if he expects me to do something and do it now.

Another second.

The copper stands, no movement at all, on the doorstep waiting for a reply.

One more second.

William opens his mouth again, wider this time, showing me he's eaten his biscuit.

And a further second.

Still the copper stands there, waiting, listening, for someone, maybe in bed, to get up and answer the doorbell.

A final second.

William shuts his mouth and opens it again.

The last second.

The copper moves, I can see the outline of his arm reaching up to ring the doorbell again.

William's face contorts.

The copper is pushing at the front door, checking it's secure.

William jumps, turning towards the noise.

I clamp a hand over his mouth, gripping him tightly with the other arm.

The copper turns away and I can hear his footsteps on the path.

I slump to the floor, loosening my grip and then cuddling William, reaching for the packet he's still holding. "Here," I say, "William, have another biscuit." I'm drenched in sweat, can feel myself shaking. That was close, the closest yet. I need to sit here for a moment or two, get my breath back, just settle myself before we take ourselves upstairs to bed down for the night.

To be expected, really – the copper. House-to-house enquiries about the woman up the street, that's all, that's what's happening now. Of course, it is – it's only to be expected. Or is it for me? Either way, there's no point in the coppers waiting until the morning. They need to walk up and down the streets, knocking on doors, asking householders if they've seen or heard anything. Stands to reason, that does. Little point in doing it in the morning.

Problem is – for the coppers – most of the people up and down this street aren't actually in. They've been down at the seafront for the fun and games. Most of them won't be coming back for another hour or so yet, later if they haven't got children. So the coppers have no one to interview about what they might or might not have seen. All the coppers can do, when they get to a darkened house, is what this one here did.

Ring the doorbell.

Wait a minute or two.

Check all is secure front and back and then go.

The copper would have scanned the front windows for a break-in as he walked up the path. He'd have listened out for sounds inside as he rang the doorbell. Checked the front door had not been broken in by pushing it with his hand.

Front and back.

He'd turn and go down the pathway to the back.

That's where he's coming now.

To the back of the house, to make sure there's no sign of any break-in. He'll check the back gate (which is shut and as it should be). He'll look up and down the garden, maybe shake the shed door (which is just fine too, all locked and undamaged). He'll walk up the back path, looking over the windows upstairs and down as he does so (nice and tickety-boo). Finally, just before he leaves, he'll look quickly through the back door (and see everything just so). Give the door a final push and away he goes.

That's the thing, though, thinking about it.

The back door has a handle he might turn.

And, for the life of me, I cannot remember if I locked the back door or not.

7.53PM SATURDAY 31 OCTOBER

Sit here and hold my breath or try to get that back door locked before the copper reaches it?

No choice.

Can't fight for my life in front of the little 'un, can I?

Just not right, is it?

I rip open the biscuits, scattering them over the hall floor.

"Tea time. Eat up, William, eat up every last one," I say, pushing William to one side so I can pull open the door into the kitchen.

(For God's sake, William, be quiet about it, though, please be silent.)

I peer cautiously round the door into the kitchen, looking up at the back-door window. I hadn't noticed before, or at least hadn't registered, but it's glass from the top to halfway down.

No blind.

No curtain.

Nothing.

If that copper looks in now, he'll see me. No doubt about that. I have to be quick. Take my chance. On my hands and knees, I crawl into the kitchen, keeping my head below the level of the back-door glass. It gives me crucial seconds while the copper comes down the back path, checks the gate, enters and, what next, looks over the shed first like I did? I have to believe that he will. If not, if he comes straight to the back door and peers in, I'm done for.

Head up slightly, looking about.

Key on side, must have put it there without thinking.

Thank God, I have a chance, a real chance if I'm fast.

I daren't look up and out of the back door as I shuffle forward as quickly as I can. If the copper's walking towards the house and sees even the top of my head, I'm fucked. He'll radio for back-up immediately and the place will be surrounded in minutes.

I'd have no chance to get away, even leaving my little lad behind. I couldn't tackle a strong young copper face to face, not without an element of surprise. If I broke out of the front door – could I leave William behind? – I'd be running into coppers to the left and coppers to the right of me.

How far would I get? I'd be hunted down in an alleyway within minutes, for sure. Know what, the police might even be armed at this stage if they've got their act together and have this down as a child abduction. I'd die fighting, but what about sweetpea? He'd end up back with the sister-in-law and Veitch. No Disneyland trip. No new life in the south of France. No happy ever after for him. Truth is we'd both be better off dead.

Key's in the lock.

I twist it ever so gently, making certain it doesn't make even the tiniest scraping sound.

There, the door's locked.

I turn, ready to crawl back out of the kitchen towards William, when I hear the click of the back gate. It's the copper, has to be. He's in the garden. Standing there, taking it all in. House to his left, dark and shut up for the winter. I will him, please, please, please, to walk down to the shed first just like I did, giving me precious seconds to get away.

But what if he comes straight to the back door, looks in and sees me crawling? Why would he check the shed first? I'm screwed, well and truly. I shrink, as far as I can, to the floor, tight up against the back door. My only chance, really it is. If the copper looks in, just a cursory, not an up and down, glance, I may get lucky. My only hope now anyway.

William calls out, more of a cry.

Dear God, sweet William, stay where you are. Please do not get up and walk into the kitchen. Do not come striding in here with your empty packet of biscuits with your mouth wide open and wanting something else to eat because, if you do, we've had it.

William's in the kitchen.

I've no choice now.

No choice at all.

I have to take the copper out as he gets to the back door or at least die trying. I struggle to my feet, turning my back to William as best I can so he won't see what's happening.

I unlock the back door as fast as I can.

Wrench it open.

Launch myself out towards the copper.

8.25PM SATURDAY 31 OCTOBER

"Nat, we have to sit down and wait like the police said." The young man looked at the young woman pacing back and forth in the small lounge of the cottage, her eyes fixed on the screen of her mobile phone. He glanced towards the policeman and woman standing and talking quietly in the kitchen and added, "There's nothing we can do ... this doesn't help."

"You should have brought your phone," she snapped. "They had your mobile number on file. If you'd brought it, we'd have known he was out immediately." She stopped and thought for a moment. "If you hadn't been in such a hurry, we'd have picked up that phone call before we left home. That would have been the police."

"We weren't to know that, Nat, how could we? How could anyone?" He looked towards his parents for some form of encouragement. "How could he have got out anyway? He was meant to be in a secure unit. Under lock and key."

His mother looked back at him, saying nothing.

The old man edged forward on his cushion, leaning towards the younger man. "Whatever's happened, happened. Nothing anyone can do about it now. There's no point in falling out. We've got to sit and wait for the family liaison officers, like the police said. They'll then keep us in touch just as soon as they have any news."

The young woman turned towards him, waving her phone at

him in frustration. "How can we just sit here and wait? While he's out there with Will doing God knows what to him..."

Both men went to answer at the same time, the younger man deferring to the older, who said, "Goodness knows, I can understand you hate him for what he did with ... did to your sister. But he's the boy's father after all ... he'll see himself as the father anyway ... and he's not going to hurt his own flesh and blood, is he?"

He looked at the old woman next to him knowing exactly what she was thinking – "Men do" – but she ignored his gaze.

He continued speaking, "Let's just think about things in a logical way..."

The young woman snorted, "He's mad, he doesn't think at all, let alone logically. Whatever comes into his head he does. If he gets angry, he hits someone. If he loses his temper ... if he really loses his temper with Will..." Her voice tailed off.

"That's all as maybe, generally, with most people, yes, but William is his son, come what may..." He went on, dropping his voice so that the policeman and woman would not hear. "What we need to do is think what he might do, where he'd go, what he'd do ... anticipate him if you like. He's obviously got enough about him to get here from wherever he was and he's going to want to get away from here again as quickly as he can."

The young man added in a low voice, "He'll have to get a car if he hasn't got one already ... but he won't come here ... not now ... when he sees the police car out front."

"Won't he?" whispered the young woman angrily. "I wouldn't put it past him, would you? A spot of vengeance? He hates you, Rick ... and me."

The old man shook his head. "He'll be out of here as fast as he possibly can. Faster than they can get roadblocks in place. He'll be heading for a back street - if he had a car he'd have left it there. If not, he'll try and steal one from somewhere quiet."

"What if he doesn't come here? What if he's gone already?" she said, her voice catching. She struggled with her composure. "It's been more than an hour since I saw him. Maybe he won't still be here … and Will's medication, he needs that, soon. What will happen if…"

The old man went to speak but paused as he heard the noise of the police radio from the kitchen. The four of them, including the old woman, turned to try to hear what was being said.

After a hurried conversation between the policeman and woman, the policeman came into the room, moved quickly to the front door and opened it. He stepped outside. More urgent words and whispers and then the policeman came back in.

"That Renault Megane over there. It's been reported stolen from Nottingham. Two officers are setting up an observation point over the way, keeping watch in case your man comes back."

The young man and woman moved towards the door.

"He's coming back," said the young man triumphantly. "He'll be here any moment. We just have to sit and wait and he'll walk straight into the trap."

The old woman spoke at last, rising stiffly to her feet. "He may, but he won't have the child with him."

They all turned to look at her.

"He wants to punish you both … for taking the child away from him; having him locked up. He has nowhere to go. Nothing to do. Nothing to offer. He will have killed the boy by now. The boy is dead. And he'll be long gone."

9.09PM SATURDAY 31 OCTOBER

"Once upon a time," I say softly, "there was a dog called … Scruffy."

(Okay, okay, I had to think for a second or two; I'm not good with bedtime stories, am I?)

"Scwuffy," repeats little William, looking up at me with a very serious expression on his face.

(We're sitting next to each other on the bed, him under the duvet, me on top, while he gets used to me.)

"Scruffy was a naughty little dog who was always getting into mischief and he..."

"Like Ben?" pipes up William. "Ben?" he repeats, twisting to face me.

(Who the fuck is Ben? Some dog he knows, maybe a neighbour's?)

"Yes," I say, "Just like Ben. What does Ben look like, William? What sort of dog is he?"

He looks at me vaguely, and settles down as if he's ready to fall asleep.

(Thinking about it, you can't really expect a little chap to know a dog's breed. Then again, maybe Ben is a cat.)

I yawn.

Ever so loudly.

(A bit faked, really, because, being a clever sort of chap, I know that, if you yawn, the other person will automatically yawn in response and, in the case of a tired little lad like William, they will probably fall gently asleep.)

William yawns.

Just like I thought.

Perfect.

You're probably wondering – as you would – how me and the little fellow are now in bed all snug as a bug.

I got it wrong.

Earlier on.

The click of the gate, remember?

The copper wasn't by the back door and he wasn't even in the garden. I reckon he opened the gate, could see all was as it should be and went out, to go on to the next house. That's what I think. The click was the copper putting the gate handle back onto the latch as he left.

Lucky fucker, I am.

No doubt about it.

Touched by Lady Luck.

I stood there, shaking – adrenalin, stress, I don't know what – in disbelief. It took me a minute or two to get my bearings, adjust myself to the silence, at least in the garden. I could hear noise, comings and goings and all sorts of revelry, in the streets beyond the house. I turned, went back in and locked the back door this time, putting the key in my pocket. Gathered up the other packet of biscuits and bits and pieces from the larder.

"Scwuffy and Ben?" says William, focusing on me again.

"Yes, Scruffy and Ben, that's right."

(I'm thinking, okay? I have to tell some sort of a story until the little laddie drops off to sleep.)

"Scruffy and Ben were best friends and they went for an adventure. In a park. And do you know what they saw there?"

William looks up at me; frankly, he's going to be no help at all with this story, no help at all.

"What ... do you think ... they saw in the park?" I say slowly.

He smiles at me, a butter-wouldn't-melt smile just like mine. I told you about them, didn't I? Yes, I'm sure I did.

(But he's not going to answer, that's for sure. He's going to sit there looking around dreamily.)

"A rabbit," I say, finally, and quite firmly so he knows it's not open for discussion. "Scruffy and Ben saw a rabbit in the park. And what do you think they did?"

(Where am I going with this? The dogs would chase the rabbit and tear it apart, wouldn't they? What sort of bedtime story is that for a little chap?)

"Jolly?" He sits up again. "Where Jolly?"

Now he's looking around. The arms go up. The hands go out. The fingers are twitching back and forth.

Who the fuck's Jolly?

Okay, I'm guessing a bunny rabbit.

Must be his bedtime toy?

I backtrack, talking over William, distracting his attention, "Scruffy and Ben – you know Ben, don't you William – went to a park and they saw a big red bouncy ball and it ... boinged up and down like this."

"Boiinng!" I go, lifting William out from the duvet and bouncing him up and down.

"Boiinng!" I go again, hoping to God this does the trick.

"Boiinng!" and William giggles. Okay, he's not going to go to sleep now but at least he's not going to have a fit of the screaming ab-dabs over some missing fluffy rabbit.

"'Gain," he laughs out loud. "Do 'gain."

And so we do, again and again and again, three, four, five times and more until he's laughing, I'm laughing and we collapse together into a heap upon the bed.

"'Gain," he says once more, but quieter this time, as if he's saying it to himself. "'Gain," he mumbles and his thumb goes slowly into his mouth.

He's asleep, bless him.

I sit here for a while; it's nice, really nice.

Peaceful it is, restful – I've never had much of that, not lately anyway.

Almost nodding off, or maybe I've been asleep, I hear the click of a gate. Footsteps on the path. A man and a woman's voice. I sit up straight. Is it that copper back? With a colleague? I hold my breath. Maybe CID has made all the local beat bobbies check all the houses again in pairs this time, one at the front, the other at the back?

Just have to sit tight.

Not a sound, little William.

Not a sound.

No, not coppers, thank God. They're arguing – the man and the woman. Quite nasty it is too, I can tell you. I can't make out the words exactly, but she's angry with him, very angry, her voice raised and accusing. He's replying, bluntly, denying whatever it is he's supposed to have done, in a deep, rumbling voice. I hear the voices coming closer now, up the path. Next, a key in the door, turning. Takes all my willpower to lie here and not move. Sounds as though it's this house. But it's the other side, it has to be the house next door. The neighbours are back from the seafront, I think.

I can still hear them. Arguing. Getting nastier too, it is. It's in the distance now, though, far off – maybe the front room of the house next door. Still arguing, on and on they go, both voices now raised to screaming pitch. They won't hear us, that's for sure – not like that. But we have to be quiet. For as long as we're here. They'll come up the stairs soon, to bed. Leastways, one of them will – I reckon the other will be on the settee tonight for certain.

I just need to make sure we don't make any noises. The lights will have to stay off. We'll have to keep away from the windows. I won't even draw the curtains. Neighbours, you see, and not just next door. All of them, both sides of the road, will be alert to what's going on by now. Will spot anything out of the ordinary, maybe be looking for it.

We're safe as snuggles here just as long as we don't make any noise.

The doors, front and back, are locked.

Everything is in its place and just as it should be.

William turns on to his side. He still has his thumb in his mouth.

That's sweet.

He's a cute child.

I move a little down the bed, just getting myself comfortable, settled into place as close to him as I can get.

I'll just sit here and mull things over for a while.

Know what? I love him.

Truly I do.

11.10PM SATURDAY 31 OCTOBER

The little boy was awake and restless. He was thinking about his mama. Sometimes at night he'd wake up, just as he'd done now, and he would see her looking down at him.

He would pretend to be asleep.

And she would bend down close to him, her hair brushing against his forehead.

He could feel the sweet smell of her breath upon his face.

And he would open his eyes as she kissed him gently.

"Night night, Will." … "Night night, Mama," he would try to answer as he faded back into sleep.

The little boy wished his mama was here now.

But he knew too that he had to be brave, what his mama called her "brave little soldier".

He had to be happy and smile and say "please" and "thank you" and not be naughty or a nuisance or anything like that to whoever was looking after him.

He had been looked after by other people many times while his mama was working and he knew it was never for very long. He did not know what it was that she did when she went up into the attic. Her office, she called it. But he knew it was important and that he had to be good for whoever was with him.

He used to like Freya best. He could never quite say the

name and it came out as "Fweya" and she would laugh and make him say it again and again. She lived over the road and would sometimes take him back there to her bedroom where she would put make-up on him and tickle him until it hurt. But she went away to a place called Cambridge and he had not seen her for ages.

There was an old lady who looked after him as well. He did not really like her so much. Her house smelled funny and she would make a fuss of him and keep dabbing at his face with her handkerchief every time he ate or sneezed or licked his lips. She could not leave him alone. Not for a single minute.

He had never been looked after by a man before. A stranger. His mama said he must always be kind and polite to strangers but that he should not talk to them. He did not really know what she meant by that. But this man – he had a scary face and a gruff voice – seemed to know him and his mama and his papa and he was trying to be nice, or so the little boy thought.

But he did miss his mama.

And he hoped, very hard, that she would be here soon.

So he shut his eyes and tried to sleep. He imagined she was here, just outside the door, waiting to come in and look down at him as he slept.

That he would feel her hair on his face and smell her sweet breath.

Any moment now.

He just had to lie here and pretend to be asleep.

And be a good boy.

11.42PM SATURDAY 31 OCTOBER

It's actually not that easy to sleep, I'll tell you that for nothing.

My nerves are all on edge.

I'm constantly listening for noises outside, the opening of a gate. A key in the door. A footstep on the stairs.

But I have to sleep.

Must have been awake on and off for the best part of three hours, I reckon.

If I don't sleep now, I'll be no good in the morning.

I have to recharge my batteries, build myself up for whatever's to come tomorrow.

He doesn't help.

The boy.

Fidgeting, he is.

Whenever I try to slip myself under the duvet, to keep myself warm, he wakes up and starts wriggling.

If I pull him close for a cuddle, he pulls away.

He's not quite the sweet little boy he was a while ago.

Don't get me wrong. I love him. I'm just saying he's not quite the perfect child I thought he was.

At one point, he sat up and looked around. Never said anything, just looked across the room, first one way, then the other.

I didn't say anything either, just waited for him to settle.

He didn't. He looked all over the room once again and finally said something. I couldn't make it out. So I ignored him, hoping he would go back down in a moment or two. He didn't. He said the word again, louder this time. He said it once more, as I was about to tell him to be quiet, and I realised what it was,

Water.

He wanted a glass of water.

He was thirsty.

I pushed him down on the bed and told him quietly but firmly to stay there and not to move. He pulled away from me quite angrily, almost nasty he was.

I crept downstairs and got a glass of water from the kitchen.

He drank it.

Wanted more.

I got one more small glass for him and he drank it down just as fast.

We had what you might call something of a stand-off at that point. He wanted another drink. I needed him to lie back down and go to sleep. It took a while, but he did as I said in the end.

Let's just leave it at that.

Say no more on the subject.

Just leave it be and let me get myself back off to sleep as quickly as I can.

12.23AM SUNDAY 1 NOVEMBER

I awake with a jolt, sitting up straight and looking around me, my mind working out where I am, how long I've been asleep.

And what it is that woke me.

I know where I am. I realise straightaway. And I guess it's now halfway through the night, maybe more. I don't know what woke me up, though. That's the thing.

I tense, listening for noise downstairs. Someone at the front door again? A copper – or was it a key in the door that woke me? I strain to hear footsteps in the hallway, the creak of the stairs, footsteps coming along the landing to the bedroom. A hand on the door.

No, nothing.

Back door? Was that the noise of the kitchen door swinging slowly open? Someone standing in the hallway, breathing quietly and listening intently? Someone who thinks maybe I am in the house. Wants to listen for me breathing deeply as I sleep. Are they waiting to hear me turn over, ready to be taken by surprise?

No, nothing.

I know what it was. I hear it again, awake this time, every nerve in my body strung out tight. The whoosh of brakes; just like the lorry I travelled in towards Nottingham in what now seems a lifetime ago. I slip out of bed, crawling on my knees across the floor towards the front window overlooking the street. Ever so carefully, I lift my head up, my eyes above the ledge, looking down.

It's the TV people: Sky, BBC. Their lorries are here, moving in as close to the police cordon as they're allowed, I reckon. They'll be broadcasting the news to the whole world in the next few hours. All about what happened. Before I got put away. There will be pictures of me. William too, I expect. They'll speculate about what I did when I escaped and at the woman's house and tell the world I've snatched my little boy. All of it designed to shock and scare.

"This man is dangerous (I'm not) and must not be approached by members of the public." "Madman on the loose", that's what the papers will say. "Child-snatcher", possibly a child you-know-what, even though William is my own dear sweet little boy. And people will remember it all, see, especially round here and for miles about. Maybe right across the country.

I duck my head down from the windowsill, crawling back to the bed, slipping up next to William, who seems to be asleep at the moment. I have to think hard and fast, maybe act soon, if I have to. I have to work out what to do. Can I still sneak away as planned on Monday? Will the news people still be here? The police? A police cordon circling the whole fucking town by then?

I'm thinking, maybe this is actually a turn for the better.

Yes, really.

Work it through for yourself like I'm doing.

The coppers think I've gone. Face facts – they don't let the TV people anywhere near a crime scene. That means they don't think I am here. They think I have got away with the little lad. That's why they've let the telly in; to let people farther away from here know what's happening so that they will keep a lookout for me and the little man.

But not round here, though.

Round here, they think I've long gone.

And that's not all.

The photo they'd have used of me would have been that old one. The one where I was all wild-eyed. With a beard and moustache. My hair swept back. Do I look like that now? No, you would not recognise me from that picture these days. Even less, if I can get this fuzz off my face before we leave.

And William? What photo will they use of him? There will be lots, I guess. The Veitchs would take pictures on birthdays, holidays and at Christmas. Yes, lots and lots to choose from. But a small lad like William? Well, their features are much of a muchness aren't they, especially at this age?

Fact is, thinking about it.

And we are talking right here and now, after all.

This town is probably the safest place to be for the moment.

We can't stay here, though. Not for ever. Not even for a few days. The longer we are here in this house, the more likely it is we'll be found out. The postman will deliver letters and maybe hear a little out-of-place giggle from William. A passer-by may glance up and see a shadow of us walking by the front door. No, we can't be here too long, safe though we are for a while.

We're safe now.

But not for long.

Anything could happen at any time.

1.07AM SUNDAY 1 NOVEMBER

The little boy was awake again and was thinking now about his papa. His papa would walk with him to Freya's or the old lady's and always say, "Be a good boy, Will."

He had a deep, booming voice like the man in that cartoon on the telly.

Sometimes, the little boy would pretend to be his papa and answer him with the same words, "Be a good papa, Papa."

And his papa would pretend to be angry, picking him up in his arms and swinging him round, high above his head and down below and the little boy would squeal with laughter.

His papa could be stern with him at times.

But he made him laugh too.

He thought about his papa saying, "Be a good boy for this man, Will."

But he was not sure if his papa liked this man. He tried to remember exactly what it was that had happened, but he was so tired he could not think what it was for sure.

He thought they had shouted at each other and his papa had fallen over and banged his head and cut himself.

He had heard his papa arguing with someone before.

And his mama had been angry with people too.

It was when Freya and the old lady had not looked after him properly. He knew his mama had shouted at Freya about something. And his papa had been angry with the old lady because she had not given him the finger-tickle thing.

But this man had not made him have that.

And he had given him biscuits, lots and lots of biscuits.

So he thought maybe he was a naughty man and that was why his papa would be unhappy.

He was not sure.

It was all so confusing.

He would have to think about it.

2.08AM SUNDAY 1 NOVEMBER

Now he's gone and wet himself.

William.

I knew he shouldn't have had any water.

I was trying to be nice and kind. It's what dads do with their little 'uns. But he's had too much. Far too much. Gone straight through him it has.

I didn't realise straightaway.

Been nodding on and off, see?

Half of me wants to sleep, the other half needs to stay on guard.

He got up by himself, William did, all as quiet as you like.

Something woke me as he walked by to the door. Instinct, I guess.

I was up and off that bed in seconds flat, I can tell you.

It's not safe, is it? At night. When it's dark. Anything could have happened to him. He might have fallen down the stairs. Got out the front door. Been halfway down the street.

I'd be fucked then, wouldn't I?

Someone would be bound to see him. A copper maybe, patrolling these back streets.

They'd know who he was immediately.

Would only have to walk a few yards down the street, see the open door and bingo. There I am stretched out half asleep, ready for the taking.

I grabbed William, asked him what he thought he was doing. You have to be firm with children at times like this. You can't have them wandering about willy-nilly at night just as they fancy. It's not right.

He struggled and squawked a bit but I shook him a couple of

times, maybe three or four, and that seemed to stop the noise. I asked him again what he thought he was doing and he finally said the word 'wee'; almost defiant, he sounded.

I took him into the bathroom just so he could do a little wee into the toilet and it was when I was helping him up and down with his pants and trousers in the dark that I felt the wetness and knew what he'd done.

I wasn't happy, I can tell you.

He should not be wetting himself at his age.

But I never said anything because we need to get back into bed and sleep as best we can so we are fresh and ready for tomorrow.

I put his wet pants over a radiator to dry out a little and, after something of a struggle, I got him back into his trousers. They are damp but they're a little loose so they can't be that uncomfortable for him. And we got back into bed, him inside, me on top again and settled down.

But I'm not very happy.

No, I am not happy at all.

I don't think I'll be sleeping much more tonight if at all.

3.09ᴀᴍ SUNDAY 1 NOVEMBER

Fuck, I must have nodded off again.

What the hell is that?

How long have I been asleep for this time?

I struggle back up, sitting upright and rubbing my eyes as the bedroom fills with the brightest light.

The air is full of a loud noise; I can't place it for the moment. Humming? Droning? Whirring?

Oh God, help me please, they've gone and found us. A neighbour, maybe a passer-by, must have looked up and seen me peering out at the news vans and reporters.

My thoughts clear as the lights and noise move slowly by. Thank God. For a few seconds, maybe longer, I thought I was in a police spotlight, trained on this house. That we'd been found. It's actually a helicopter, most likely two, and they are sweeping their way over and above and along the streets and towards, I think, the far end of the town and away. They're searching for me and the little lad obviously.

That's good news if you think about it.

Just like I said.

They think we're on the streets, out and away from the town.

They think they're going to track us down – with spotlights, sensors, God knows what they have these days – as we flee.

But, guess what, fuckers?

We're here.

Hidden away, safe as can be in this dinky little house.

Come Monday, when it's all nice and dark and the circus has ridden out of town, we'll go, picking up the car from along the seafront and driving away down the side roads by the sea to the coaches near Dartford, and away to Shangri-fucking-la.

Until then? A little snooze I think.

Just me and the little fellow.

I'm so tired, so very tired. But I know I really should try and stay awake, just in case.

4.11AM SUNDAY 1 NOVEMBER

The little boy was thinking about his little bicycle and was wondering where it was.

He had seen his papa take it out to the car when they left home.

And he had seen his papa carry it into the house with the lion on the door.

But he did not know if this man next to him now had it and whether he would get to ride on it soon.

He hoped this man had it.

But the man was angry with him.

So he knew he would have to be a good boy if he was to get a go on it.

The little boy liked to think about riding his bike in Brockwell Park.

Papa would put his stripy helmet carefully on his head and do up the straps.

His mama would check they were nice and tight.

Papa would then help him onto the bike and make sure he was steady.

His mama would ask if his feet could touch the ground.

Papa would stand behind and put his hands on his back and push him along as he went faster and faster. Sometimes, his papa would push so hard that he could not move his feet fast enough on the pedals.

His mama would call out to be careful!

Papa would then push a little slower and they would all laugh as he pedalled off down the slope with his papa and mama running after him.

Sometimes, the little boy imagined that the pedals would go very, very fast on their own and his legs would be all of a blur and the bike would take off and swoop and soar into the sky.

He'd look down as he flew above the lido and the café and the trees and far, far away over Chestnut Road where Charlie lived and into Rosendale Road where he'd wave at Pari playing in her garden and on until eventually he'd reach the park at Crystal Palace where he'd see all the statues of the dinosaurs.

He imagined them moving about, roaring up at him, but he'd be too high, even as he dipped up and down just as close to them as he could get. Round and round he'd go with the dinosaurs chasing him over and over until they all bumped into each other and fell down into a big heap.

Then he'd wave goodbye to them as he turned and flew for

home and tea with his mama and papa. If he had been good, he knew he'd get a chocolate treat. A big sloppy, squashy one.

He loved his little bike.

And his mama and papa.

But he did not like this man at all.

5.35AM SUNDAY 1 NOVEMBER

It's been an arsehole of a night.

I don't know how much sleep I've had.

Fuck diddly-squit, frankly.

When I got under the duvet, William seemed to wake up and struggle. When I lay on top of the duvet, I didn't seem to sleep. Too cold.

Then he'd wanted water.

And he'd wet himself.

Every time he turns or sits up and does that looking around thing he does, I'm awake.

It's non-stop.

Not a wink.

We've had the TV people arrive.

And the helicopters go over.

No, not a peaceful night at all, not for either of us.

William seems to be quiet at last, though. At peace, finally. I am just going to lie here, try to relax, shut my eyes.

I'll not fall asleep now.

Too late for that.

Or is it too early?

Still dark but sunrise soon, for sure. I will just lie here quietly and work out what we're going to do today. I've got to keep the little fellow quiet for quite some time, that's for sure. I don't know how I am going to do it.

Play games I suppose.

Not sure what.

Will need to give it some thought.

It's nice now, with William. We had one or two troubles in the night, him and me, but all is well. We have made our peace, I think. We're pals again, just like a daddy and his little boy should be.

I will have to see if I can find some paper in the house.

And pens, or something like that.

We can do some drawing.

I've always liked drawing, had something of an eye for it, you might say. I drew in the annexe, sketches of how I imagined William would look. And views of the south of France. Beach and sea sketches were more trouble than they were worth, though, to be honest. Sprake and Ainsley would find whatever it was I had drawn and I'd come back to find a naked man with a huge swollen penis etched into the middle of it. Every single time.

William would want to draw rocket ships, I think.

Or maybe cars.

Or boats or trains, I don't know, I can't think straight at the moment, I'm so tired.

Just need to shut my eyes.

Have a little rest.

Catch up on my sleep.

I've never been to the south of France, you know. I've got it all worked out, though. What we're going to do. It's all in my head; I can shut my eyes and imagine it now. We'll spend a week or two in a villa down by the beach. There are bound to be some holiday ones empty at this time of year. We'll just relax, putting all of what's happened behind us once and for all.

I can see it in my mind's eye. I'm outside by the pool, stretched out on a sun lounger, just catching the last few rays of the year.

William is playing by my feet. I shut my eyes, snoozing for a moment or two, not really thinking of anything. My mind drifts and floats away and I feel totally relaxed. I've not felt like this for ages. It's just like a lovely warm dream where everyone is happy.

A man leans over the sun lounger.

I hear him say something to me.

He's offering me a job!

He must think I'm here as a caretaker for holiday homes owned by Brits across the south of France. I go in and check empty properties daily, clean out the pool now and then and just double-check everything is safe and secure. The man would like me to do the same for his holiday home and wants to know how much I charge.

That's got me! How much do you charge to check a property regularly? I don't know what to say. I hesitate, thinking. I must say something. Got to think of a price. Hurry now. I hear the man's voice asking me something again, angry this time. He asks me again how much I'll charge. Still I don't answer. I don't know! He shouts now and I hear William stirring and moving; he's being frightened by the man's loud voice.

I wake – in the bed next to William.

Looking up, there's a man staring down at me.

As I come to and focus, he swings round to run away.

10.40ᴀᴍ SUNDAY 1 NOVEMBER

I reach out to grab the man, too late – he is up and by the bedroom door, pulling it open.

As he does so, he turns, wasting precious seconds, glancing back at me. He's scared, knows who I am. I can tell.

I'm up and out of the bed and after him, almost without thinking – he's the owner, I know instinctively, and I have to get to him before he's down the stairs and out the front door, screaming for help.

At the top of the stairs, he hesitates, looking down and then back at me for a second or so, deciding whether or not he can outrun me.

Too late now, he stops, turns back round and says to me, almost defiantly, "I know who you are. You and the boy."

"It's not what you think," I answer, keeping my distance from him.

"The police stopped me on the way in. I never dreamed for a minute ..." He holds my gaze for a second, then drops it, not knowing what to do next.

He seems to rally in confidence, what with me unsure what to say and not replying. "Give yourself up. The police are all over the place. You won't get away."

"We were going to stay here for a day or two, that's all, until it blows over. I've got it all figured."

He nods, trying to look calm and thoughtful, his hand going up to his chin. How he must yearn to wipe those pinpricks of sweat from his face.

"I have to stay here. We have to stay here. Me and my son. For a day or two longer, that's all."

"Yes, yes, I can see that. Yes, that makes sense." He nods slowly and then stops, not certain what to say or do next. It's as though he's about to turn and walk away as if nothing out of the ordinary was happening. As if this were a perfectly normal conversation.

He looks at me again, eye to eye this time. He's terrified, I can see.

I look back at him, working out how to tell him he has to stay here too.

"I ... I can't let you leave the house." My voice cracks, it comes out sounding more like a nervous request than a statement of fact.

He looks around, swallowing on a dry throat.

"My partner's coming up," he whispers. I have to strain to hear him. "He'll be here soon."

We look at each other.

Neither of us knows what to do next.

I can't keep two of them here and quiet until we leave, that's for sure.

"Papa?"

It all happens so fast. We both hear William call out at the same moment, the rustling as the duvet is pushed back followed by the soft sound of footsteps on the floor. The man takes his chance as I turn to look towards the bedroom. He twists round, ready to run down the stairs. In the split second he stands there, with his back to me, I lift my foot, put it in the small of his back and push him with all of my might out and over the stairs.

He seems to hang in mid-air for a second.

Falls forward, hitting the banister, once, twice and again as the momentum of his weight carries him downwards.

Hits his head hard on the wall near the bottom and lies dead still.

"Papa?" says William, coming out of the bedroom. He's rubbing his eyes. "Wee?"

I watch and wait. A moment. Maybe a minute. There's no movement from the man. I take William by the hand, steering him away from the staircase and gently towards the bathroom.

We stand there, by the toilet, me straining to hear something, anything, maybe the sound of the man twitching, even struggling painfully to his feet.

I'm distracted.

William reaches to flush it.

"No," I shout suddenly, reaching out and hitting his hand away, instinctively.

I stand there for a moment longer in the terrible, strained silence, hoping to God no one has heard me next door or outside on the street. It's all quiet – I think. I've no real way of knowing now. Just have to take my chance and carry on. William turns his face up at me, his bottom lip pushed out. I pick him up, making soothing sounds and noises as I sweep him back into the bedroom. I've got to get him to lie down or at least sit quietly, keeping to himself, while I check the man at the bottom of the stairs.

Is he dead?

Stunned and about to wake up?

What do I do with him if he's dead – or close to it?

William does not want to sit quietly. He certainly does not want to lie down. He doesn't even want to be on the bed. However much I cajole and jolly him along, he struggles and simply won't stay put. I hold him in place on the bed with one hand, an angry, almost buzzing noise coming from him, as I rummage by the side of the bed for the biscuits.

"Here," I say, sounding more angry than I should, as I thrust a handful of broken-up biscuits at him. "Here's your food, eat it all up now. Come on."

That seems to settle him, at least for a moment, as I move across the bedroom to the door.

Do I shut it?

So I can deal with the man without William seeing?

But what if William yells out and they hear him next door?

I leave the door half-open, taking a quick glance back at William, head down and chewing on the biscuits, as I step back onto the landing. I look down the stairs. The man hasn't moved, not a flicker. He's still and utterly lifeless.

Know what?

He's stone-cold dead.

I wish he wasn't. I'd not hurt a fly except in self-defence, that's for sure. You know that, don't you? Yes, of course you do.

No one will know what happened; not if I leave him there as he is. When someone eventually comes, they'll just think he fell down the stairs. A tragic accident. I'll tidy up behind us. Leave everything as we found it – even put the key back by the shed – and no one will know we've been here at all.

I pause, listening for William, maybe next door too.

All quiet.

Two, three, four steps down I go at a time.

Only problem is this, I realise, standing over the man's dead body – if someone comes up to the front door, a neighbour maybe, and looks in, they'll see the man's body on the staircase. But how likely is it that someone will come up the path, let alone peer through the glass on the door, on a Sunday?

Not very.

But if they do?

Before we've had a chance to get away.

I could move him. Maybe drag him into the living room or the kitchen? No good – anyone glancing into either, maybe that beat bobby on his rounds again, will see the body straightaway.

Can I drag him upstairs? I'd have to keep him out of the bedroom and bathroom; I can't have William seeing him. It wouldn't be right and proper, would it?

The spare room? It's full of boxes and household things; maybe this man and his partner have been moving themselves in from London over a few weekends. It's probably the best place – only thing is, I'd need to arrange things so that it looked as though he'd had an accident there. Clean up the mess here on the stairs too.

There's a smear of blood on the paintwork by the side of his head.

Have to lift him up, off the stairs, to drag him upwards.

I put my hands round his shoulders and head, ready to lift him.

He's still breathing.

Fuck's sake, he's still alive.

I turn him slowly over, so he's lying on his back stretched out down at the bottom of the stairs. His head falls back; a dark trickle of blood, more black than red, runs from his temple to the lid of his right eye. He's spark out, that's for sure. But, moving my head closer to his mouth, he is breathing. It sounds shallow but steady. There's life in him for certain. I feel over his skull, not sure what it is I am doing or looking for; some sign, maybe, that he has cracked it and is going to die anyway, no matter what I do. It feels, well, as it should, I guess. He's alive and is going to stay that way.

Now what?

You tell me.

I'm damned every which way.

Leaving him where he is for now, I move quickly back up the stairs and into the spare room. Remember? Boxes and bags and all sorts? I crouch down – just in case – and shuffle across the floor. Men's clothes – casual stuff, nightwear, some shoes and slippers – are in the first few bags. Towels and fabrics in the next two. A box with curtains and various knick-knacks wrapped in newspaper. I open these carefully; a couple of pieces of china, a heavy doorstop in the shape of a dog and a garish, multi-coloured glass ashtray. I pick the last two items up, one in each hand, to work out which is the heaviest.

It's got to be done.

What choice do I have?

You tell me. There's no choice at all.

I glance back into the front bedroom, checking William's still there – he is, lying on his back now sucking his thumb content-edly and staring into space. Not for long, though. He'll be up and about any moment. Little children don't sit still forever even if they're well-behaved like William is. I have to be quick.

I walk to the staircase and down towards the man. I stand over him again, steeling myself this time to raise the heavy glass ashtray up and then, I'll have to shut my eyes, bringing it down as hard on his head as I can.

I look down.

A bloodshot eye stares back at me, focusing on my face.

He whispers something, so quietly I almost can't hear him.

"Help me," that's what it is. I stop, thinking for a moment. I have to work things through in my head. Think on my feet, as it were. Thing is, he's no threat. He can't be. Not really. He's not going to live that long. I don't think so anyway.

I put the ashtray carefully on the stairs beside his feet. Moving behind him, I lean forward, wrapping my arms around his chest, heaving him, as slowly and as gently as I can, back up the stairs, one step at a time. Now we are at the top and it's easier as I pull him as carefully as I can into the spare room.

I lay him on the floor.

Put towels and fabrics under his head.

Prop him up slightly.

He's okay to be left for a minute or two as I pull a small hand towel from a bag and walk carefully to the bathroom. I need to wet it, maybe wipe the man's face, squeeze some water over his lips. Need to be careful, though. I turn the cold water tap slightly, pushing the edge of the towel below it to catch and soak up the running water. There's a second or two's hesitation, a knocking and a clanking from somewhere up above and then the water runs freely.

I wipe the blood from the man's face.

Can't have William seeing him like that.

Cradle his head as I squeeze water from the towel into his mouth.

He tries to struggle up, is too weak, and settles for a brief smile, of sorts, as he slips back down. He focuses on me again – and I take in his appearance as I look back at him. An older man, maybe late 50s or early 60s, dressed in a black suit, white shirt, free, amazingly, from blood. Thin, what they call wiry. His hair dyed black, too dark for his lined face. But it is a kind face.

Sitting here quietly, it hits me suddenly.

What he said earlier.

"My partner's coming up . . . he'll be here soon."

"Look at me," I say to the man, as forcefully as I can without William hearing. I lean forward, pulling him up by the arms so our faces are inches from each other. "What did you mean, when is your partner coming up?"

His head lolls back, as he slips in and out of consciousness.

"Listen," I say, laying him back down and shaking his face to wake him. "What did you mean about your partner? When is he coming?"

No good, he's unconscious again. I use the wet towel to wipe his face, will have to wait until he comes to once more. Will ask him then.

Meanwhile, I search his pockets, see what there is. Inside his jacket pocket is a thin, black leather wallet. I empty it, spreading the contents by the side of his body. A driving licence – his name is Gerald something-cwski – has a small photo stuck to the back of it, showing him as a much younger man with an older, bald-headed man and a small white terrier between them, its tongue out as if it's panting.

"Is this him?" I say louder again, shaking the man by the arm and putting the photo close to his face. "Is this your partner?" No use, he's still not there.

I rummage through his trouser pockets. A handkerchief in one, a small key ring, with two keys on it, in the other. I study the key ring, with a Mini logo. One key is an old Yale – the front door of this house, I'd guess – while the other is a car key, presumably for a Mini. So, out there, probably just outside the front door and no more than 12 feet away, is our getaway.

"Go," replies the man suddenly. He's laid back, his eyes shut, his face twisted in pain. "Go!" he says again, as strongly as he can.

"Gerald?" I say sweetly, leaning forward so our heads are almost touching, so he can be sure to hear me. "Can you hear me?"

He nods, painfully, his lips twisting. I push the corner of the towel into his mouth and he sucks on it slowly, like a baby. "Better?" I ask nicely. He nods, almost imperceptibly. "What did you say about your partner coming up? When will he arrive?"

It seems to agitate him. "Go!" he says again. "Go … please." It strikes me that he's frightened, not of me, nor for himself – he must surely know his life is ebbing away – but for his partner. He's worried that I will kill him too.

"We'll go, me and my little boy, later; when it's dark. We can't go before then. It's not safe. When is your partner due here?"

This time, a huge effort, I don't know how he does it, he somehow struggles upwards onto his elbows, as I support him by the arms. His eyes open, he struggles to focus now, his eyes rolling back and he almost spits out the words, "Go … now … Go … now."

He slumps back.

God forgive me.

I've killed again.

11.20ᴀᴍ SUNDAY 1 NOVEMBER

The four of them, the young couple and the old couple, flanked by two police family liaison officers, one man and one woman, looked at the older plain-clothes officer who stood before them in the doorway of the cottage.

The young man and woman went to speak, both of them getting to their feet as the older officer turned to face them.

She spoke, her hands gesturing them to sit down. "We've no news yet, I'm afraid. I've just come over to tell you what we know, to put you in the picture."

"No one's told us anything, it's been ages ... I've been using this ... my phone ... to see if there is any news, on Sky."

"Kept us in the dark ... we should be the first to know, not the last."

"And you will be, just as soon as we have something to report. Let me tell you what's been happening."

The two police officers, responding to the senior officer's nods and movements, stepped back towards the kitchen. The two couples sat and waited for the senior officer to speak.

"May I ...?" She sat down on an armchair, leaning forward. "Orrey – Raymond John Orrey – has been at a unit near Nottingham for the past 18 months or so and escaped on Friday night at about midnight. He stole a car from Nottingham and drove here yesterday morning. It's the one you have outside ... we're keeping watch with officers ... but we think he's long gone."

"With Will?" asked the young woman. "He still has Will?"

"We assume so ... as his biological father ... we have no reason to suppose otherwise. But he is on foot, so far as we know. There have been no reports of stolen cars in this vicinity in the past 24 hours or anything out of the ordinary. There has been a domestic incident – I understand you're aware of that, Mrs Veitch – and we are still looking into that matter and trying to contact the estranged husband. The car for that household remains there, which may mean Orrey had no involvement. That's now been immobilised. We have this one to do, outside here, at some stage, but we've officers at an observation point for the time being."

The old man spoke up, "It said on ... Natalie's telephone that you've been searching for him and we saw, well we heard, lots of activity in the night, with helicopters. Did they see anything?"

"We had roadblocks on the main roads after you reported to the station. And officers from the parade were deployed to check houses in the area where you last saw him. We think he is somewhere outside of Aldeburgh. We had helicopters up and they've not seen anything yet. We suspect they'll be hiding in a farmer's barn somewhere. They may have hitched a lift. We've let the TV people in to get the news out there far and wide and our officers are searching farms and outbuildings. We still have roadblocks on the main roads, checking cars going out just in case."

"If the boy is alive, officer, and I very much doubt that knowing what we do about Raymond Orrey, but if he is, you had better be quicker than that," responded the older woman, standing up.

The old man interrupted, "William is a type one diabetic and without his medication, and proper food and care, which he won't get, he will become seriously ill very soon. It could even be fatal. You must hurry."

12.32PM SUNDAY 1 NOVEMBER

Me and my boy, little William, are sitting on the floor, just as we were; best place for us, I reckon. For now anyway. I've been thinking things through carefully, long and hard, you might say, and have decided it's too risky to wait here until Monday. We're going to go tonight, just as soon as it gets dark.

I can't bear it here.

I feel trapped; too much is going on around us.

I want to be out of here as soon as I can, free, and on the way to France.

I've the ashtray on the floor next to me – if the dead man's partner comes in before we leave when it gets dark, well, let's just say I'm ready for him. I don't want to, mind. But I'd have no choice. What else can I do?

I'd hear the key in the front door first.

The partner would come in, probably shouting a cheery "Hello."

He'd look round, downstairs to begin with.

Nothing to see there. I've cleaned up the stairs. Front room? Well, I've not even opened the door to that, let alone been in there – it's too easy to be seen from the street outside. I've straightened up the kitchen, though, left it as it was.

Maybe he'd be puzzled.

Call upstairs, thinking the dead man – I can't bring myself to use his name, not now – may be lying down.

Up he'd come, a big smile on his face as he swings open the door.

I'd have to be quick, very quick, with my back to little William so he did not see me raise my arm and bring the ashtray down on the man's head … again … and again. God knows how many times I'd need to do it. I'd have to drag him back outside, along to the spare room where I've covered the dead man's body with towels and curtains. Finish him off there if I had to. Not what I want to do. But I'd have no choice.

Then back to waiting again.

Until it gets dark.

When it's safe to leave.

William's humming to himself. He does that, I've noticed. Just sits there, when he's awake, and hums different tunes. He's a self-contained, happy sort of chap. Some songs I know. Others I don't. I join in humming when I know it. We daren't sing, of course, not with people next door.

It's been a good hour or more, since the man died.

Just sitting here, waiting.

The neighbours – did they hear anything?

I run through it in my mind again. The man's voice, raised, as he stood above me. Footsteps as we ran to the staircase. Voices at the top of the stairs. William calling out. The man falling down, once, twice, three times and hitting his head. Me shouting at William in the bathroom. The bump-bump-bump as I dragged the man up the stairs and along the corridor.

Did next door hear something?

A sudden, unexpected noise. Had to, surely?

Uncertain though, imagining things?

Maybe they are there now, on the other side of this wall. Ears pressed to it, just listening, checking if what they thought they heard was real. Whispering their thoughts to each other. We have to be silent, no matter what. I daren't let William sing out in happiness or cry or shout out in anger. Anything like that, when everything else is quiet, would be sure to be heard by next door. We can't have that happen.

Did they see anything, have they spotted something odd, out-of-the-ordinary?

I've kept away from the front windows, haven't even touched the curtains.

It's been tempting to close them, pull them to, hide away. But what if someone in the houses opposite noticed, knew the owners were away and put two and two together and dialled 999? I daren't risk it.

Thing is, I'm careful, me.

And smart, see?

I think about things no one else would. I'm clever like that. The first thing most people would do would be to close the curtains. Next thing you know, the police are smashing down the front door.

There are noises now, though. Out on the street. A hubbub,

that's what they call it. The police vans, maybe? Sky and the BBC on the move? Are they leaving? On their way to the next big story? All done and dusted and nothing to see here, so on your way please so everything can start getting back to normal? I'd say so. Yes, for sure. The vans are rumbling and tooting and making their way back out of town. Good news, I reckon. I can't look out, though, can't risk being seen by anyone on the outside. I don't even sit up straight in case I'm seen from the windows of the houses opposite.

Have they seen something already?

The man standing over me as I slept.

Me jumping to my feet and chasing him.

I rerun exactly what happened in my head. They – anyone looking out of the windows of the houses opposite – could have seen the man in the bedroom, looking down at me. Nothing to worry about there; they'd be alert for me, a younger, bigger man, and a little boy. Would they have seen me jumping up? Maybe mistaken me for the man's partner, at least from a distance? The little chap is the key, of course; if they saw him, they'd raise the alarm. First thing I'd know, the police would be breaking down the door. Guns, dogs, Christ knows what. No, I've not been seen. Must be careful not to let him be seen, little William.

Still waiting, me and the little fellow.

Rats in a trap, that's what we are, thinking about it. At least until it's dark in, what, four or five hours?

A long wait for us.

I've found paper and pens. A Basildon Bond notepad, for writing letters, really. And a fountain pen and pencil set, like you'd give as a gift for Christmas.

All unused and tucked in one of the boxes in the spare room. In among bank statements and other paperwork.

We've been drawing, him with the pencil and me with the pen, all sorts of things. Cats, dogs, you name it, we've drawn it.

I can't sit up straight. I'm sure I said. We may be seen. We can't even talk, let alone move about much. We may be heard. And I know the dead man's partner is coming at any moment. "My partner's coming up ... he'll be here soon." That's what the man said. Not just "My partner's coming up", not "My partner's coming up, he'll be here tonight" or "at 2pm" or whatever (so that I could be prepared), but "My partner's coming up ... he'll be here soon." Soon. That's the thing, see? That's the worry and what sets me all on edge. It's the not knowing of it all. Here soon. How soon is soon?

This evening?

An hour?

Any moment now?

William shifts uncomfortably next to me. He pulls a face. I know what that is. Dads just do. It's an instinct with us. Have to get him to the bathroom quickly. Crouched over, making encouraging noises, I hurry him out of the room and along the landing.

Too fucking late.

I clean him up as best I can. I put his pants back on him from the radiator and pull his trousers up. Will have to do for now. I've done my best but daren't wash him properly or give him a bath. The noise of the water tank, the banging of the pipes, the running of the water – will all give us away to the people next door.

This isn't easy, you know.

Sitting here, fiddling about doing next to nothing to keep a child quiet.

Listening out for the dead man's partner to arrive at any moment.

It's enough to drive you mad, it is.

1.00PM SUNDAY 1 NOVEMBER

"He's missed last night's, Rick, and this morning's and the one now; what's going to happen to him?" The young woman looked up from the sofa.

"Ssshhh," he hushed her down, even though they were alone in the cottage while the family liaison officers had stepped outside and his parents had taken the opportunity to go for a "a well-deserved breath of fresh air", as the old woman put it. "He'll be fine for a while. It's not an instant thing, he will have some insulin in his system ... keep him going for a bit."

"How do we know that ... how do we know how long he'll be fine? He wasn't before, was he ... at the start. Look ..." she added, showing him the screen of her mobile phone. She read, "This is what this American site says, 'Man with type one diabetes found dead in the morning after having been observed in apparently good health the day before.'" She choked through the last few words.

"That's just America ... it's all scare stories over there ... they might have had something else wrong with them anyway, their heart or something ... drugs." He moved to the front door to check again on the car that had been left there. "Will ... he'll just get tired and a bit scratchy today, that's all. That's probably for the best ... he won't trouble Orrey."

"Won't he? If he gets scratchy? Remember what Orrey used to do to Kate? She could never say what she thought, had to agree with everything he ever said. Bow and bloody scrape to him. And she had to creep around the house in absolute silence so as not to anger him. How can you even think Will's safe ... if he cries when he's hungry, or misses us?" She paused, struggling again with her composure.

"Thing is, Rick, you know this – if Orrey has to ... If Orrey has to, he'll do whatever he needs to do to get away. Will's safe only while he's no trouble. When he becomes a nuisance ..." She sat down, her head dropping, fiddling with her phone again as she had all night long and for most of the morning.

"They're saying on this newspaper site that we left him on his own and that we deserve to lose him ... that he's not ours anyway ... look at the comments after this news story ..." She went to pass the phone to the young man. "Know-All247 writes, 'I'm very sorry but they should not have let the poor child out of their sight' ... what do they know, all these people? What's it got to do with them?"

He brushed the phone away. "We need to do what the police say, just wait ... there's no point in keeping on checking these sites, upsetting yourself; they don't know, do they? And people who email comments about things they know nothing about aren't worth listening to ... Nat, here, come and look."

She jumped up, panic rising within her as she crossed to the front door. "What is it, what do you see?"

"Nothing ... nobody. Don't worry. The family liaison officers are over by the sea. I don't see any other police any more. I think there was someone over there by the road in a green car. That's gone. So too is that plain-clothes policewoman who was walking about by the prom. The car Orrey drove is still there, though ... whether they secured that, I don't know. I'm not sure where their observation place is ... was; one of the houses I think. Perhaps they're looking elsewhere now ... he must have gone."

In the distance, they saw the old man walking back towards them from the far side of the car park. He waved at them, attracting their attention. The old woman was some way behind him as he hurried forward as best he could on aching legs and feet.

The young man strained to hear what the older man was saying, was mouthing at them.

The young woman looked at the young man. "Maybe they've found him, Rick, maybe they've got him back."

The young man went to speak as she hurried off across the car park. "It doesn't seem ... I don't think my dad looks as though ..." He stopped as he watched the young woman reach the old man and they exchanged words. As he saw her shoulders slump and she put her hands to her face, he ran across towards them.

"They're leaving town, Richard," said the old man, reaching out to touch his arm. "They're going. All the television and radio people. I spoke to one of them and there have been sightings of Orrey and William ... lots of sightings ... on the roads into London. They're heading off that way we think. They are closing in on them. We need to sit and wait for the police to come back and tell us they have got William back. It won't be long now, I'm sure." He turned and waved the family liaison officers over to tell them.

2.15PM SUNDAY 1 NOVEMBER

Hours it's been.

Just sitting here.

Me and the little 'un.

God knows I've done everything to keep him quiet. We've hummed. We've sung (ever so quietly). We've drawn pictures. Loads and loads of pictures. We've done the water and wee routine again. And for good measure he's been sick too. More than once. I don't know why, he's only been eating plain biscuits. Digestives and custard creams. Not much wrong with them.

We've had one or two tense moments, shall we say.

He can be tricky, I'll tell you that.

He won't just sit there and behave like a good little boy.

I've tried so hard. I have told him stories but he pulls away when I put my arm around him. He makes that angry, buzzing noise now and then for no good reason. I have played all sorts of games. I Spy seemed to keep him quiet for a little bit. Then I did this thing where you go "round and round the garden" on his hand then go "one step, two step and tickly under there" under his arm, but he pulled his hand back the moment I reached for his armpit. He's an awkward so-and-so and that's a fact.

But he's just started to settle at last.

Become a little sleepy-headed even.

It's about time.

I lift him onto the bed, give him a chance to have a sleep. And he does. I pull the duvet over him and he turns on his side with his thumb in his mouth again. It gives me a while to relax, shut my eyes for a minute or two; not that I dare fall asleep with the dead man's partner due at any time. I check the glass paperweight is close by. I'll need that. Now would be a good time for him to arrive, while William is asleep on the bed. Yes, a very good time.

Then it starts.

Quiet but persistent.

The tapping.

At first, I thought, straining to listen and to hear every noise, that I was imagining it. Assumed maybe it was the creak of the rafters of an old house or the knocking of a water pipe. That, somehow, my mind in a heightened state of awareness was playing tricks and taking an ordinary noise and turning it into something more sinister.

Tap . . .

Silence.

Tap . . .

Silence.

Tap . . .

There it goes again. Quite unmistakable. Not a random noise at all. But something real and steady.

Silence.

Longer this time.

Tap ... tap ... tap.

My mind is playing tricks on me. I can't work out where it's coming from. Maybe the back door of this house? Is it a neighbour? From next door? They've seen the Mini outside, think the man has arrived from, where, London maybe and have come to the back door with, what, an apple pie, cake, some home-made biscuits? They're tapping on the glass with their fingernails to attract attention.

Who knows?

Silence again.

No more tapping.

Quiet for a few minutes. Then I hear creaking, no imagining there. Quite the opposite. There is clear and definite creaking somewhere above my head over towards next door. I strain to listen. Someone next door – the man I heard talking outside last night I suspect – is very carefully and very gently moving his weight across the loft, joist to joist, from his side of the roof to ours. I can hear the creaking – quite clear, quite definite – as he does it.

There's a reward, I reckon.

For me.

This guy's a fucking have-a-go hero.

I guess this row of old terraced houses shares some sort of communal loft. This fucker next door is going to have a go at capturing me. I think he's heard something – maybe me shouting out, perhaps William calling "Papa" – and has put two and two together and made four.

He's smart, I'll give him that.

If he goes to the police and tells them what he's heard and they believe him, they'll storm the place and he and the reward will soon be forgotten. He'll not get his money. But, here's the thing, if he captures me and comes out of the front door – in front of the police, Joe Public and any BBC and Sky reporters who are still hanging about – well, they can't avoid the payout then. Maybe he can even sell his story to the papers, make himself some extra cash.

There it goes again.

The creaking.

Directly above me now.

I turn, gently hushing William, who has woken up again and is now making some sort of retching noise in his throat. I need him to be quiet, dead quiet, and now, so I can listen and see which way the next-door neighbour is going. But I daren't clamp my hand over William's mouth to keep him quiet. He'll struggle in my arms, maybe make that furious buzzing noise again. I'll not be able to hear. I leave William be. His gagging noises make it harder, though. I sit up straight, straining to hear.

"Oran," says William, sitting up slowly. He looks dazed.

Oran? What the hell is oran?

"Shhh," I say, "yes, yes, in a minute, in a minute."

"Oran?" he repeats sluggishly.

Christ's sake, I can't hear. Does he realise I'm trying to listen? It's all for his sake, after all.

"Yes," I say, as firmly but as quietly as I can. "In a minute, William."

God almighty, he rolls off the bed and, after a moment or two, gets unsteadily to his feet and moves slowly towards the door.

I'm up too and after him, almost without thinking, grabbing him by the shoulders as he reaches the door. I spin him round, hold him tight in a hug – harder than it needs to be but I want him to know, it has to get through somehow, that he must be quiet. Now he's struggling again and I can't hear the man above me.

For God's sake, be quiet, William, please.

The man will have heard what's happening. He'll have taken advantage, moved swiftly across, from one joist to another, to the loft hatch in this house. Where the hell is that? I have to think fast. It has to be on the landing, doesn't it? At the top of the stairs? I don't know, I really don't. I never looked. Well, you wouldn't, would you?

I hold William down, God help me, what else can I do.

Somehow, I swing the bedroom door open and look up. I can see it on the landing above the staircase. The loft hatch. Just as I thought. Never noticed it before. I hold William still and quiet – he's passive in my grip – as I watch the hatch. No sounds of creaking or movement now.

The man – the next-door neighbour – is in the loft by the hatch, listening and waiting. He's going to open it at any moment, pull back the hatch, drop down onto the landing and go for me.

I push the door to. Let's not make it easy for him to know exactly where I am. I need to retain some sort of element of surprise. Give myself a chance. He'll be armed in some way, for sure.

Kitchen knife? Hammer? I don't know.

It's going to happen.

Any second now.

William twitches; some sort of spasm runs through his body. I let go of him, look down in horror. His head tips back as what looks like an electric current jerks its way up and down his body. Some kind of fit. I don't know what to do. I lift him up, hold him to me, as gently as I can this time, making soothing noises. I don't know how I'm supposed to help. I hold him close. Love him. It's all I can do.

What else is there?

I cry out.

No thought for anything but my little boy.

Moments pass, seconds, maybe minutes. William twitches two, three times more and then seems to slow and relax and is eventually still. I lay him out carefully on the bedroom floor, leaning forward, my ear close to his nose and mouth. He is breathing, no doubt about that. He is alive. He is well. He has just had some sort of sudden fit. But he's okay. I just need to leave him be, let him sleep now, recover his strength.

The man?

From next door?

At the hatch?

I tense. With me distracted by William, he would have carefully opened the hatch, moved the cover to one side and dropped quietly onto the landing below. He is there now, I can sense it, almost feel his presence, on the other side of the bedroom door. He's heard William writhing about, my cry of fear and knows exactly where we are. I could not help myself. It was instinctive. The man is listening and waiting, ready, after a few moments' silence, to storm in.

So be it.

I get to my feet.

And wrench open the door.

3.22PM SUNDAY 1 NOVEMBER

The policeman, a new one to the young couple, said a few words to the family liaison officers who opened the door and invited him in. He sat down with a heavy sigh, as if he had been on his feet too long and it was close to the end of his shift.

The young man and the young woman exchanged glances.

The old man, sitting alongside the old woman, spoke first.

"Aren't you PC O'Keefe? We haven't seen you for a while."

"I've been off sick. But they've brought everyone in today as back-up. I've been asked to give you an update." He opened his notebook. "We also need to get you …"

"Where's the plain-clothes officer, the older woman, the one in charge? Where's everyone gone?" said the young woman.

The policeman shook his head. "They're all following leads, it's still our priority and will be until you get your boy back. The Met are now involved too. Your ex-husband and your son have been seen …"

"He's not my ex-husband," answered the young woman angrily. "He was married to … and he killed … he killed … my sister. This isn't some sort of domestic squabble. The man has taken our son and he's a murderer … and our son – Rick and mine – is not well."

The policeman paused and continued. "A man and a young boy answering the descriptions given have been seen in various locations in and around Suffolk, mainly Ipswich. I've been asked if you – Mr and Mrs Veitch – would come with me so you can see the footage from a CCTV camera by the railway station and make a positive identification. We think they may be heading to London."

The young couple got to their feet, with the young man looking towards the older couple, "Will you be …"

"We'll be fine," answered the old man as the younger woman, pulling on her coat, moved to the front door. She turned.

"Hurry, Rick, we need to see if Will's on the train for London. Won't we lose him again, officer, if they get that far?"

"If we can get a positive identification from you and we know where they're going … to London … we can pick them up on CCTV as they move through the Tube network. The Met are pretty good at this sort of thing. Once we've tracked them, we can pick them up."

"Go, Richard, and good luck."

"Will you be alright, Dad? Safe?" The young man looked first towards the family liaison officers and then at the policeman for reassurance.

"They'll be safe, sir. Your man has long since gone. Your parents have nothing to worry about at all. And we still have police officers out and about just in case."

The old woman spoke up, "It might be better if you let him go, officer. If you catch him, he'll kill the boy on the spot ... if he hasn't done so already."

3.30PM SUNDAY 1 NOVEMBER

Funny thing, you know – imagination.

When your nerves are shredded like mine.

I can't hear that creaking any more.

Just my mind playing tricks. Hard to believe, but there was no neighbour with a kitchen knife crouched on the landing, waiting to go for me.

Old houses, see? That's the thing. They're almost alive, creaking and clanking away in the cold weather. Wood stretches and shrinks. Pipes knock against each other. That's all it was. Just the house going about its business. I stood there on the landing shaking for a while, I can tell you. Can you blame me? Stood there listening for an age, as a matter of fact.

Just in case.

You never know.

Best to be careful.

Me and my sleepy-headed little boy are back in bed now, though, snuggled up this time and just waiting for the hours to pass oh-so-slowly.

The house is still playing its little mind games with me, though.

Tap ... tap ... tap. There it goes again.

I ignore it now. I know it for what it is. Old pipes. My imagination. I just blot it out. All we need to do is sit here and wait for the next three or four hours or so and then we go – off to the Mini and away. I reckon by then all the police will have left, other than a few beat bobbies to placate the locals. Yes, it's going to be easy, the next stage. Easier anyway. A drive to Thurrock, coach, France and off we go.

Tap.

Long pause.

Tap.

Long pause.

Tap.

I just ignore it, really I do. I cuddle my little William instead. He seems to be calm now, settled in himself and alright with me at last, his ever-loving dad. I don't know if somehow his fit – if that is what it was – has quietened him down. It seems to have knocked the stuffing out of him. He's breathing steadily, not really moving and not focusing on anything. I gently move his head so it is facing me and smile at him, trying to make eye contact. He seems to look right through me.

Worried?

No, not at all.

It's just been a shock to his system, all of this. That's the thing. He looks a good colour and is breathing properly. Those are the main things, aren't they?

Quiet now.

No tapping.

Just a trick that's all, like the creaking.

I've worked it through carefully. In my head. How we are going to get out when it's getting dark. I have to bluff big-time. I can't afford to sneak about or look shifty or hesitate in any way. I need William to be quiet and docile, just like he is now. I'm going to wrap some curtain fabric from the spare room around him. Just enough to make it look like a bundle of fabrics rather than a little boy. I'll open the front door, lift him up, walk confidently down the path, open the car door and lay William across the back seats. In the car, start up, drive away.

There it is again.

The tapping.

Tap … tap … tap.

I don't know if the noise is in my head – whether I am imagining it – or if it is a real noise. The water pipes maybe? The tank in the loft? Perhaps that's what I heard before when I thought it was creaking; it was the tapping from the pipes going into the water tank. It's funny, though. It seems to come and go. Different taps. A definite rhythm to it. I'm sure of it. Would drive you mad if you lived here, that's for certain.

Shit, I've been asleep again.

How long this time? An hour?

Not sure, it's growing dark now, though.

William is asleep too. I'm not sure if I should wake him, check he's okay. I move my hand up to his nose and mouth. He is breathing and it still seems to be steady enough, not laboured or anything. He looks peaceful, as though he doesn't have a care in the world. I'll leave him as he is for now. If in an hour or so's time, I can lift him as he is, half-asleep, to the car that will be easier.

I'm so exhausted, I couldn't help myself nodding off.

No sign of the man's partner.

Reckon I'd have woken up automatically if the front door had opened.

Has it, though? Is that what just woke me? Something must have done. Is the man's partner now in the house? Did he call out as he came in the front door, just like I said he would? Is that what woke me up?

I slip my arm out from under little William, pins and needles in it, move out from the bed and go over to the door, opening it gently so I can hear all over the house.

Quiet as I can, I stand there, crouched and listening. I can't hear anything. Nothing at all. It's quiet now, except for that one thing starting up again.

Tap tap tap.

Rapid now, in quick succession.

Stronger, more insistent this time.

I stand and listen, trying to work out where it's coming from. Not from the loft? No. Surely not from downstairs? It's hard to tell. There's a pause for a moment and then another three taps, spaced out more evenly this time. Still strong and definite, though.

This is odd.

Another pause, and I am waiting for the next three, which, if I'm correct and this is real and not my imagination, will be three taps in rapid succession again. Long pause. Tap tap tap. There it goes again. What makes a noise like that?

Tap tap tap.

Tap. Pause. Tap. Pause. Tap.

What the hell is that? And then it dawns on me. It's not tap … tap … tap, followed by tap, pause, tap, pause, tap.

It's actually tap tap tap.

Tap. Pause. Tap. Pause. Tap.

Tap tap tap.

Put another way, it's meant to be dot dot dot, dash dash dash, dot dot dot. Or the other way round. I don't know. I do know it's Morse code, though. For SOS. That man's not fucking dead at all. He's very much alive and in the spare room tapping SOS on the wall to the neighbours. And it's taken me fuck knows how long to realise it.

Right on cue.

There's a knocking on the front door.

And, seconds later, the man calls out feebly from the spare room, "Help."

4.24PM SUNDAY 1 NOVEMBER

God help me, what do I do now?

Think quickly, have to think fast.

Who's at the front door?

Man from next door who's heard the tapping? Maybe; but would he have called the police first? Probably. Is it the police? No, they'd storm the place. They'd not send one copper round to knock politely on the front door. That man's partner? Most likely, but wouldn't he have a key?

I hear a movement at the letterbox.

"Gerry, are you there? Can you let me in, please?"

The man's partner.

But he can't get in. The man – Gerald – must have had the only front-door key. He came ahead. His partner followed. What now? He'll know Gerald is here; the Mini is outside – somewhere anyway, I'm not sure where exactly. Directly outside or – given the police and TV crews that were here – has he parked someway down the street or round a corner?

"Help," I hear Gerald call out again. It's weak and it's oh-so-faint but will his partner downstairs, the letterbox flap pushed open, hear it?

An agonising moment. Is this how it all ends?

I wait to hear "Gerry, is that you?" followed by the crunch of the door as the man breaks it in, believing Gerald is lying there, a heart attack victim.

A pause, lengthening – as if we are all waiting for each other to do something. I hold my breath for what seems a minute or two more, my nerves stretched taut, not sure what to do, until I hear the sudden, blessed relief of the flap of the letterbox clanging shut and the man walking away.

We have to get out of here now. The man will think Gerald's popped out and has forgotten to leave a key. That doesn't matter because the man knows there's that spare key in the garden by the side of the shed. At least there was. It's now in my pocket, remember? So what does he do when he realises that Gerald's arrived but is not answering the door, the back-door key has disappeared and there is, according to the television, a madman on the loose? He goes straight to the police, that's what.

I'm trapped in here with William. Game over.

Unless I'm fast, really fast. I've got a minute, little more.

Got to get out of this house straightaway.

I sweep back into the bedroom, dragging William up and out of the bed by his arms. He lolls for a moment, opens his eyes and falls forward into my shoulder, trying to get back to sleep, thumb moving instinctively into his mouth.

Back onto the landing, I move towards the spare room to fetch something to disguise William as best I can. "Help me," I hear a barely audible whisper and turn back round immediately – I don't want William to see that man, who can only just be alive, with barely enough strength to tap on the walls and call out in little more than a whisper.

At the top of the stairs, I loosen my grip on William to double-check the key for the Mini is there in the jumble in my pocket. It is. As I come down the stairs, I have two choices. Out the front door and straight to the car, assuming it's outside. Or I wait a moment or two longer for the partner to come back round to the front and we then slip out of the back and into the side streets and alleyways that take us to the car I left in the car park down by the Veitch cottage.

I stand, William in my arms, at the bottom of the stairs now. I know I have to take two, three, four steps to the front door, open it as if it's the most normal thing in the world, and step confidently onto the path down to the gate and to the car. But I can't do it. I just can't bring myself to move forward. My nerve, which has held for so long and so far, fails me now.

I don't know what's out the front.

Daren't look. I cannot take the chance of being seen by anyone at all.

Fact is, I'm scared, I don't mind telling you.

I turn at the bottom of the stairs – quickly, as I could be seen through the glass – and move to the back of the hall by the kitchen door. Someone would have to press up close against the front door to see me there. I know, or at least I'm pretty sure, that the man is going round the back of the house to get the key by the shed.

Not there? What next? Would he assume the worst and break in or go for the police? Or he might just think that Gerald had lost his key, taken the back-door one and had then gone out to the shops to get milk and bread? How likely is that? Not very, but it's what I'm going to go with. It's all I've got.

I stand and listen for the back garden gate for what seems an age.

Not sure what to do. God's sake, now William is becoming restless in my arms, close to waking.

I have to do something, and fast, rather than just standing here with the minutes passing, waiting to be discovered.

At last, so suddenly that I jump as if I was not expecting it, I hear one, two heavy footsteps on the patio. A long pause (as the man looks into the kitchen)? The rattle of the handle (thank God I locked the back door). Pause again. Then the voice once more.

"Gerry, Gerry? Are you there?"

He's puzzled, perhaps a little anxious, but there's no sound of panic rising in his voice. He sees this as an inconvenience, a nuisance, not as anything untoward or sinister.

I hear him standing by the back door, scuffling his feet and coughing now, clearing his throat. What's he doing, calling Gerald on a mobile phone? Stands to reason, doesn't it? Wants to know where he is. Out to get supplies? But Gerald didn't have a mobile phone on him. Did he? No, I checked each pocket in turn. Did he leave it in his car? If he had a phone on him and I had missed it, he'd not have been tapping SOS on the wall, would have reached for the phone, no matter how much pain he was in, and pressed 9 ... 9 ... 9. That's for certain.

I strain, listening to hear sounds from upstairs.

An ever-fainter "Help" or, God help us, the beeping of a phone. Nothing, thank goodness.

A moment or two of silence; I suddenly realise I am holding my breath again. The man at the back door swears to himself – just annoyed now, not anxious at all – and I hear his footsteps, moving away. Now's my chance. I have to time this just so. In my head, I count his footsteps to the back gate: six, seven, eight? The gate's pulled open. Was that a click or am I imagining it?

Wait: two, three, four seconds. Not sure.

The gate is slammed shut. No mistaking that. As he goes back round to the front of the house, I have to slip out the back and disappear into the alleyways.

I listen, straining for any sound at the back of the house.

It's over for us here; it's time to leave. I nudge William and his eyes open wearily and he coughs and splutters, almost retching.

"We're on our way, little William, come on – we're on our way to a new life in the south of France!"

Part 3

THE DEPARTURE

4.56PM SUNDAY 1 NOVEMBER

It's dusk and a sea mist is rolling in, giving us cover to get away.

We're in the back alleys, heads down and hurrying along.

Going back to the car park at the far end of the seafront.

With the man gone looking for Gerald, I reckon it will take 30 minutes, maybe more, before his anger turns to worry. He'll walk to the shops, check out the nearest pub and call on any neighbours he knows first. Then someone will tell him what they've seen on the news, repeating what's been put out about me.

Lies mostly, if not all of it.

But I've told you that before, haven't I?

Remember?

Eventually, the man, troubled now, would stop a policeman and explain Gerald's car was parked outside but the house was locked and dark, the back-door key was missing and Gerald was nowhere to be seen.

Him and the copper would knock on the front door.

They'd check the back door, each pulling at the handle.

Then they'd look at each other. The man would nod firmly and the copper would put his elbow to the glass, push hard, and in it goes.

Room to room they'd move downstairs. The man would hurry upstairs, calling Gerald's name. The policeman would be at his shoulder, pushing by to the bedroom, checking. Last of all, one of them would open the door to the box room.

That's it then, now they'd know.

Dead? Alive?

Either way, it doesn't really matter. I'm fucked – no disguising what I've done.

We hurry on, as quickly as we can, through the alleyways. I think we have 25 minutes, tops.

Did I say? I'm sure I did.

Listen, why don't you?

We've 25 minutes to get to the car and away, out of the town and on the road down to Thurrock. Back roads will be safest. The police may still have cars stationed, ready and waiting, along the main roads, maybe even roadblocks, especially on the way out of town.

Not been seen yet.

Our luck holds.

For now anyway.

I carry William, his body turned towards me, so his face cannot be spotted easily. If no one sees his face – his angelic cherub face – and my head is down, I might just get away with it all the way to the car.

It's darker now and I'm getting into my stride. Dirty alleyways, full of bins and bottles and carrier bags overflowing with rubbish. Need to be careful not to stumble. I focus on walking briskly, one step firmly in front of the other.

I hear noises ahead and a gaggle of girls appears out of the mist, all laughing, each trying to out-talk the others. Coming towards me, I drop my gaze, my hand reaching up to stroke William's head so he can't turn and be seen.

There are four or five of them, teens, maybe 14 or 15. None of them will look at me. A man of my age is invisible to them.

They move alongside. The smallest, a slight, dark-haired pixie dressed in black, is pushed towards me by one of the others. She bumps into me, stumbles back and the others erupt into laughter.

I glance down as she hits the ground, a startled look on her face.

As she turns to glare up at me – seriously, as if it's my fucking fault – I look away and hurry on. I really want to break into a run but know I dare not. I just keep walking, as steady as I can. I mustn't look back, can't risk them all seeing my face, recognising me.

There is another burst of laughter and I imagine the other girls reaching down to help her up. There's an angry shout. "Hey, Hey," one of them cries, the bravest of them all.

They're lucky I don't have time to stop, that's all I'll say.

They'd not be so happy then.

I move on as quickly as I can until all I can hear in the distance is a mix of shouts and obscenities as they watch me fading into the mist.

Did they realise who I was? I don't think so – if they'd known anything, they'd not have been laughing and joking and pushing each other into me, would they?

I'm safe, still.

I press on. No time to waste.

Have to be quick.

A sharp right and I'm walking along the back of the buildings fronting the high street.

How far now? Half a mile maybe? Does this run the full length? Easy if it does.

No one about to see me until I come out of the other end by the car park.

I slip suddenly on the path, my left leg sliding away from me. I manage to stay upright. I need to slow a little, can't risk falling over with the little 'un in my arms.

Now he's awake, struggling upwards.

Hands to his eyes, rubbing them.

Here we go. God hope he doesn't start retching again.

Like he has something stuck in his throat.

It's a nervous thing I reckon, a tic.

I keep on moving. If I stop and try to soothe him, we'll waste valuable minutes. I reckon we now have no more than 20 minutes to get to the car.

As we move along, ever-slowing, with William heavy in my arms, I listen for the giveaway sounds of discovery: the police car sirens as they race to the house or the wail of the ambulance. Not long now.

Ahead of me.

100 yards or so.

A man steps out.

I stop dead in my tracks, taken by surprise. Not sure what to do. There's a turning to my left, about 30 or so yards up, between us, which may take me out on the high street. I can use that if need be.

The rattle of a bin lid.

Glance up.

The man has turned and gone.

I hurry on, past the turning, moving towards where the man dumped his rubbish in the bin. William's making some sort of grumbling noise in his throat, almost a growl, with every step I take.

We move parallel to the man's back gate. Left it wide open. Without thinking, I stop to close it.

He is standing there.

In silence, just inside the gate.

Our eyes meet.

"Hello," I say, without thinking. He does not reply. Just looks back without acknowledgement. An old man, 80, maybe even older. Bald, a fringe of white hair. Dark cardigan, white vest, dark trousers. He stands there expressionless.

Slowly, I turn away.

Hold William tighter.

Move on quickly.

20, 30 yards on, I force myself to look back. The man has stepped out again. Turned towards us. I raise my hand as if I am a neighbour out and about with his little boy, maybe going for a fish and chips supper.

Does he know who I am?

Has he seen the television news?

If so, I am surely done for.

He will turn and go indoors, making for an old-fashioned telephone sitting on a table in the hallway. Dialling 9 ... 9 ... 9, he'll say in a low mutter, clearing his throat of phlegm, "Hello ... police? I've just seen that madman (I am not) and the boy, come quick."

Ten minutes, then.

Is that what I've got left?

Ten minutes to get back to the car and away.

40, 50 yards farther on now.

There is another turning just ahead, 10 yards or so, and that leads us out to the high street and the car park.

A final glance back.

The man has gone.

How long do I have?

Five minutes? How long does it take to dial 999, be put through to the police and for them to arrive, cars, dogs, marksmen, the whole works? I have to get to the car and drive off down one of the lanes that lead out of the town. I daren't try the main roads, not now.

I turn into the passageway to the high street and the car park. So heavy in my arms, I drop William to his feet. He trips and falls on his knees. Now he's crying, slowly at first and then rising into what is close to an angry scream. I think he's hungry, plain and simple.

I'm not giving him anything.

He'd only throw it back up.

Probably over me.

I lift him, try wiping him down, but I don't know what else to do – I can't have him screaming like this; he'll be heard and people will put two and two together.

I clamp my hand over his mouth again.

Leave his nose free this time. (I didn't last time, okay?)

He struggles, his face reddening.

I bend over, fearing he will twist and twitch in my arms and collapse into another fit. But I cannot risk everything – our freedom, our happiness, our new life together – by letting him go as he will scream and scream. We are so close to the high street that he could so easily be heard.

"Be quiet," I say, furiously. "Be quiet and I will put you down and you can walk."

He takes no notice; it's as if I am not there, as he struggles more and gets redder still. He's about to black out, I can tell.

"Walk, William, walk," I urge. "William, walk like a big boy."

Something seems to get through to him as he stops, looks at me – through me, as though I am not there – and then takes a long, deep breath.

"That's it, William, good boy," I say. He's come to his senses and is going to walk nicely for Daddy. I slip him down to the ground and, holding his hand, turn him round to walk on.

He is rigid.

White-faced and as stiff as a board.

Not moving at all.

He's holding his breath, I think. Or so it seems. I can't tell. It's dark now and there is very little light in this passageway. I'm not sure if he's angry or if he has simply seized up, in another sort of fit. I drop to my knees and turn him round to see.

Jesus, I can't tell in this light.

He is ramrod stiff, eyes rolled upwards.

He does not seem to be breathing.

I pull him down onto his back and crouch over him, my mouth moving to his. Don't know what to do, but have to get some air into him for sure. I blow, pause, blow again. I don't think this is a fit, not this time. More like a temper tantrum. Blow, pause, blow. Have to get some oxygen in there fast.

He's still and breathing quietly.

Not sure if he is awake or asleep.

I stand there, for a second or two, listening for sounds behind me, to the sides, and to the pathway ahead. Nothing. I leave William there on the ground, safe for a minute with no one about, as I stride the 10 yards to the top and peer out; the high street is to my left, the car park down to the right.

There are street lights and parked cars dotted here and there, but, so far as I can see, there isn't anyone on the street. All clear. For the moment.

Got to do it.

Take my chance.

Go right now.

I turn and race back to William, lifting him up again into my arms. He's still semi-conscious and sinks easily into me. Seconds later, all still quiet, I am back at the high street. I check once again to my left. Once more to my right. Still clear. I have to go, while it stays that way.

I am walking purposefully. A glance around. I take a step onto the slight, grassy slope, over a low metal rail and I am on the shingle of the car park. I stand there for a moment.

Not sure what to expect.

Some sort of police presence?

Lights, guards, everyone waiting for me?

It's just as it was, as if nothing out of place has happened here at all. I step out confidently, William snuggled close. Two, three, four steps towards the car. It's hard not to break into a run, even though I know I can take my time now. Home and dry. Almost, anyway.

Five, six, seven steps.

Now halfway there.

I check back, just in case. No one there – obviously.

Eight, nine, ten steps and I am at the car, ready to open it and slip William next to me onto the passenger seat so I can keep hold of him. Rummaging for the key, I glance up, towards the cottage, which I can now see clearly, top and bottom. It's still dark and I'd say that it looks as if no one is inside.

Only thing, though, there is a policewoman on the doorstep.

I stand there gazing at her.

As she looks up and across at me.

5.16PM SUNDAY 1 NOVEMBER

"So, other than her," the young woman glanced towards the front door where a female police officer was keeping watch outside, "the police have now all gone from here and we're supposed to just sit here, hour after hour, waiting for something to happen ... for some news." She put her phone into her handbag. "There's still nothing new on any of the news channels."

"There won't be, Nat," answered the young man, sitting back on the sofa. "That last officer said, didn't he? They were sifting through the responses before they ... or we ... do an appeal. Sort what they've got, see if there are any good leads. And they've not all gone. It's still their priority, but they have to change shifts and bring everyone up-to-date and compare notes. They'll be back soon."

"How long's it going to take ... William wants help. He needs us, Rick. Now." The young woman dropped her head forward.

The old woman, carrying two mugs of tea, came back into the front room followed by the old man, who had a tray with two more mugs and a plate of biscuits. The old woman passed the drinks to the younger couple and sat down in the chair. The old man put the tray on the coffee table and moved to the window.

"Let's hope these leads are better than the CCTV one. Was the man an Asian, did you say?" The old woman pursed her lips into the semblance of a smile.

"That's not fair, mum," answered the younger man. "He did have a child of about Will's age and was acting oddly. Hiding in the corner. It did look strange. He was an Eastern European, we think. Not Asian."

"Probably an illegal immigrant ..." laughed the old man, sipping at his tea. "Trying to buy the cheapest train ticket to London for his whole family ... one on the ticket in the compartment, 16 taking it in turns to hide in the toilet."

The young woman looked at the young man and raised her eyebrows.

He shook his head.

"You can't say that sort of thing these days, Dad. You shouldn't even think it."

The old man continued, "You're always going to get plenty of calls. Lots of sightings. One or two mischief-makers with nothing better to do. Trolls they call them. You just have to wait for the police to uncover the genuine lead and then they'll act fast. You wait ... you'll get a call suddenly ... out of the blue ... any moment, to say they've got William back."

The old woman finished her tea and motioned to the old man

to sit down. "He'll be long gone now and it would be best to let him go. What do you think he would do if he were cornered? He would hold the boy as a hostage at best. At worst ..." She let her words tail away.

"For Christ's sake, why can't you be supportive for once," the younger woman shouted. "We all know what could happen. Will could go into a coma if he's not looked after. And he could be ... we know what Orrey is like. He tormented Katie ... near enough tortured her at times. But it doesn't help ... we know that Will could now be ..." She stuttered over her words, falling silent.

"It doesn't help, Mum, really," added the young man. "Please. We know it's frustrating and worrying. But we all want Will to be found safe and well. I'm sure if we can find Orrey before Will falls ill and reason with him, we can get Will back with no real harm done."

"And if not ..." said the old woman.

"Well, once he knows Will is not well, he'll take him somewhere; he'll leave Will where he'll be found easily. Outside a supermarket or somewhere like that."

The old man watched the old woman pull a face of disbelief. He turned away as he felt a surge of anger, something close to hatred in that instant. There really was no talking to the dreadful old cow at times.

5.17pm SUNDAY 1 NOVEMBER

I blank her. The policewoman.

Well what do you expect?

What else can I do? You tell me.

I tug open the passenger door, climbing in and over and dragging William behind me onto the passenger seat. I hear the policewoman call out politely as I lean across to pull the door shut. I ignore her again, pretending I have not heard, that I'm just an ordinary fellow.

But she must have seen William, mustn't she?

Not sure, can't tell.

The car was between us, after all.

I'm now fumbling with the key, trying to put it into the ignition, but my hand is shaking. She calls once more, louder this time, more emphatic, and I can't help but look across. God almighty, she is moving purposefully towards me. Still some distance away, though.

Key's in. Lights kept off.

The car fires up.

I rev the engine, far too hard.

I reverse the car and turn around, 180 degrees, so I can drive straight for the exit and away. The force as I hit the brakes jolts me back and then forward. William is thrown hard against the dashboard and tumbles into the footwell of the passenger seat.

Maybe the policewoman hasn't seen him. She won't now anyway. Perhaps she was just there, outside the house, to question passers-by, her first call to me nothing more than a polite request to ask for information. Too late now, though, my reaction giving it all away.

I look up, steadying myself to accelerate off.

She is still coming towards me, walking, but quickly now, about to run.

Her hand is up in front of her, signalling me to stop.

I only have seconds to decide, but I have no choice. If I stay, I'm done for. She's a big, muscular woman, as big as me, and fighting fit.

End of the road.

I have to go.

Right now.

I rev the car loudly, deliberately, so she hears it, giving her the chance to jump out of the way. Still she comes striding forward. I see her mouthing "Stop now" at me, her face contorting as she tries to shout above the noise of the engine.

She's reaching for her radio, even though I'm about to drive straight at her. I ease off the clutch, pressing down on the accelerator. Hard, so the car moves loud and fast towards her. She knows she has to jump out of the way. Now. For fuck's sake, jump now, you stupid ….

She doesn't.

The car slams into her as she is about to shout into her radio.

Knocks her onto the bonnet.

I panic, first touching the brake, then pressing back hard on the accelerator. It throws the policewoman off and in front of the car, which hits her again with its full force. This time I stop; I can't bring myself to run over her.

I've cut my forehead and William lies lifeless by the passenger seat. The policewoman is sprawled out in front of the car.

Shakily, I reverse so I can see her. Utterly still. I can hear noise – static, an enquiring voice? – from her radio. Maybe I'm imagining it. Hard to tell. Difficult to think straight. Have to pull myself together. I look round. No one in sight.

Draw breath, calming myself for a moment or two.

Reach forward for William.

Dazed I reckon, but better left there, unseen.

Life or death now, well and truly. If the policewoman's dead, the coppers won't let me live if they catch me. Any excuse will do. They'll bring in the marksmen and take me out no matter what. Even if I surrender. They'll think of something.

That's what they're like, see: an eye for an eye. Take down a copper and it becomes a death race when you're on the run. I have to go. I start the car up, inch slowly around the policewoman's lifeless body, lights off, and drive to the exit of the car park.

Lights on.

Where now?

I have to get out of town as fast as I can.

5.19PM SUNDAY 1 NOVEMBER

"What's that noise ... what the hell is it?" The young woman was first to her feet and across to the window, pulling back the curtains to look out.

"My God!" she said. "God, Rick, it's Orrey. Look, it's Orrey."

The young man was at the door, snatching at the latch to open it.

"Dad, Dad. How do I...?" He pulled at the latch and swung the door open so he could see outside.

The policewoman down, spread out across the ground.

Her radio crackling.

The blue car moving away to the car park entrance.

The young woman pushed by him, running barefoot after the car.

"Nat, Nat, wait...hold on," cried the young man. "You'll never catch him on foot. We'll use the car. Where are the keys?"

He turned to the older couple coming up behind him, gesturing towards the policewoman on the ground in front of them.

"Quickly, Mum...Dad, help her. I need to find my car keys."

He ran back into the cottage as the old man bent over the policewoman's body.

"Help me ... help me get her head up." The old man lifted the policewoman's head, looking at the old woman for support. "Your cardigan, let me have your cardigan."

He leaned close to the policewoman's face, her head to one

side, trying to tell if she were breathing. He moved his head as close as he could to her mouth.

"Feel for her pulse ... here." The old woman reached for the policewoman's wrist. She shook her head. "I'll get a mirror, from my handbag, you can use that to see if she's breathing."

A blur of confusion.

The young man coming back out, without his misplaced keys but with a mobile phone, gesturing towards the older man to take it and use it. Then running after his wife.

The old woman behind the old man, holding a mirror.

The old man looking down at the lifeless body of the police-woman – dead, surely.

Then the angry cry from the young woman from the far side of the car park.

"Rick, oh God, it's him, Orrey. I saw him. I can't see if Will is with him, but it's definitely him. Your car keys are in my bag somewhere. We have to go after him ... before he disappears..."

They turned together towards the cottage.

5.20PM SUNDAY 1 NOVEMBER

I've got to get away.

Out of town, and quickly.

No need to pretend any more.

I am at the exit. No one to be seen nor any cars driving on the road. I can turn right, up and out of town. Probably the fastest route; but most likely to have a police presence?

Or I can turn left, the road running along the seashore, up to the side roads half a mile or so on and then beyond that into a maze of lanes. Longer but safer, less likely to be coppers there?

I choose the fastest option – right, no time for delay. I turn and smile down at William next to me. "Here we go, little fellow, here we go – to Disneyland!"

I accelerate the car to 20, 30, 40 miles per hour down the high street. I daren't look back, don't need to. The policewoman's lying there. I have to go, be gone, before she's found.

By the fish and chip shop.

By the cinema.

Left, and up the hill.

A mini-roundabout some way ahead. Two or three coppers stopping cars as they come in and out. I pull over to the side. Have they seen me? I don't think so. There's a car coming into town and another that pulled out ahead of me that's going out of town. These cars have the coppers' full attention. I swing the car round.

Stop.

Three-point turn.

Go.

I leave the lights on – daren't dim them in case that attracts attention. Would look odd. A tell-tale sign. The coppers are behind me now and I glance in the rear-view mirror – don't want to risk turning around in case they see me. It's dark and still a little misty but a sharp-eyed copper might well see me watching, what with the street lights along here.

No one seems to have noticed.

Back to the seafront.

Straight across to turn left and away along the beach road towards Thorpeness and a mass of hidden lanes beyond.

Fields to the left of me, the beach and sea to my right. It's darker here. Easier to disappear into the night. Again, 100, 200 yards distant, I see coppers. Two of them on either side of the road. There to check cars going out and coming in.

My luck still holds. The coppers are distracted again.

It looks like they are in conversation with a group of youths who want to walk along the road out of town but are being turned back, from what I can make out.

No way past for me then.

Once more, I pull over.

Start to do a three-point turn.

William makes a noise, a sudden rush of breath. Seems to be coming to. No time for that now. I hush him, watching the coppers and youths in the distance. I keep the lights on again, to avoid suspicion – and reverse the car back so I am side-on now to the coppers.

William makes a gagging noise again. I push him to make sure he stays down and out of sight but then let go, hoping he won't sit up. I can't keep holding him. It will be near-impossible for me to complete the turn and drive away using only one hand.

Jesus help me now.

I need you.

Have to take my chance.

Back into first gear, I edge the car forward, turning it away from the police as I do so. It's all I can do to stay calm and not rev the engine, which would surely have the coppers looking up and over.

Easy does it, oh-so-slowly we go.

There. At last.

It seemed to take an age, but I've done it.

The car is facing away from the coppers. William is below the height of the headrest; no chance of being spotted. I know I should drive away nice and steady. But I can't help myself, can't help but stop for a moment and take a look in the rear-view mirror.

One of the coppers is still talking to the youths. He's facing me but doesn't seem to have looked across, absorbed in what the youths, almost dancing around him now, are saying. Some sort of argument, for sure.

The other copper is a woman. She's not looking at the youths. No, not at all. She is gazing up and along the road at me. Stopping and turning must have caught her eye. She has her head crooked at a funny angle.

I can see what she is doing.

She is talking, saying something about the car, into a radio resting on her shoulder, as I pull away.

Has she seen the number plate?

I don't think so, not from that distance. I think she will just alert other coppers – who and where? – telling those on the roads out of town to keep watch for this type and colour of car.

No choice now. Have to go right the way back along the seafront.

Make my way into those lanes at the far end.

Have to see how far they will take me out of town.

Back I drive, nice and steady, the same way that I came. By the bookshop. By the cinema. By the fish and chip shop. The town is still quiet and lifeless. Hardly anyone about. No cars on the move. One or two pedestrians, that's all. Nothing out of the ordinary.

Maybe those lanes are the best place for us, after all.

Get as far as we can out of sight. Then dump the car in a barn or a field behind a spread of trees.

See what we can do from there and where we go.

I'm approaching the car park now, where I left the police-woman for dead. I can see lights on at the cottage and one or two of the houses. I slow further, edging by the car park. I guess one of the neighbours must have discovered the policewoman, alerted others.

I stop the car a little way up the road just by the exit to the car park. Looking across, I can see a small crowd – three, four people – standing around the body. Dead? Alive?

I see it before I hear it.

Glancing in my rear-view mirror.

The police car, coming like the wind towards me, all lights flashing.

5.33PM SUNDAY 1 NOVEMBER

The old woman, kneeling by the side of the policewoman, made a huffing noise as she looked up at the sight of flashing lights. She turned to the old man, now speaking softly to two elderly dog-walkers he'd called over to as they'd crossed the car park with their Labrador.

"Police car," she said, getting carefully to her feet. "She needs an ambulance, not the police ... she'll need a hearse soon enough."

"They'll have medical training, will know what to do. We never learned," he replied, looking at the dog-walking couple.

"We did a first aid course years ago," said the male dog-walker. "Just keep her comfortable, head raised. It's all you can do."

"Mouth-to-mouth, mainly," the female dog-walker explained. "For drownings ... children on the beach. We were volunteers. I think we're too late for this lady. Is there a pulse? I saw you checking."

"It's very faint. And there's some breath, but very shallow."

"What happened, did you say she was run over?" asked the male dog-walker.

"Has she spoken?" said the female dog-walker.

The old man and the old woman shook their heads – no nothing – as a policeman came sprinting over. He bent down, touched the policewoman's neck and arm and then spoke urgently into his radio, calling for help.

Another policeman approached, looking at the old couple and the dog-walkers as he ran up to them. "What happened?"

"It's Orrey," the old woman answered. "He came back for the car – you said you'd been keeping watch since last night but you obviously weren't any more. He's knocked your colleague out … and driven off in the car."

"What car is he driving?"

The old woman stared back at him, snapping, "It's the one that's been sitting here for the past 24 hours while you chased all over the countryside on a wild goose chase. The one you were supposed to still have under observation in case he returned."

The old man stepped forward, trying to soothe matters. "Listen. Orrey. Raymond Orrey – the man you've been looking for – came back, we think with … with our grandson, William, and stole the blue Renault that's been parked out the front here."

The policeman gazed down at the fallen policewoman as the old man went on, "Your colleague must have tried to stop him. We don't know the number of it, the car; we never thought to look. Our son and his wife will have it. They've gone after him. To stop him."

"Which way did he go, Orrey?"

The old woman answered this time. "We didn't see, we were tending to your colleague. We thought she was dead. She nearly was. She's just about breathing. He would have driven out that way …"

The old man pointed to the exit to emphasise the old woman's comment. His eyesight wasn't so good these days. He could swear that was a Renault over there. But it couldn't be, could it?

" …and then headed out of town as quickly as he could, I imagine. Wouldn't you?" The old woman finished speaking. "Well, wouldn't you?" she added, turning towards the old man.

The old man, distracted by his thoughts, turned to her to answer.

5.34PM SUNDAY 1 NOVEMBER

Engine and lights off.

I drop down, pulling William towards me so we are both below window level.

He makes a squawking noise.

Daren't look up and back, to see where the police car is going. Left, into the car park to the huddle of neighbours around the fallen policewoman? Or behind my car, coppers out, running up to us, wrenching open the doors to arrest me and snatch back little William?

I wait, face pressed close to William's.

He struggles a little.

I pull a silly face and make a funny noise. He watches me.

Is this how it ends? Right here and now? Locked in a sweet embrace with William, me gurning and whistling gently, him reaching out to touch my raspberry-blowing lips? All the while, me straining to hear the sound of the police car stopping, doors opening, coppers' footsteps approaching my car?

William doesn't look very well, to be honest.

Car sick, I reckon.

I can't bear it. Is it all over now, is this it?

I wait, stiff and tense. Not wanting William to see how I feel, scared and frightened. What do I do if the coppers rip open the doors? All over in seconds, no chance to get to my feet and fight, just dragged out onto the pavement, in front of my sweet, gentle little boy, and manhandled away, never to see him again.

I am not going to give up without a fight. I've come too far.

Moving my arm, I reach out and press down the lock on the door.

As the coppers reach for the doors, I'll sit up and drive off.

It would be the end, of course; I know that, deep down. The coppers, struggling to break open the doors as I move over to the driver's seat and fire the car up, would soon be racing back to their own car.

How far would I get?

I'd have to take my chances – driving into the lanes with my lights off, taking the car up as fast as I could, 40, 50, 60 miles per hour and more, trying to shake them off. I'd not get far, not up against an experienced police driver. But I'd have a last few minutes with my dear, sweet William and we would have the choice of living or going out together. I'd not want to go on without my little boy. Nor him without his loving daddy.

William looks at me. He's troubled, a daddy can tell.

I go to kiss him.

His breath smells sweet and sickly.

Clumsily, he pulls away.

I hear footsteps and am ready to react, while treasuring our last few seconds of happiness.

"I love you, William." The first time I have said that to anyone in my life and meant it, really meant it, with all of my heart. I look at him, gaze into his soft blue eyes and will him to say the same back to me. If he could say it, just once, before the coppers get to the doors, it would mean everything, the whole wide world, to me.

"William...?"

5.36PM SUNDAY 1 NOVEMBER

"Rick, where is he? Where's he gone? You've lost him. How could you lose him?" The young woman cried out.

"Because he could have gone either way and anywhere from there ... so many turnings." The young man tried to keep the mounting panic out of his voice. "He's not going to go the obvious way, is he?"

He banged the steering wheel with his fist in frustration.

He slowed the car. Came to a halt.

Looked back towards the way he had come.

"What are you stopping for? Rick! Don't stop ... just keep driving, go and find him." She rubbed furiously at the windows, trying to see out more clearly.

He revved the engine.

Began to turn the car around.

Then stopped, thinking.

"Nat, think for a minute ... work it out; what would you do?"

"I'd be driving at 90 miles an hour looking for Orrey. Why don't you? For fuck's sake, Rick, this might be our only chance."

She punched him on the arm.

"No, Nat, stop, listen."

She punched him again. "Drive, Rick, for fuck's sake, drive."

He grabbed her hands, pushing his face close to hers.

"Listen," he said, "listen to me. I've worked it out. I know what he's going to do. If we wait here, we'll catch him. Trust me, Nat, I've worked it all through."

She sat back, wrestling her hands free and turning away from him. She leaned her head against the passenger window. "You idiot, Rick, you fucking stupid idiot."

"Nat, listen. Orrey will try to head out of town down the high street. It's by far the quickest way from the cottage. But they will still have roadblocks up. That's what they said."

The young woman turned back to look at him.

"He'll be forced to come this way, towards the lanes. Eventually, anyway. There are too many lanes to block off. And so ..."

She nodded.

"And so ..." she repeated, " ...if we sit here and wait, I'll either get a phone call on the mobile any minute to say he's been arrested at one of the roadblocks or, once he's driven himself round and round in circles, he'll come back down here and try to make his way out down the lanes."

The young man nodded.

He began to drive.

Reversed the car onto the side of the road, so it would not be seen.

They waited.

5.37PM SUNDAY 1 NOVEMBER

William looks back at me with a serious look on his face. I lean forward to kiss him another time but he pulls further away, starts struggling. He can sense, I think, that the coppers are upon us.

I sit up sharply.

Nobody there. My overactive imagination, hearing footsteps where there aren't any; the mind plays tricks when it's under pressure. God knows, but you should know that by now, shouldn't you?

I slide across, pulling William back onto the passenger seat.

I look over towards where the policewoman lies, surrounded by people. The police car is there, two coppers out by the small crowd. I see the coppers bending over. Is she dead? I can't tell. I think so. She has to be, given the force of the car hitting her.

Glance around, as I reach to start the car up again.

I cannot stay here a moment longer. It can only be a matter of time before the coppers start looking for this car. If the policewoman is alive, the coppers will lean forward and she will sit up as best she can and whisper urgently to them, "Renault Megane, blue, registration..."

All they have to do is look across.

And see it here, a blue Renault Megane...

With me sitting and watching, just asking to be caught.

I turn on the lights, start to drive, everything nice and normal, just as it should be. William sits in the passenger seat next to me. I turn and say, "Sing?", nodding and smiling. He looks back at me but does not respond. I answer for him. Daddy – he now thinks of me as Daddy, you know – just needs to drive out of town and then we'll have a sing-song. William watches me as I look back – a final check – towards the crowd.

In the distance, I hear what sounds like an ambulance, coming in from out of town. Would they call an ambulance for someone who's dead? If she's alive, I need to be quick, have to get out of here before the ambulance arrives and the coppers turn towards it. Maybe, just maybe, they will notice this car almost right in front of them. Even if they don't, every fucking copper for miles around will soon know what I'm driving and they'll all be watching out for me.

I tug at the handbrake.

Off we go slowly.

Into the night.

I drive steadily, just like it's any other car journey. Beyond the houses that peter out as the road turns eventually into an untreated track, wide enough for one car, tight for two, with the beach to the left and the harbour, speckled with lights, a way ahead. There are turnings, some lanes, a few dirt tracks, I think, to the right.

I need to make the correct choice, picking a bigger lane that will lead out and join up with other lanes into a bigger road and on, eventually, to the A12 and away. It's quiet here, as the street lights fade, with just a few cars and boats parked up higgledy-piggledy by the beach. I slow further, looking for the turning to my right.

Nothing yet. I nudge the car on, telling William to think of some songs he'd like us to sing.

"In a minute," I then hush, "Daddy's looking for a turning." He repeats the word. "Turr'ing," it sounds like. "Road," I say. "We are looking for a road ... a road to take us to Disneyland."

"Dis'land?" he replies slowly.

"Yes, we have to drive down this road and get a coach and then a boat and we will, if we're very good and very, very lucky, get to meet Micky and Donald and ... the dog (or whatever the fuck it is). Are you going to be good, William?" I turn and look solemnly at him.

He looks back. No triumphant hands in the air this time. He knows he has to be on his best behaviour and that's what we need if we are going to get away.

"William has to be good. A good boy for his daddy. Can you do that for me, William, be a good little boy?"

He looks away, out of the window, as if something has caught his eye.

I turn, just in time to see a car's lights turn on, and watch in my rear-view mirror as the car rolls forward and onto the track behind me. I accelerate smoothly forward. It seems to do the same, sitting close to my tail. So close its lights almost disappear out of view.

Coincidence? Just a regular guy, a fisherman going down to the harbour? Or a plain-clothes CID copper in a car, covering this end of town? I slow my car, watching all the time in my rear-view mirror. The car does exactly the same.

"Be a good boy now, William, just sit nicely for Daddy." My heart is in my mouth. What do I do if it's a copper? Drive on to the harbour? What then? A boat? Can I get that far ahead? Even if I could, what would I do with a boat – I've no fucking idea.

I check the mirror again; the car is close behind and all I can see are its lights bouncing up and down on the uneven track keeping pace with me. I can't tell who's in it or how many there are. One?

Two? I have a chance if it's one and I can get him alone before the other cars follow him down here.

Should I stop, pull over, get out of the car, ready to take him on?

Or keep going to the harbour and confront him there?

Whatever happens, I have to do it with no one about, that's for sure.

Suddenly I see, some way ahead, close to the harbour, the lights of another car being switched on. The car swings out, 100, 150 yards or so away. It's coming towards me. The track now seems so narrow and I don't know if there is enough room for us to pass without one of us pulling over to the side. Is that the plan, though? To force me off? Do I now have a copper behind and a copper racing towards me?

We'll know in a minute or so; I have no choice but to keep going.

The car behind stays close – too close for my liking if I have to brake suddenly.

The car ahead is still coming at me and one of us needs to give way, I think. I'm sure it's too tight for us to both to pass by at the same time.

Is that how coppers work? One in front, the other behind? The one in front forcing me off the road, the coppers in the car behind racing to drag me out? Would they dare do that, though, risk injuring or even killing an innocent little boy in a head-on collision.

I don't think so.

But I'm not 100 per cent sure.

What the hell do I do?

Thank God, the turning I want is just ahead of me. I think I can get there, before the car in front of me does.

If I accelerate now.

Hard and fast.

I press my foot down.

5.40PM SUNDAY 1 NOVEMBER

"Rick-k-k," screamed the young woman, "too near."

The young man eased his foot fractionally off the accelerator.

"I have to ram him. Off the road. Do your belt u..."

They both saw – at the same time – the car on the far side coming towards them.

"Will," she shouted, "you'll kill him."

He hesitated.

Eased back.

Saw the car in front swing at speed, almost swerving off the road, into the lane to the right.

The car on the far side now almost upon them.

It swerved towards the lane to avoid them.

"Brake Rick, brake," she cried, drawing in her breath.

Too late.

The cars collided.

A long silence.

The door by the young man wrenched open.

"You stupid..."

The young man, dazed, struggled up, reaching for his seat belt, unhooking it.

"I'm sorry, so sorry ... He's got our son, Will. Was getting away."

"What the hell were you thinking, driving so fast, have you seen what you've done to my new..."

The young man pushed by, moving around the other car, skewed and blocking the lane, the front crushed inwards, lights broken.

"He's getting away, I have to stop him. He has our son."

The other driver, younger and more physical, glared at him in anger. Bemused. Not understanding.

The young man turned back, glanced at his wife.

"Nat, Christ, Nat..."

She lay there, head against the dashboard. Blood trickling down her forehead. Unconscious.

"Please," he said to the angry man. "You have a phone? Please call the ambulance. I have to..."

The young man turned away and moved off on foot.

Hoping somehow that the car he was chasing, which had swung and swerved at speed into the lane, might have lost control and crashed just a very little way away.

That the driver too may be stunned and dazed.

The little boy unharmed somehow.

The young man reunited with the little boy and returned to the young woman waking up back at the car.

Together again.

As a family.

5.42PM SUNDAY 1 NOVEMBER

It's dark.

In the lane.

I accelerate away.

Looking back, I see the two cars, the one behind me and the one ahead, crashed into each other at the entrance to the turning. I see what looks like a man – hard to tell from the distance – running down the lane. As if he might catch me. I watch as he slows, stops and raises his hands towards me.

Dear God.

It's Veitch, I swear it is.

How can that be?

I drive on, as fast as possible. The lane, unlit, twists to the left and then to the right before resuming its straight, long path.

I cannot see the cars any more. I assume Veitch will be running back, getting the other car to reverse, allowing him to get into the lane, to chase me down.

How could this happen?

Why is he there?

How could he know?

I accelerate up to 20, 30 miles per hour, as fast as I dare. There are hedgerows to either side, high, far too high for me to see the fields beyond. If anyone or anything comes out of a side gate, they've no chance. I daren't slow down, though, not now. Veitch will never give up, I know that.

I look back, expecting, at any moment, the lights of the car behind me to come bobbing and weaving into my rear-view mirror. And when I do? The track is straight and far too narrow for him to overtake. I will accelerate, that's all. Faster and faster. On and on.

Until I outpace him and break free or he catches up and it's all over. One way or the other, he will never take me. I swear that to you, on my little boy's life.

Any second now, I will see the lights of the car. I'm waiting. He's coming at any moment. I am not even breathing.

Nothing yet. But by God, it's any second.

On I go. The track runs into and through scrubland to either side, then dips down and back up into woodland. Should I pull over, hide the car in the trees, snatching William up and making a run for it? How far would I get? I'd only have a minute or two's head start and could never outrun Veitch, not with William in my arms.

Is he behind me? I can't tell, not with the trees in the way.

Is that a beam of light from a car, shining between the trees? A trick of the light? My car headlights reflecting off some long-abandoned, broken-down wreck in the woods?

I have to keep going, just keep on.

The lane opens up into a wider road, enough for two cars to go side by side, and I can see ahead for a short stretch. I jiggle the rear-view mirror, lining it up with the spread of trees I've just driven through. I'm waiting for the tell-tale pin-pricks of light that reveal the car closing in on us, signalling that we're coming to the end of it all.

Nothing, no car in sight.

I keep watch, shushing William to soothe him, adjusting the mirror as the lane eases first to the left and then to the right.

Still nothing there.

Should have been by now.

Where is he?

And then I get to a crossroads. Perfect, just fucking perfect. I can turn left, right or go straight on. I've lost my sense of direction, not sure which way to go. Straight on is too obvious. Right might double-back. I go left, into a long sweeping arc of a lane.

I dim the lights.

Go on.

A two-to-one chance of getting away; and better, with every minute that passes.

One minute.

Two minutes.

Three, four and eventually five.

I'm breathing again; it's as if I have held my breath since that turning. I'm sweating too, can feel it in the small of my back. I hadn't realised how hard I had been gripping the steering wheel, a real white-knuckle ride.

I sink back into my seat, breathing a sigh of relief. I feel my confidence surging. Fact is, we're going to do this, we are going to get away. No ifs or buts or maybes about it any more. We've got out of that shithole of a town and are now putting miles and miles between us as the minutes pass and nobody and nothing is on our tail.

Done and dusted?

Not quite – but we're going to go free.

I can tell you that with cast-iron certainty.

5.58PM SUNDAY 1 NOVEMBER

"Go?" asked the old man, his voice shaking with anger. "I don't believe this. How can we just go? Now, of all times? They've only just taken that poor police girl away."

"We always planned to leave this afternoon – and we are leaving much later than we planned." The old woman stood at the foot of the stairs, looking into the lounge where the old man sat, breathing heavily. "I'm going to pack. Start tidying up."

He struggled to his feet, exhausted suddenly from recent events. "How can you possibly leave with all of this going on? William goodness knows where. Richard and Natalie chasing him. We can't just go ... go? Anything could happen."

"That's as maybe," she shouted back down the stairs, "but it won't happen here. Everyone has now gone ... the police. Ambulance. We're left on our own. The police will attend to matters."

She moved out of earshot but he could hear her above, walking about, pulling clothes out of drawers and cupboards, packing them into suitcases.

He sat back down, cursing under his breath. "We can't just go," he said loudly, shouting back. "Richard and Natalie will come here if they cannot find him. They will want to tell the police where they looked. They'll expect us to ..."

He stopped talking, looking about the room at all the things he'd need to pick up and tidy away if they were to go. He swore, suddenly sick of it all, of everything, as he got to his feet, moving to the kitchen to get carrier bags to collect the bits and pieces and throw away the rubbish.

She came back down the stairs as he started to stuff leftover food and old newspapers into a carrier bag. He looked at her and she stared back at him, waiting for him to glance away as he always did eventually.

He didn't this time.

"I've had enough," he said flatly.

"I've had enough of it all." He repeated himself, almost absent-mindedly.

"It's over."

She ignored him and carried on talking.

"You'll need to go upstairs and get the suitcases for me. They're too heavy to carry down, with my wrists. You do that while I tidy up properly here."

She passed him a pile of board games. "Take these up as you go."

He stopped, thinking for a minute before speaking as calmly as he could. "We cannot possibly leave here while Richard and Natalie have gone. Anything could have happened. We have to sit here and wait. They might need us ... to help."

She placed a half-empty cup of tea on top of the board games. "Tip this down the sink and wash it up," she said.

"And put the boy's bicycle outside the back door, save us tripping over it every two minutes."

"We cannot go now just so we can get home at a decent time. It is not fair on Richard or Natalie. And think about the kiddie, little William, about what might possibly be happening to him."

"And that dirty old thing," she added, pointing to the axe by the fire. "Needs to go back into the shed."

He looked at the axe.

And at the old woman.

And came to a decision.

6.02PM SUNDAY 1 NOVEMBER

I need to think through a new plan.

Give me a minute, why don't you?

I have to get my thoughts straight.

I daren't risk taking this car back on to the A12 to Thurrock and the coaches. That policewoman on the seafront could have been radioing the car details through to CID when I swung the car around. And the other policewoman in the car park – alive or dead now, I don't know – may have done the same. And there's Veitch; he knows what I'm driving.

All of the coppers for miles around will have the car, the colour and the number plate. Could I tear off the plates? That's an automatic police chase in my book. No, I need to be cleverer than that. I've got to out-think them.

I lean across and give little William a playful shove with my elbow. He pulls away, looking up at me. He has a white-faced look about him that I hadn't noticed until now, like he's dead tired. I wink at him to be cheerful, so he knows we're going to have some fun. It's me and him now. All the way to the south of France.

"The wheels on the bus," I sing, encouraging him to join in with me. I repeat it and then carry on the tune. "The wheels on the bus go round and round, round and round, round and round, the wheels on the bus go round and round, all day long."

The little chap seems to be trying to focus on me.

He's smiling now, a bit anyway I think. He loves his daddy.

Know what? I'll do some special effects.

"Here we go again, William, come on, join in ... the wheels on the bus go round and round (circular motion with my left arm), round and round (do it again), round and round (fuck me, it's tiring), the wheels on the bus go round and round (I do it again), all day long."

William tries to move an arm back and forth.

Not sure what that's meant to be.

Will try something else.

"The dog on the bus goes woof woof woof, woof woof woof, woof woof woof, the dog on the bus goes woof woof woof, all day long ... again, William, come on, join in." We try it again ... "The dog on the bus goes woof woof woof, woof woof woof, woof woof woof, the dog on the bus goes woof woof woof, all day long."

"Woo ..." goes William, eventually. A bit half-heartedly to be honest.

"Woof woof," I go, leaning towards him and pretending to bite.

He's got it, even if he is a little sleepy. We're off and singing.

As I sing different songs, my mind runs through the various options. I can try and drive the car all the way to Thurrock via the back lanes. We can drive to the nearest town, tuck the car out of the way somewhere and try to get hold of another. We can go to a big town, hide the car in a back street and maybe see if we can get a coach first thing to London where we'll disappear into the crowds.

"Itsy-bitsy spider climbed up the water spout."

God almighty, what's next? (no idea).

"Humpty Dumpty sat on a wall, Humpty Dumpty had a great fall."

Can I take the back lanes all the way to the coaches at Thurrock? It has to be 60 or 70 miles, surely? An hour or so on the main roads, three to four hours at least, going round in circles, on these back ways. I doubt I could do it. I certainly couldn't do it without getting lost. It's south, I know that, but that's about it. I don't even know if it's this side of the Thames or the other. Either way, I would have to go on a main road somewhere in this car and I'd be picked up by the CCTV cameras straightaway. The coppers will be keeping watch, no doubt about that.

"I'm a little teapot, short and stout.

"Here's my handle, here's my spout.

"Lift me up and pour me out." (That doesn't make sense.)

"I'm a little teapot, short and stout."

Can I drive to the nearest town, park in the back of beyond and try to steal a car? It would be close to impossible to break into one without drawing attention to myself. But if I found one with the doors left unlocked?

Ainsley, back in the annexe, once told me – for what seemed like hours, on and on, as he twitched and gibbered and stumbled over his words – how to hotwire a car, firing it up if you didn't have a key.

But I can barely remember what he said, much beyond ripping off the cover behind the steering wheel to get to the wiring. What then? How do you find the two wires to be stripped back and joined together from a tangled mass of wiring?

"Hickory dickory dock.

"The mouse ran up the clock.

"The clock struck one and..." (Bollocks to that, I've no idea.)

"William sing?" I say (I've no idea how these old songs go much beyond the first line or two). "What would you like to sing, William?" He's quiet for a moment or two, thoughtful, like. I'm not sure if he heard me or whether he is going to do anything.

He looks car sick again so I give him a minute or two, gently encouraging him, until eventually he starts moving his lips. He's so quiet that I can barely hear him. I lean forward, trying to make out the words or the tune. I can't hear what he's singing to start with, the words don't make sense, and there's no tune that I can hear. Then he puts his finger carefully into his mouth and makes some sort of spluttering sound. He then says "pop".

What the hell is that about?

I lean in closer.

He stops and looks at me.

"Go on, William, go on." But he doesn't, he looks instead down into his lap and it's as if he is somehow disappointed in me. It's as if I have let him down. I wrack my brain trying to think of a song that ends with children making a popping noise.

My mind – like I've nothing else to worry about right now, for fuck's sake – runs through all the nursery rhymes I can remember from my childhood. We sit there for three or four minutes driving along quietly – another mile or two away from the coppers and closer to freedom – before it strikes me what it is. I'm not sure of the exact words but I sing it anyway for my little William.

"Half a pound of tuppenny rice, half a pound of treacle.

"That's the way the money goes.

"Pop goes the weasel."

William tries to make a popping noise, his finger pulling at his cheek.

"Again?" I ask. I do it slower this time, singing the words – right or wrong – carefully and clearly so that he can join in. I'm not sure that he does; he just seems to be moving his lips.

"Half a pound of tuppenny rice, half a pound of treacle.

"That's the way the money goes.

"Pop goes the weasel."

I shout "pop" to make him chuckle but he does not respond, tired again now. I show him how to make a proper popping noise with his mouth rather than saying "pop". I mime hooking my finger into my cheek and pulling it out to make a "pop". William tries, bless him, his fingers – at least two if not three – slipping wetly out of his mouth each time. I give up.

"Pop," I say.

And I look at him and smile contentedly.

6.10PM SUNDAY 1 NOVEMBER

"Nat, oh Nat." The young man sat in the driver's seat of his car, cradling the young woman's head in his hands. "He's got away, Nat, can you hear me, my love? Orrey, with William. I couldn't stop him. I tried. I did my best," he whispered.

He brushed aside the woman's hair that had fallen across her face. Dabbed gently at the blood on her forehead with the sleeve of his jacket.

He'd been driving too fast, too angry, trying to get close enough to push the bumper of the car in front, to nudge it again and again, harder and harder, forcing it to stop.

But Orrey never would; why should he?

He ought to have tailed him, just kept him in sight, made sure he didn't get away.

Got Nat to call 999 while they followed him; could have got police cars in place, roadblocks, to force him to a halt.

That's what he should have done. Left it to the professionals. Not tried to do it all himself. Wanting to be a hero for his wife and son.

He had failed them both.

Too late now.

Orrey was gone. Will too.

Had to hope that his mother was right, that letting them get away was best, rather than forcing Orrey into a corner. He was his biological father after all. Had to hold on to that uneasy hope.

Just the two of them left now, for the time being anyway, him dazed and shaken, her unconscious.

He looked down at his wife.

Alive.

But bloodied and damaged somehow.

There was something about her. He was not sure what. He could not tell. But it felt as though something were not quite right.

She was still and she was breathing. But it was laboured. He did not like the way her breaths rasped, as if reaching for something, then stopped and started again, after a moment's silence, as if straining for even more air.

He looked up, out of the car. The other car driver, now less aggressive, had retreated to his own vehicle. Sat there, fiddling with his mobile phone, waiting for the police and the ambulance he'd called to arrive. Where were they? He wanted to be on his way.

Others had gathered, half a dozen men and women, out of cars that were queuing, waiting to pass, at either end of the crashed cars.

"Just sit there and the ambulance will be here in a minute. We've moved our cars to the verges so they can get to you," one woman offered reassurance.

"You should lay her flat, not hold her at an angle like that, give her a chance to breathe clearly" said a man.

Another, older man, leaned further in. "It's been years since I did first aid training at work, but if you don't mind me saying your wife's head is at a very strange angle to her neck."

He looked down at his wife again, beyond her cut and battered face.

He ran his hands over her neck and shoulders.

Was it broken? Her neck?

Can you die from that, he wondered suddenly?

The young man tried to speak, to answer, but was choking on his words. "We ... Nat and me ... we ... chasing our son."

He stopped.

A terrible sense of realisation. Was his beautiful, darling wife now dying in his arms?

"Nat ..." he sobbed, "oh, Nat ..."

6.32PM SUNDAY 1 NOVEMBER

Me and sweetpea drive on in silence now, both of us exhausted. I don't know how far we've driven, by fields and farmhouses in this flat and desolate place, but we've yet to see any cars driving towards us or behind us.

Know what?

We're safe, for sure.

Together at last.

Whenever the road splits in two or reaches a crossroads, I take the one that takes us southwards, towards Thurrock. All I know is we've got away and, if I'm careful, there is nothing to stop us now. Nothing at all. No police cars in these back roads. No helicopters flying above. All we have to do is keep going.

Five, ten minutes later, I can sense William is a little restless. He's moving a bit. Wee? Poo? Not yet, little man, not just yet. I want to get as far as we can.

I distract him by singing. "The daddies on the bus (I'm thinking quickly alright?) go ho ho ho (I shake like Father Christmas), ho ho ho (I do it again), ho ho ho (why did I start this?). The daddies on the bus go ho ho ho (I do it again), all day long."

Next I do mummies who chatter.

(I thought he might get upset at the mention of Mummy but he does not seem to have thought about that one.)

Then, and I have enough to keep us going for a while, we can do cats, birds and monkeys (well it's not meant to be realistic is it?).

I have, while all this is going on, worked out what we are going to do.

Taking this car on a main road – with police cars, CCTV cameras and what have you – is too risky.

Trying to get another car – short of using violence, which I cannot bring myself to do again with my little lad beside me – is out of the question.

So we are going to drive to the nearest big town, leave the car in a tucked-away street and get a coach to London. I still have cash and a card, remember – 1106, that's the number. It will be easier to disappear into the crowds in the city and I think there may well be coaches from Victoria station that take us all the way to Disneyland in Paris.

Ipswich, Woodbridge or Felixstowe?

I slow to read a sign.

Not much more than 30 minutes now, I reckon.

We'll hole up somewhere for the night; sleeping in the car is too risky. Then we'll make our way to the nearest bus station for half six or seven. That's about the time they'll run buses down to London. Arriving by eight thirty for people to get to work or have a day out doing some shopping and a trip to the theatre before getting the return coach at half-ten or eleven.

"The donkeys on the bus..."

(Yes, I know, but we've covered most farm and zoo animals now.)

"...eee-aaw, eee-aaw."

On and on we go.

Long and endless lanes.

Mile upon mile of fields.

Another crossroads, almost identical to the last. I've the same three choices again. Ipswich. Woodbridge. Felixstowe. All sound like big towns to me, big enough to run a daily coach service to London anyway. I slow to check the distances. Ipswich is the closest. We'll head for that. I check all ways are clear – again, no people, no traffic, nothing overhead – and accelerate smoothly away.

10 miles, that's all.

Not long now.

And then the car, moving slowly, starts to cough and judder.

I look at the dashboard, leaning forward to see it clearly between the spokes of the steering wheel. Shit, I'd forgotten all about that. The car had fuck-all petrol left. A red light, the petrol gauge now sat stubborn and unyielding below zero.

The car jerks and judders a little way further as I press my foot down on the accelerator to try to get as far along the road in it as I can.

Not far.

Maybe I should have eased off the accelerator instead.

No matter now.

The car comes to a halt. We're stuck – in the middle of fucking nowhere.

8.27PM SUNDAY 1 NOVEMBER

I don't know how long I've been walking now.

Nor how far.

Two hours? I've near enough carried William the whole fucking way.

Not much longer.

To a town.

I left it where it was, the car, on that back road of endless rolling fields. Nowhere to hide it. We – me walking, my little boy in my arms – doubled back as quickly as we could to the crossroads to take a new road towards one of the other towns. If the car was seen – when the car is seen – the coppers would put two and two together and move off down towards Ipswich. We, in the mean-time, are now moving away in another direction.

At first, I tried to make William walk alongside me. I started singing the wheels on the bus again, but the little fellow stumbled and fell almost straightaway. I swooped and picked him up in my arms for a cuddle but he pulled away from me.

After a brief struggle, we sat at the side of the road and I tried to feed him the last of the biscuits. But he didn't want them. Before we set off again, he did a wee and a little bit of a poo and I cleaned him up as best I could.

I've been walking ever since, up and down the dark lanes, cutting through the fields now and then, heading ever south, but staying to the road when it seemed the straightest route.

I carried William with his head resting on my shoulder for a while. He seemed restless, though, not wanting me to carry him that way. I tried making him walk side by side again, but he didn't seem to be able to manage it, and slipped over two or three times; every time I tried to make him walk, really.

I'd carry him again and we repeated this up-down, on-off process for what seemed like miles until eventually he fell asleep. I then alternated between carrying him upright against my shoulder and horizontally across my chest.

I stopped twice, taking cover the first time behind a spread of trees when I saw car lights in the distance some way ahead of us. I watched as they seemed to flicker and dart to and fro as they came towards us.

I held my breath as the lights dipped down out of sight into a valley and waited for them to come back up and reappear in the road right in front of us. I waited, five, maybe ten minutes out of sight, my darling boy stretched out tired and exhausted behind me, but the lights did not appear again.

I assumed the car stopped off at one of the farmhouses that I see now and again at the far end of the fields, accessed by single-lane tracks.

The second time, an hour or so later, was when I saw a small deer, not much more than a fawn on spindly legs, appear from a copse and run out into the road in front of us. I stopped and slipped William down onto his feet, shaking him gently awake. He struggled to come round, but then, as he stood there, his hand in mine, with both of us no more than 20 yards away, the deer stood equally still, watching us.

It seemed as though minutes passed, me holding my breath in this magical moment, until I foolishly pulled William's hand and took a single step forward. In that instant, the deer raised its head, hot, misty breath steaming from its nostrils, and slipped silently away into the trees to our right.

After that, we sat there a while, by a tree at the side of the road, waiting and hoping that the deer might return or that we might see others. Maybe a herd, led by a majestic stag. William, his weight against me, then seemed to roll forward until he was asleep with his head on my lap.

I could have stayed there all night – I could have stopped here forever, died there together – with William asleep, with my arm around him and me leaning against the tree. It was if we were the only people in the world.

But I knew, deep down, we could not stay long, no more than a few minutes at most. If we were to fall asleep and wake up in the morning, it would give the police another eight or nine hours to find us. It is only a matter of time before they come down this road.

If we stayed there a while, we would not have time to get into the nearest town and get on a 6am or 7am bus into London. So we stopped there for maybe 10 or 15 minutes more and then carried on our way.

William has not moved a muscle for ages now, seems to be fast asleep.

I can feel the warmth of his body, which seems heavier with each passing minute, against my stomach.

On and on I walk, slower and slower. I cannot walk much farther. At some point soon, I need to stop.

8.35PM SUNDAY 1 NOVEMBER

The little boy was trying hard to remember when he last saw his mama and what it was she had said to him. He thought she had been laughing but he was not sure.

He felt so tired.

It was something nice, what she had said, but he could not recall what it was at all.

He could not really think.

He tried again, as hard as possible, to remember because he missed his mama very much.

But he could not do it.

He thought about his papa instead, but that was not a happy thought. Papa had had an argument with this man with the staring eyes and there was a fight.

He did not like that.

The fighting was not like it was in *Kung Fu Panda*.

But he liked thinking about *Kung Fu Panda* a lot. His papa always called it *Kung Poo Panda* and that made him chuckle.

And his mama would tell his papa off. But sometimes she would chuckle too. He liked it when they all laughed and they would then have a tickling fight. That was funny.

He wanted to see his mama again.

And his papa, soon.

He hoped that when he woke up they would be there and papa would throw him high in the air.

He knew he had to be mama's brave soldier until then and he would be.

He would be a good boy for this man with the torn face.

He had been on his own before with other people so many times and he knew he just had to wait until his mama and papa came back.

It could be any moment.

He had to be good until then.

But he really missed his papa and his mama.

Sometimes his papa would be away for a little while for something called work and his mama would look after him on her own.

And his mama had been gone for some time not so very long ago when she had had to go to hospital.

He did not really want a baby brother or sister.

But he remembered his mama crying. And his papa too.

So he tried to look sad. And he hugged his mama. That had made her cry even more.

Yes, he wanted to see them again very much.

Hopefully, when he woke up they would be there for him and they would have a tickling fight and they would all laugh.

And this man with the staring eyes and torn face would go away and leave them alone.

8.57PM SUNDAY 1 NOVEMBER

As the road eases slightly to the left and straightens, I see a house at the side of the road, or at least, I can see a light from an upstairs room, like the beacon of a lighthouse.

I walk on.

Ever closer.

500 yards now, maybe 300?

I do not have the strength to take us much farther on foot but dare not stop and rest. I would fall asleep and that would be the end of us. This house may have a car. Has to, surely, this far out. One way or the other, that could be just what we need.

Have to try to break in.

Jump-start the car.

Get away without the owners noticing until morning.

Our only chance.

It's an old, run-down cottage, a single dormer window in the loft, alight as the owner gets ready for bed. The cottage looks unchanged since the 1950s. Most of it is bottle green, from the front door to the window frames to the driveway gate.

At the end of the driveway, adjacent to the cottage's back gate, is a stand-alone garage, green-fronted too. If my luck's in, there will be a car there that I can get into without being heard by whoever's in that dormer-bedroom.

It's an old woman, up there, I reckon. She lived here with her old man when they were first married, him cycling to work in sleepy old Ipswich, her at home keeping chickens in the back garden for eggs to sell by the roadside. He's long dead, leaving her alone and in her 80s. She goes to bed early, huddled in blankets to keep herself warm.

This is going to be so, so easy. Don't worry. Don't even think about it. She'll not need to come to any harm.

She won't hear a thing and I'll be long gone by the morning.

It'll be an old relic of a car but it will get us from here to where we want to go.

Most people – stupid people – would wait for that light to go out, leave it a while until the old woman fell asleep, and would then make their move.

Not me.

I'm smart, see?

But you know that by now, don't you?

Say she's lying there and hears a noise. What's she going to do? She'll have a phone for sure, even in this out-of-the-way place. She'll dial 999. "Hello," she'll say in a wobbly-chinned voice. "Is that the police? There's someone in my house, come quickly."

Can't have that.

Far too risky.

No, what I'll do is to make my move while that light is still on and she's pottering about, getting ready for bed, folding back the sheets, winding up the clock and hanging up her clothes for the morning. She won't hear anything outside then. She'll be too preoccupied.

I lay William carefully down by the side of the road, taking off my jacket and rolling it up under his head. I move forward and undo the latch on the front gate.

Swinging the gate back, I wait for the scree-eech of unoiled hinges, but it makes no sound at all. The garage is 10 yards in front of me. I look up. The light is still on, curtains yet to be drawn. There are net curtains at the window. I cannot see anyone moving about. I go back for William, carrying him up the driveway, just in case a police car drives by.

I lay William back down on the driveway and slip my jacket on again. He shifts restlessly in his sleep, close to the garage door, safely out of sight of the cottage window and any passing car.

With luck, the garage door will be unlocked and it will be a simple matter of opening and closing it behind me. I can then break into the car and get it started quietly. Any noises will be muffled by the garage doors pulled to behind me.

Shit.

I'm out of luck.

It's locked.

I pull at it. The wood and the lock are old and it would be easy enough to force the door open. But the crack and tear of breaking wood would be too noisy. I look around to see if there are any gardening tools at the side of the garage that I can use to maybe pop open the lock. Nothing.

I open the garden gate, quickly and without thinking.

It makes a sharp screech, loud but lasting only a few seconds.

I stop, standing still, listening and looking up at the cottage.

Nothing, no downstairs lights going on, no sounds of move-ment, it's as still as the night. I move into the garden – a nice old picture postcard of apple trees, bird baths and hedgehogs.

Another fucking world, this is.

A gardening fork is stuck in the ground next to my feet. I hold it in one hand, testing the prongs with the other. It's a strong one, tough enough for me to push it into the door and force open that lock.

I move back out, leaving the screeching garden gate open – no point in pushing my luck – and check William is okay. He's sleeping. I move to the garage door, forcing the gardening fork into the side by the lock. I apply pressure, as carefully as I can.

I'm straining as hard as I can now, using all of my strength.

Something's going to give: the door or the fork.

Can't tell which, just push the fork further in, leveraging it again.

With a loud splintering noise, deafening in the silence, the garage door gives way under the force. It's open. I stand there for a moment or two, listening and looking for signs of life from the cottage. Nothing.

Know what? I reckon the old woman will be tucked up nice and warm in bed by now, teeth in a glass, hot water bottle by her feet, drifting away into sleep.

I wait a moment or two, then notice I'm panting, my breath like white smoke in the cold air. I decide to leave William on the driveway while I sort out the car. It's going to be cramped in the garage and I don't want him waking up and struggling and calling out in the quiet of the night.

I swing open the garage door, the lock now hanging loose from the wood.

It opens silently. I'm charmed, me. Told you that, didn't I?

Expect to see an old car, a relic of a bygone age.

It's a newish car, though. Three, four years old. Yellow, another of those Japanese ones. The old woman must have a son, maybe a daughter, who told her she had to sell her old Morris Minor. "Mum," they'd have said, "you can't be living out there with that old car of dad's. We've got you a new one, from the two of us." And they'd all beam with pride and happiness and love for one another.

Seems a shame to damage it, forcing it open.

Maybe the old dear has left it unlocked – it doesn't need to be kept locked in a secure garage, does it?

I try the door handle – shit, it's locked.

It's dark in here, hard to see much, and I check the floor and the shelves at the back of the garage, shuffling into darkness, for a torch and, if I am really lucky, a spare key hanging up on a hook or a nail banged into a shelf.

I run my fingers along the shelf, by a row of paint pots and other half-used, might-be-useful-one-day bits and bobs. My finger catches what feels like an empty tin and it tumbles off the shelf, bouncing onto the car bonnet and down to the floor, its lid coming off and spinning against the wall.

Going to have to force the car door.

Don't want to; have no choice.

I force the fork into the gap by the side of the door.

There's no give in the car door at all. I push the fork in as far as I can into the gap and pull at it with all my strength. Something's happening, I can tell – there is some movement; not much, but I can feel something giving, reluctantly and oh-so-slowly.

I pull harder, my head now beaded with sweat, a tight feeling in my chest, and then, suddenly, as I was about to give up, the prongs of the fork bend so that they are now almost at right angles to the handle.

Nothing else for it.

Will have to break a car window.

I need to find something big and heavy.

I move quickly out of the garage, no time to waste, but stop as I get to William. He is awake and sitting up, his hands to his head. He can only just have come to, maybe wakened by my attempts to break into the car.

I bend over to whisper some warm and comforting words and, as I do so, he reaches his arms up, wanting me to lift him and give him a cuddle.

I do so, but have to be fast – no time to waste. He's blurry-eyed and not really awake. I kiss him on the cheek and make gentle murmuring noises.

"Stand right where you are."

A voice from behind me. Deep and authoritative, a man's voice.

"Move and I'll shoot you dead."

9.17PM SUNDAY 1 NOVEMBER

A long silence.

No one moves for what seems like minutes.

I say, finally, into the silence, "Don't shoot ... my little boy."

I shift William a little so that his head, which he struggles to keep upright, is just above my shoulder. I want the man behind me – whoever he is – to see I have William in my arms.

"Put him down and walk away."

If I put William down, the man could simply shoot me where I stand. I think quickly, not sure what to say. What can I say? I hesitate. And then it comes to me suddenly. An excuse.

"Our car packed up . . . we need some petrol to get home."

"I know who you are; you've been on the telly. You killed your wife."

"No," I say, still thinking fast. "No, I didn't." He knows who I am. My words tail off, I'm not sure what else to add. "Not really . . ."

"You're violent, it said so on the telly. A danger to the public, the BBC said."

"I just want to leave with my little boy."

"I can't let you do that. Put him down and you can walk away. Or else I'll shoot you where you're standing."

I stand there, not knowing what to do. Christ help me, I cannot give William up. Not like this. And, if I put him down, I'll be shot for sure. If the man shoots me while I'm holding William, the chances are the gunshot will kill both of us. What do I do?

"You're a murderer, I can't let you go with the boy."

"I didn't kill my wife . . . she was mentally ill . . . a depressive . . . she threw herself in front of a car."

"They said you killed her. And more. I've seen it all on the telly. I can't let you go."

There, he's given himself away. His exact words, "I can't let you go" – as soon as he has William, he'll shoot me.

"If I put my boy down, you'll shoot me."

"Not in front of the boy. I'll call the police when I take the boy indoors. You'll get a sporting chance over the fields before the police get here. You're two miles from the bypass that way; five or six miles from anywhere in any other direction. I'll give you a sporting chance. Like we do with foxes."

"I can't give up my boy."

"Then I'll have to shoot you where you stand."

"And you call me a murderer?" I can feel the anger rising; I have to control it. "You'd kill me and my son in cold blood, just shoot me in my back?"

"Put your boy down on the ground and walk away."

You know what? I won't do it.

"Your boy's ill. It said so on the BBC. He needs his medication every day. If he doesn't have it, he could go into a coma. Did you know that?"

I shake my head, don't believe it's true. Just a nasty, vicious trick, something to try and make me give up my little William.

"Look at his head, he can't even keep it upright. Has he been sick? You need to let him go. I'll call an ambulance for you, get help for him."

"He's just tired, that's all. He's only little. It's past his bedtime."

"Look at him, look at his face. He needs help. You'll lose him otherwise."

I'll lose him anyway. I turn slowly, ever so slowly, so that I'm now facing the man, with William's body cradled upright in my arms. The man is older and shorter than I thought; well into his 70s and whippet-thin. He looks as scared as I feel. But he has one thing I don't. A shotgun. It looks as ancient as him and I can't help but wonder if it's actually loaded. Maybe it is – he talked of foxes.

"That's the ticket, just put the boy down there between us and you can go." There's a half-smile on his lips. Encouraging me? No. If that gun is loaded, he won't be letting me go, I don't reckon.

"No," I say. "He's coming with me."

"Then I will shoot you as you walk off."

Know what? I don't think he will. As William moves, half-asleep and trying to get comfortable in my arms, I take a step back, not taking my eyes off the old man. He watches me.

"I've a gun myself," I lie, to scare him. "In my pocket."

"Put your boy down and take your chances with me then," he answers.

I take another step backwards.

And another. He says nothing else, just watches me.

One more away from the man.

"I'm going to turn and walk with my boy. We're no trouble to you. Leave us alone."

"I can't let you leave. The boy needs help. And you're dangerous. And you've just told me you're armed."

Our eyes meet.

A battle of wills. He lifts the gun higher, levels it towards my head.

I have to go, see what happens.

"You'll have to shoot us both then."

I turn, almost stumbling, and take a step farther away from the man. I do not know what he is going to do. Shoot me? With William in my arms? I adjust his position carefully. Can the man see William clearly now?

There is silence.

I wait to hear the cocking of the gun.

Or has he done that already; is he about to shoot?

I hold my breath, take one more step and another. Part of my mind is screaming at me to stop, look and see what he's doing. The other tells me to keep going, to take one careful step after the other, down to the gate and away.

It is now just a few steps to the gate.

Six, five, four.

Three, two, one.

I stop at the gate. My back to the man. William still in my arms. This is it. The moment. Make or break. Life or death. I have to know which. I turn my head slowly, looking back at the man. Will he shoot me? Me and William?

He has gone, I broke his nerve.

But he will be inside now, calling the police.

And I think, dear God, my time with William is almost up.

9.36PM SUNDAY 1 NOVEMBER

The little boy did not feel very well. He wanted to tell the man with the staring eyes and the torn face but did not seem able to do so.

He kept falling asleep and, when he did, the angry man would shake him awake every time when all he wanted to do was sleep; he could not say anything.

He did not like the angry man. He was a little scared of him.

His lips felt cracked and dry and he thought he might be sick again.

He wanted to say he felt ill so the man would fetch his mama and papa. He did not want to be with the man any more. He did not want to be on his best behaviour. But he could not seem to think of the words to say. They would not come to him.

When he felt unwell, usually his mama would somehow know and make him feel better.

Or his papa would.

He did not miss having the finger tickles and the injections. He did not like those. But he knew, somehow, that he had to have them.

He could not remember when he last had anything like that.

The angry man did not do them.

And he let him have biscuits, as many as he wanted. He liked biscuits but his mama and papa would only let him have them now and then.

The little boy felt hot.

And he felt sick all the time.

And what he really wanted now, more than anything, even more than seeing his mama and his papa again, was to go back to sleep.

He felt a little better as he started falling asleep. The ache in his stomach seemed a bit less painful.

But then the man would shake him awake again. Or drop him to the ground. Make him try to walk on hurting legs.

He liked it best when the man carried him, even though he did not like the smell of the man.

It was a nasty smell, like he smelled on his papa when he had been out running on a hot day.

And there was another smell on the man.

He did not know what it was but he did not like it.

It was a sour and dirty smell.

He felt sleep coming on again, as the man carried him, walking steadily now, into a rhythm.

A falling-asleep pattern.

It would be nice to sleep.

Just sleep and sleep and sleep.

9.52PM SUNDAY 1 NOVEMBER

I headed towards the bypass – two miles, or so the man said. Better than five or six across the fields to anywhere else.

Was he telling the truth?

I don't know, I'd have thought we've walked more than two miles by now. Off the road, out of sight, and across fields and ditches and tracks.

Maybe the man said it was two miles just so I'd go that way. Then, when he called the coppers, he could tell them exactly which way I was heading. I should have gone the other way. Tried to outwit them. But I am tired now, too tired – dog-tired, in fact.

The bypass is safer anyway. I can hide in a ditch there. A lay-by. Like I did when I got out of the annexe, remember? It seems so long ago now. The annexe. Spink. The big house. Sprake and Ainsley and Tosser Gibson.

I was safe there.

In the annexe.

No one would hurt me.

If a car pulls over, we could hitch a ride. Leastways, I guess I could on my own. I reckon everyone everywhere, round here at least, will be on the lookout for a man and a boy together. Maybe we'd have to try something else.

Must have been a half-hour now since I left the old man at that cottage.

Longer probably. I'm tiring so much.

Not seen or heard anything yet.

I'd have expected to hear police cars by now. Sirens. Behind me. Going to the cottage to speak to the man with the shotgun. And then helicopters overhead, searchlights picking us out as we criss-crossed our way across fields and over gates. Then dogs – like I had before – but not in the distance this time, right here and now and all around us.

William's asleep again. He has a troubled look on his face, I think. He's not warm, and that's a fact; it seems to be getting colder step by step. My body heats up, though, breath and sweat almost creating a fog around me. Poor little lamb is having a bad dream. I think I should wake him but he's probably better off asleep.

I stop, for no more than a second or two, exhausted.

Bent double almost, William squeezed tight between my chest and stomach.

He does not move, asleep in the land of nod.

We cross a field. Crops or livestock, I don't know. Crops, I'd guess – I see no animals. There is a fence ahead of me and another gate – always another gate, one after the other – and, beyond that, some more trees.

God, it's like hell, just walking the same empty and identical fields one after the other, over and over again. This bleak and relentless landscape.

We may have to rest there, by those trees, for a while, out in the middle of nowhere. But it will give us a little shelter and some cover from the skies above.

Is that where it all ends?

I can't go on much further.

Really I can't. I'm close to giving up now.

I lift William up and over the gate, laying him down carefully on the ground. As I climb the gate, I look back automatically – still nothing and no one in sight. I listen again – no police sirens, barking dogs or the whirring of helicopters in the distance.

I've done well really.

To get this far.

Have ridden my luck for so long now, it has to break some time.

Picking William up, we make for the trees. Two long neat rows of them. I walk through them, almost at the point of exhaustion, and then, in the distance, close enough to see the cars and the lights, I spot that bypass.

At last.

Thank you.

God, bless you.

If we can just press on for half a mile more to get there,

maybe slide into and hide in a ditch by a lay-by, we might still have a chance. If a car, any car, pulls in, we could do something, anything, to get away.

We go into the next field, me striding straight across as best I can rather than skirting round the edges as we have done with some of the muddier ones. My feet sink in places in the thick, squelchy ground.

I stumble once, then again, struggling to stay upright and keep my trainers on. I drop William as I stumble but he does not seem to notice. I cuddle him quickly, as we keep moving, licking the back of my hand and wiping a smear of mud from his cheek.

Closer now. To the bypass.

I can hear the roar of the cars.

Four, five minutes away, I'd say.

Is that a police siren? In the distance behind me? I've been expecting that. But I can't tell – with the noise of the road in front of me – if it's real or my imagination, waiting for the sound this past half-hour or more, and conjuring it up in my mind.

I stop for a second or two, drawing breath, and I hear it more clearly now, carried on the wind first this way, a little weaker, and that way, a little stronger.

Not long now then. The old man with the shotgun will be telling them what happened, that I had a gun and saying he'd seen me head off towards the bypass.

I'd cut through the fields, though, thank God – not stayed on the road, where they'll look first.

On we go, across the fields, towards that bypass, not so very far.

One step in front of the other, left then right, left then right. On and on.

We're off the fields now, they are all behind us, and we are on a track that runs along the side of the bypass with trees – planted years ago for soundproofing I guess – between the track and the bypass.

On the other side of the bypass is a housing estate. I glimpsed it as I came to the end of the field and passed half walking, half slipping, my arms tight around William, down a slope and onto the track.

I've seen something else too.

On the outskirts, not far away.

Some sort of tower, maybe for phone masts?

Somewhere I can hide, that is.

Think about it, why don't you?

The coppers are behind me now, in their car at the cottage and, in five or ten minutes, there will be more coppers and cars and dogs and Heaven knows what flooding the roads, the bypass and that housing estate.

They won't know where I've gone. But they'll be sure of one thing – that I've kept going; up or down the bypass, across into the housing estate to steal a car. Anywhere, but always away, ever on the move.

We need to hide and sit tight. If we can get to that tower and climb it and lie low there until morning – while the coppers, dogs and helicopters buzz angrily around us – we might still have a chance.

You just watch me.

Despite everything, we're going to get away.

Just you see if we don't. Just you wait and see.

All of this – the running, the hiding, the chasing – will end once we are at the tower. It will all be over.

A nice sleep.

Waking to a sunny day in the morning.

The end of this nightmare and the start of our new life.

9.59PM SUNDAY 1 NOVEMBER

I move along the track, looking for a path through the trees that will lead me to a bridge over or a tunnel under the bypass and into the housing estate. All I can hear now is the sound of the traffic – if there are police cars, dogs and helicopters behind me, I cannot tell. Thing is, I don't want to hear them. I want to press on and get to that tower and some cover for the night.

I've found it.

A tunnel, an underpass – just like I said.

We're down it now and cutting through.

Out the other side and all clear, I walk up and on to the border of the housing estate. I need to be careful here; have to make sure no one spots us and recognises who we are.

I lift William up again and lean him against my shoulder so that, if we see anyone, I can put my head down close to his as if we are talking. It will shield my face and his; we'll just be like any other daddy and little boy going home from an evening at a neighbour's house. Maybe a family party to celebrate a birthday.

A much-loved uncle perhaps.

Sweet William's favourite.

Now it's time to go home to bed.

From what I can make out, the housing estate is one long curving road.

Various avenues and closes come off it. Fancy names for a shit place like this.

I have to walk, so far as I can see, right along the curving road and somewhere ahead, some way to the left, there will be an avenue or close that will take me to the tower.

Off I go, my head close to William's, in case anyone sees us. I feel exposed here, on this housing estate. There are houses to my left and to my right, lights on, cars in the driveway, music and noises and the occasional shout or ripple of laughter breaking the night air.

Further up the road, to my left, I see a young girl, late teens maybe, coming out of the front door of a house. She turns, as I hang back, pretending to talk to little William, and says something, laughing, to whoever is still indoors. She teeters off on heels, her back to me, on her way out for an evening.

A car comes past me from behind, a silver Peugeot.

Full of boys, out on the piss. The car slows as it comes alongside the girl up ahead of me.

Raucous laughter this time, something shouted from the car window; she feigns deafness.

I carry on walking as the car roars away, keeping in step with the girl, but holding back, 100 yards away, so that, if she looks round, she won't think I'm following her. I look up, two or three minutes later, and see the girl has gone, must have turned into one of the avenues up ahead of me, maybe going to meet a friend, share a taxi into town.

It's busier now, the estate. Cars go by me both ways, ordinary cars but no police cars, thank God.

One car pulls up on a driveway ahead of me and a couple, holding bottles and takeaway bags, get out and disappear into the house.

Head down, I keep up my bizarre walk-stop-walk-stop pattern, striding out and then slowing and stopping and pretending to talk to my sleepy boy whenever anyone is in sight. On we go, as quickly as we can.

Halfway to the tower, I see a parade of shops and a children's playground next to it with a slide and broken-down swings. Youths sprawl, two on the swings, another on the slide. Two more, on bikes, wheeling back and forth. Another, younger boy, by the look of it, has a skateboard that he's pushing up and down with his foot.

Aimless, they are, and spoiling for trouble. I daren't risk it. I have to cross the road before they see me, can't have them looking too closely at me and William, dirty now and splattered with mud from the fields. It only takes one of them to pull out his mobile phone.

Over we go, before they look over and spot us approaching. God, please let them leave us be, let us be on our way around this endless road on this ghastly shithole of an estate.

We're alongside them now, these yobs, on the other side of the road. Just keep looking ahead, daren't glance across, attracting their attention. If they know they bother me, that I'm worried or frightened by them, they'll call out, taunting and jeering. Any sign of weakness, that's all they need to see.

Maybe the braver ones, the ones on bikes, will come over, following me, wanting to know who I am, where I'm going, demanding money to leave us alone.

I hold my breath, keep going. I put my head down a little as if I am talking to William, fast asleep now in my arms. They're almost behind me. We've nearly made it. And then one of them, I don't know which, makes a meowing noise, like a cat. Quiet at first, then louder, howling on and on. Others laugh and one or two join in with the caterwauling.

It's clearly directed at me, this mocking, echoing noise. As if to say they've seen me and know I'm scared of them, that I'm chicken. Kids today, eh? Perhaps the ignorant fuckers think it's chickens that meow.

On we go, not so far now; the tower is in sight.

I can see it down at the far end of this curving road.

On the home straight, and then to the left, at the end of an avenue.

As I walk, I am listening all the time, a sixth sense, hearing beyond the noises from the houses, the comings and goings of cars, the people moving about ahead and behind us, all taking little or no notice as they go about their business. I'm tuned into the sounds of pursuit – the sirens of the police cars, the whirring of the helicopters, the barking of the dogs. And I don't hear anything.

Thing is, they've gone the other way.

For sure. No doubt about it at all.

They've headed back out, down those country lanes and fields, back towards Ipswich or Woodbridge.

But not here. If they were coming this way, they'd be here by now. I'd have heard sirens, coming ever closer. I'd have seen the lights of the helicopters. As they drew nearer, I'd have had to drop off this road and out of sight, maybe looked for a house that was dark, with the owners out, and broken into a back-garden shed, hiding out there until daybreak.

But there's been nothing, no sign at all, since I came to the bypass. Even then, thinking about it, I only heard a police car siren – thought I heard a police car siren – back towards that cottage.

Maybe I imagined it all. Easy to do when you're under so much stress. Thinking about it a little more, that man with the shotgun may not even have had a telephone. It was just a bluff, that's all, to make me give up the little 'un.

Yes, we're almost home and dry.

Good job too – have to say I'm exhausted and William is as well; he hasn't moved a muscle for ages now.

We'll hide in the tower until the morning.

We turn into the little avenue that leads us to it. I can see it at the far end, behind a wall and a gate; simple to climb that, and there may even be an easier way in if I scout round the back. It's dead quiet here; just four or five houses to either side. Some lit up, others dark and empty. I stand for a second, just listening again – no noise at all, not that I can hear, from any of the houses.

We move forward, past one house, all lit up.

Then the second, this one in darkness.

A third, all lit up, a woman at the kitchen window, washing up at the sink, I reckon.

She's looking out towards me but she won't see me. Lights on in the house, dark outside, see? Makes it impossible to see anyone that does. I should know. I spent hours at the annexe, planning my escape, watching what was happening outdoors, and just working out exactly what I was going to do when I got the chance to get away.

I had to do all of that when the lights were out, though, that's the thing. When the lights were on, I couldn't see anything outside. But people could look in and see me and what I was doing. I didn't realise that straightaway, to be honest. In fact, we had a bit of trouble about that in the early days when I first arrived, but that's another story and not a very nice one actually. Let's not talk about that. Don't even think about it.

As I said, the woman in that house, looking out, cannot see us. Know what? I'll prove it to you.

I give her a little wave. Then a big one.

Nothing, not a glimmer. I can't help but chuckle to myself. I could be stark naked for all she knew. But as I say, let's not go there. Just forget I mentioned anything.

On we go, by the fourth and fifth houses, some sort of sensor lights going on as I pass by, and on to the wall surrounding the tower. I walk slowly around it, so that I'm out of sight of the houses, just looking for a way in.

At the back, where youths have obviously been hanging out, judging by what's on the ground (don't ask), there's been some damage to the wall; enough for me, holding William carefully, to climb over and in.

I take off my jacket, using it to wrap around little William, strapping him to my body, just in case. It's a long way up, for sure.

We start climbing the steps, up and up we go to the platform near the top.

It's cold.

And the steps are slippery.

But I need to do this.

We need to be safe.

And we will be.

At last, we're here. We're safe now. About time too. We can get some peace for once. We can settle down and get some rest until daybreak.

I unstrap William, still deep in sleep, and lay him down carefully, my jacket rolled up beneath his head. I move to the edge of the platform, peeking over.

It's all quiet down below in the avenue, other than a woman walking quickly from one house to another. No more signs of life anywhere at all. I look up into the dark, clear sky and gaze around me 360 degrees. No signs of any helicopters.

I sit for a while and listen. No sounds of sirens. I look down again over the housing estate. All is just as it should be. Nice and quiet. The world is at peace. And so, I have to say, are we, me and my beautiful little boy.

He means more to me than anything, but then I have told you that, haven't I?

Yes, I'm sure I did.

He means the world to me.

I settle back, am going to snooze gently for a little while. Not too long, mind, and not too deeply – I need to be alert, just in case.

After all, you never know, do you?

Better safe than sorry, that's what I say.

I'm not home and dry yet. Not quite.

I can't tell you how exhausted I am. And we have a long day ahead of us again tomorrow, don't we? Up at six, a coach to London, then, one way or the other, on to France and away to our new life together forever.

A villa in the south of France.

Paddling in the pool. Stretching out in the sun.

Our life will be just perfect. For ever and ever.

Yes, it's all coming together very nicely now, extremely well indeed. We've had some trouble along the way, for sure we have – but nothing I couldn't handle. From here, though, it's all going to be plain sailing. But you know that by now, don't you?

I've told you that.

Yes, I definitely have.

We're looking at a very happy ending. What you might call a happy ever after. And it all starts when we wake up in the morning.

11.44PM SUNDAY 1 NOVEMBER

God almighty, what was that? I've been fast asleep.

Night-time surely? But it's as bright as day.

The tower is ablaze with lights.

I sit up, checking William is still next to me. He is. The tower is brightly lit and I can hear someone shouting, from somewhere far away, but can't make out the words. The wind blows the voice this way and that.

I crawl on my hands and knees to the edge of the tower – I daren't stand up and be seen – and peer down towards the ground below. In the distance, a line of police cars blocks the top of the avenue. There's an ambulance there too, with paramedics, ready and waiting. I see one or two coppers stopping people from coming in. The houses and bungalows to either side are dark. I can make out an elderly man here and a young family there being ushered away by even more police.

There are a lot of them down there.

All with their eyes on me.

And guns? Yes, I reckon so.

In front of that line of police cars, in the dead centre of the road, is a cluster of five or six policemen, between two spotlights aimed up at the tower, all clearly talking among themselves and deciding what to do. One has a megaphone and that, I assume, is the voice that woke me. Here he goes again. I still cannot make out what he's saying. But these are angry, demanding words.

Do I need to make them out?

What he's saying is directed at me and obvious.

"Give yourself up." No more, no less.

I crawl back and look down at my little boy with his soft and gentle face, his features not yet properly formed. He's still not much more than a baby, really, untouched by life. He lies there, asleep, not moving at all. I crawl away. I just have to think, get my head straight, and decide as fast as I can what to do next.

I run quickly through the options.

Any which way, it's the end.

One way or the other, it's over.

If I stand up now, straight and tall, as proud as a daddy should be, with my head and shoulders in view, I have no doubt the police marksmen, out there somewhere, will shoot me dead where I stand. The houses are dark, but I know, deep down, that there must be police with guns at the windows.

I thought I was safe here.

I did not think things through. Someone must have seen me, reported it to the police.

The coppers with guns are there, somewhere, just waiting.

I could stand up, with my beautiful William in my arms; they daren't shoot me then. And we could, dad and his little lad, go together. Over the side and into the night forever.

Can I do that?

I could make my way down to the ground alone and give myself up. But they've got me marked down as a cop killer by now. And they think I have a gun. They'd shoot me as I got to the bottom of the steps. Will say they thought I was armed. That they had to kill me.

That would leave William an orphan.

Even if they didn't kill me – if that policewoman back in that seafront car park is still alive – they'd hustle me down to the floor, with other coppers and the paramedics rushing by me to get to William. He'd be terrified, he would, poor little mite. And I'd never get to see him again, to say goodbye, and would spend the rest of my life locked up; what with Smith in the annexe and that woman from Nottingham and the one from Aldeburgh. There was that man in the house too, wasn't there? And the policewoman. So many. Too many. God forgive me, what have I become? I have done some terrible things.

Would I want to go on without William?

Would he want to go on without me, his daddy?

I know the answer to that, you don't have to tell me.

I could lift William up and we could go down the steps together, a last cuddle and maybe, somehow, if we could slip out over the back steps, we might still have a chance to get away.

There's always a way, isn't there?

It's worth trying, isn't it? Surely?

I'd rather die than leave William alone.

Suddenly, happening quickly now, I hear, down below, two or three police cars revving their engines, moving into different positions in the avenue, I'd guess. I'm not sure why. Then, a louder, more aggressive engine noise coming in – a van, coming to a halt; policemen, armed and ready to attack, leaping out of the doors at the back, waiting for instructions, ready to strike.

It's almost over, when all's said and done.

I have to make my decision.

For both of us.

Live or die.

The two spotlights, aimed at the tower, seem brighter somehow, or maybe that's just my imagination. Driven by fear and panic. I hear the copper with the megaphone shouting up at me again. I can make out some of the words now, " ...yourself up ... last chance". They're getting ready to storm the tower, that's what, are now ready to take me out if I don't come down with my darling little boy.

I've decided.

I know what we are going to do.

It's the end.

I crawl on my hands and knees back to William. I turn him gently over onto his back. I am going to kiss him and give him one last cuddle. He is pale and still, moving beyond sleep I think. And then I see him twitch and spasm and I think there is some sort of froth around his bottom lip. He's still alive but dying, just like the man with the shotgun said.

My boy is dying. My beautiful, dear sweet little William.

I lift him up in my arms. Stand upright and turn around.

Move to the edge and hold him high so the coppers can see him.

I'm shouting now, but I'm not sure what I'm saying; it all pours out of me in fear and anger and hatred and built-up fury. If they'd just left us alone, let us go. We'd have gone away, been no trouble to anyone. We'd have started our new life together in the south of France and no one would have heard from us ever again. We'd have been happy, my little boy and me. I'd have brought him up properly, to be a good, kind person. Leave us alone, just leave us alone, that's what I wanted to say.

He's awake now, William, or so it seems.

His head lolling to one side. Frothing at the mouth.

They must see that in the spotlight, must see what a terrible state he's in.

I have to put my William down by my feet. I need to be fast now, before the police storm the tower. I must be quick. I have to clear my head and calm my voice and move to the edge of the tower again and say what I have to say in a loud and steady voice. I have to tell them what I am going to do. They have to hear me. They have to know.

I lay sweet William down.

I know what I am going to do.

I step forward into the light.

Author's Notes

I should begin by stating that, unlike Raymond Orrey, I love all of the locations in *Sweet William*. My grandparents and mother, Charles, Edna and Maureen Gayther, came from Nottingham before they moved to London for my grandpa's work in 1940. I was brought up in south London on stories of Balfour Road, the Palais and my great-grandmother's offal shop. Fifty or so years on, when our children, Michael, Sophie and Adam, were small, my wife Tracey and I, now living in Suffolk, would go up to Nottingham for shows at the Arena and plays and pantomimes at the Theatre Royal. We visited Sherwood Forest in the spring and summer and running through the woods, what's left of the forest, was the inspiration for the start of the book.

The big house and annexe are imagined as being close to Clumber Park. It's not meant to be Rampton, which is 15 to 20 miles or so away. Orrey hides in a ditch – I've been in it myself – on the Ollerton Road near Edwinstowe and then makes his way across to the A614 where he hitches a lift in the lorry. There are many ways over the Trent and plenty of housing estates similar to the one where Orrey enters the house. You probably won't find any that are exactly as I've described them. If you do, it's coincidence.

We've been going to Aldeburgh for the best part of 30 years. Michael pedalled his little red bicycle along the prom when he was about three years old. All these years on, we still visit regularly. We always go to the bookshop and have fish and chips upstairs at the Golden Galleon. A walk round the shops, up and down the beach, a coffee or an ice cream up by the boating lake, depending on the time of year; a perfect afternoon out.

Those of you who know Aldeburgh will realise that I have moved the carnival from August to Halloween. I had the fairground scene of Hitchcock's *Strangers on a Train* movie in my head when writing and I think a cold and misty October night works better than a warm summer's evening for this story.

Much of Aldeburgh remains the same – you can work your way from the car park along the front to the boating lake and back up to Chopping's Hill and into the roads behind. The park and promenade are a little different, but not so you'd notice too much. The rest of it – the toilets, the hut where Orrey snatches William, the terraced houses above the town – is all there. Maybe not the exact terraced houses, but as near as makes no difference. The way out of town? If you know Aldeburgh, you'll know where the marshes are as well as I do. If not, it doesn't really matter.

Eventually, Orrey makes his way with William to a housing estate outside of Felixstowe in Suffolk and on to the tower. If you drive along the long A14 road, you will, just before you reach Felixstowe, see the tower to your right and the fields that Orrey crossed to the left. I've walked our dog Bernard, a Jack Russell terrier, around these fields for many years and they are much as they are presented in the book. The housing estate exists and you can walk in the footsteps of Raymond Orrey. The tower is there at the end of The Langstons, which is, give or take, much as I have described it.

Going back to the big house and annexe where Orrey was, after sentencing, detained under section 37, the scenario and those living there and the escape are all broadly accurate; the text was read by a number of hugely experienced people who work in such a system, and with a range of what might be described as heavy-duty prisoners. People like Orrey can and do escape in the way described.

Type one diabetes – not to be confused with type two – is a serious condition and can be fatal. The US story referred to in the book is a real one. The symptoms and effects shown in the book are much as you might expect, but they are, of course, seen through Orrey's eyes. He sees his child, becoming ill, as being little more than sleepy-headed. We had the book read by those with long experience of type one diabetes, including a doctor and a parent of a child with type one diabetes. Personal experiences can all be different, of course.

The police procedures were checked over carefully and we had plenty of assistance from, among others, an ex-Met police detective who has worked on similar cases. There is a fairly typical, I think, sense of confusion early on that allows Orrey to get away, but, once it has become clear that a child has been taken, it's all hands on deck after that and the police are coordinated in what they are doing. Mistakes do happen and those on the run do slip through the net. I have tried to reflect this mix in the book.

This is, or is meant to be, a thriller, a page-turner, a 'what happens next?' story. I have tried to write it instinctively without stopping and starting to check nitty-gritty facts such as which way the wind was blowing on a particular night. I hope it is read in the same way. For those readers who enjoy spotting errors, such as anachronisms in a period drama, I am sure there is something for you to enjoy here too. Please note though that the story is seen through the eyes of Raymond Orrey and, to a lesser degree, the other characters. Orrey is, to put it politely, an unreliable narrator.

Iain Maitland
www.iainmaitland.net
www.twitter.com/iainmaitland

Acknowledgements

A book does not, of course, go from the author's mind to the printed page without the help of very many people in between. *Sweet William* is no exception.

Thank you, Saraband, for publishing *Sweet William*. You've been just brilliant.

Special thanks to Craig, who first read the manuscript and made that fateful, late Sunday-night call to Sara.

Sara, I knew from your first words that I wanted you to publish *Sweet William*. It then got better and better and better.

Thanks as always to my agent-nurse-cheerleader Clare for everything you do for me. Clare suggested the title – the closest I got was *Sweety Pie* – and one or two key changes to William and Raymond Orrey.

Ali, your nit-picking copy-editing made *Sweet William* clearer and stronger. I thank you for it.

I must thank those who read the book at an early stage. Your input was invaluable. In particular, Dr Sheena Meredith, Martin Brennan, Jeannie Lumb and David Burgess and one or two others who wish to remain anonymous; thank you very much for reading the book and for your help in getting prison, medical, police and other scenarios and procedures as accurate as possible.

Scott Smyth – I love your cover, thank you.

Angie Harms – thank you for your proof-reading and for going the extra yard.

Tracey, Michael, Sophie and Adam – my family. I doubt anyone will recognise you anywhere in *Sweet William*. That's not to say you're not in there. I'm sure you spotted yourselves.